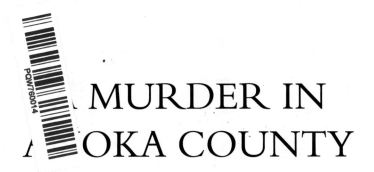

# A MURDER IN ANOKA COUNTY

# A MURDER IN ANOKA COUNTY

EDDIE JANE GAVIN

Rev. date: 05/09/2014

**To order additional copies of this book, contact:**
Xlibris LLC
1-888-795-4274
www.Xlibris.com
Orders@Xlibris.com
540488

# ACKNOWLEDGEMENTS

Veronica Fenice for her invaluable assistance in manuscript preparation. You are such an asset.

This book is dedicated to all those Law Enforcement personnel who keep us safe.

# CHAPTER ONE

Mildred leaned back in the saddle, enjoying Maud's even canter. The movement of air was pleasant on her neck. Her back still felt ramrod stiff from the remembered dreams.

The heat was intense. While she was leery about the possibility of someone breaking into the house, she slept each night with the windows opened wide to the night breeze. This morning's wind had brought with it the soft sound of horses nickering in the night. That sound usually encouraged her to turn on her side and return to sleep. Today had been different. Something was wrong.

A sound awakened her. It was early. Mildred had always been up with the birds; this was different. Now, 'four in the morning' was not too early to consider getting up for the day. This morning she was especially edgy. Something had nagged at her.

She wondered if it was because of the many months spent in the hospital recovering from the accident. She had thought hospitals were quiet havens of healing until she spent almost a year in various institutions. Early morning awakening was pure reality, if you lived in a small room whose sole function was to sustain your own body functions.

Now, as the soft wind teased around her, remembrance came. It was the anniversary of the accident, May 3, 1998. Maud's feet pounded a pattern on the soft earth as Mildred urged her forward in an effort to block the thoughts, before they had an opportunity to gather into a concerto of pain.

Too late. With the memory came a vivid sense of loss. Not only had the accident disrupted forever the sanctity of Mildred's life, but it had also taken the life of her husband, Emil. The accident, as it was so loosely referred to by the press at the time, seemed an ill-disguised attempt to murder her.

Mildred Smythe had been the Nursing Director of a Psychiatric Hospital. The principle witness in a very important drug and prostitution case in Federal Court was one of the patients. The prosecution was ready to present their case. Mildred had been working with the patient and was aware of his testimony. On the day of the accident, the final pieces of the investigation had fallen into place for the prosecuting Attorneys.

It had been a long day at the hospital. Late in the afternoon, Mildred had received a call from an old colleague, Fred Gorman. "Mildred, we've got to talk. I've found the missing piece!"

Fred was the investigator in the case. He was an old friend of Mildred's. She knew what he was talking about in his brief statement. "Can you be at the farm by eight thirty this evening?" She asked.

"Absolutely!" He countered.

She'd called home to let Emil know the plan. He hadn't been happy about it, but after 26 years of marriage, Emil knew Mildred had a primary love in her life. It was Psychiatry. He came second, yet was not jealous of it. His relationship with her stood outside the realm of her career. When they married, he told her he understood. She never doubted it. He was a successful contractor. He spent long hours outside the home. This combination of commitment to career, coupled with the long hours spent apart, enhanced their relationship instead of destroying it.

Fred arrived at the E. Bethel farm. Mildred did not. At 8:22 PM, a concrete truck surged into the intersection of Constance Blvd. and Lexington Avenue, forcing Mildred's classic Triumph TR 3 into a deep drainage ditch on the east side of Lexington Avenue. The car was crushed and broken. Later Mildred learned the Anoka County Sheriff at the scene had said to the Minneapolis Star Tribune reporter, "it's the worst car crumpling I ever saw, with a live body attached to it."

Attached she had been. Her left leg was impaled by a metal rod and the steering column pinned her into the leather bucket seat. Her left pelvis was fractured and her right leg had multiple injuries. Her last thoughts had been, "this is no accident!" The next thought was, "Oh shit, I'm dead!" She lost consciousness.

Many months later she pieced the story together. On May 4th, Jeffrey Fancher had been working in his 60 acre field with the John Deere. At 8:22 PM he was ready to pack it in for the night and eat some supper. He sensed the crash before he heard it. Mildred's car had caught his eye many evenings as she sped past his property. This particular evening, the hair on the back of his neck prickled and he started the tractor at the moment of impact.

He was already moving to the scene, praying he had that length of tow chain on the back of the cab. In a minute he scurried down the incline of the drainage ditch and hooked the chain to the frame of the car. It was already filling with filthy water.

Minutes after he pulled the car out of the ditch, he heard the sirens. His radio message to his wife in the house, had been a garbled plea to call the police. A neighbor had also heard the crash and called. Three squads arrived in tandem. The deputies had just finished their meeting and a cup of coffee at the Tom Thumb. Farewell words had barely been out of Deputy Samuelson's mouth when the emergency call came.

Mildred's life, that fragile thread of spirit, clung to her body by virtue of the incredible action of these four people, a hobby farmer and three cops. They were good. Actually, more than good, they were excellent. The first responders of Anoka County earned their pay that night. They saved her life.

She was unconscious for several days. When she awoke she was told that Emil had died of a massive heart attack the evening of the accident. When the Sheriff notified him of Mildred's accident he had collapsed. She hadn't been able to be there for him, when he needed her most. Mildred suffered with intermittent depression as a result.

Maud stopped under a large tree. Shade graciously spread over her shoulders. The dawning sun spread pools of light along the curve of trees and shrubs. Emil had diligently planted them when they first bought this property. He wanted her to have a place to ride her horse and relax from the stresses of Psychiatry. The beauty he'd planned cast a spell in this woodsy place. He had created a gift of love that transcended time and space. Today, it felt invaded.

Mildred drew a deep breath and dismounted. She pressed her face into Maud's mane, then stood a minute. The pungent, sweaty smell of the horse's neck filled her nostrils with the present. She needed to ground herself in the here and now.

The fact that she could walk, ride, and climb stairs was nothing short of a miracle. When she arrived at the emergency department of Mercy Hospital that long ago evening, from the Emergency Room Doctors to the Orthopedic Surgeon, no-one thought she would live, much less walk again.

"Tenacity!" The word came unbidden to her lips, as she rested against the large Tennessee Walker's sturdy body. When Mildred told her orthopedic surgeon she planned to ride horses again, he threatened her with a commitment hearing. "It would be physically compromising for you to even think such a thing! Jesus, Mary, and Joseph! You can't be serious, Mildred!"

But, she was. She pushed herself through the long recovery and the bone infection that plagued her and arrested her healing. That damned drainage ditch was full of every germ known to mankind. Mildred knew she had taken every one of them on-board physically.

Antibiotics triumphed, but just barely. The experience left her with great respect for the evasiveness of the bacteria's defense against the antibiotic. She never underestimated germs again and she hadn't taken Penicillin or any other antibiotic since her recovery. She was convinced the only reason the drugs finally cured her infection, was the fact that she rarely had used antibiotics, and her immune system had been in excellent shape. Mildred was no medical genius, but she was well aware of 'saving the big guns for when you need 'em', so to speak.

The art of medicine sometimes called upon every natural process, to win the fight for life. Mildred survived. Emil didn't. His death was instant and mercilessly brief.

Mildred pulled her thoughts together. She was on her way down the road to pick up the newspaper. She needed to keep focused on the here and how, not past pain. She was expecting to find an article in the Star Tribune about women's issues today. Mildred did Psychiatric Nursing for a local woman's shelter. She was a major proponent for enforceable protection laws for victims. Since her retirement, this was an important part of her life. The article was written by one of her colleagues.

Mildred climbed up on Maud's back and continued around the curve of the driveway toward the mailbox. She saw the paper sticking out of the box. Emil had built a small bridge to span the wide drainage ditch. The effect heightened the beauty of the entrance to the driveway. Both the mailbox and the paper box were built on the bridge facing the road. It was picturesque and inviting.

Maud clamored over the bridge, then shied to the side. "What!" Mildred was jerked in the saddle. She looked around. Immediately the image of a body filled her consciousness. She began to retch uncontrollably.

A body was splayed in the water. She knew who it was. He was partially anchored to the very edge of the water, just barely at surface level. His face was etched in her mind. Dino Manuchi had been the key witness for the Prosecution. He had been Mildred's patient.

His injuries, however, were what fixated her vision, bringing a scream of anguish to her lips. His pelvis was obviously crushed. His right leg was twisted to the side, most certainly broken in several places. A steel rod was impaled in the upper thigh. The similarity to her own trauma was not lost to her. She felt herself slipping down from the saddle. Maud reacted and reared back twenty feet after Mildred dismounted.

She felt shaky and rooted to the spot. As if in answer to her thoughts, a car stopped. "Mildred, what's wrong?" A neighbor called. "What's going on over there? Something fall in the ditch?"

"Harry." Mildred's relief at seeing another person was dramatic. "Have you got your cell phone?"

"Sure thing. What da ya need?"

"Call the sheriff! 911! There's a dead body here." She wiped her hand over her forehead. "I don't think there's any question that he's dead. We need to get the Sheriff and the crime lab here as soon as possible."

Harry's answer was to pull over and pull the phone from his pocket. Within minutes he was at Mildred's side peering into the ditch. Mildred restrained him as he started to head down the incline toward the body.

"No! You can't do that! This looks like a crime scene. We're already too close to it. The sheriff will need every piece of evidence he can find here. I don't want us to muck up the scene!" She emphasized.

"Oh, shit! You're right! Sorry Mildred. I just thought maybe there was something we could do for him. It's indecent for anyone to be displayed like that guy is."

Indecent yes, but Mildred got the picture. The message was patently clear, "there but for the grace of God, . . . ." She took in several deep breaths. It helped to steady her.

The trial of Dino Manuchi collapsed while Mildred was in the hospital. The major pieces of evidence did not bear the weight previously given them. Most of the witnesses refused to testify. Dino's information lost credibility. The case was history in two months. Dino Manuchi went back to his 120 acre farm in Anoka County. Peace descended on his homestead.

Now Dino was dead. Mildred knew with clarity, born of years of quantum leap thinking, she was on someone's hit list of 'who's who?'

The first county car arrived. It was Deputy Samuelson who stepped out of the squad. "Miz Smythe, I got the call and was just a couple of miles from here at the fire barn. A rig is coming ASAP."

"I don't think you'll need a rig, you're going to need the coroner and the Murder Squad." She pointed into the ditch. Samuelson ran down the incline and looked at the body.

"You're right. No way is this guy gonna wake up and smell the roses. I better call in and get Lt. Jacobs outta bed. He needs to get over here for this." He walked up the incline and called the dispatcher. The rig arrived as he completed the call.

Mildred could hardly believe only 7 minutes or so had passed since she had Harry call 911. In that amount of time, several more cars had stopped and people wanted to know what was going on. The second squad on the scene began to direct traffic and send drivers on their way. "You gotta move on. We've got an accident here. The sheriff' needs to be able to get in here."

It worked. The precision traffic control was a major help. Mildred's surprise was that so many people were awake and on E. Bethel Blvd. at six in the morning.

She took another look at Dino Manuchi. Her eyes traveled over his entire body, recording every possible thing she could perceive.

"The same old Mildred." His voice was soft in her right ear. She didn't have to turn or face him. The familiar scent of his jacket permeated the space between them. The close proximity was unnerving.

"John." Her voice wasn't exactly steely in tone, but close. It was flat. She was afraid to say very much. Every time this man came near, she felt the rise of emotion. She was a barometer of feelings.

There was a time when John Jacobs and Mildred Smythe were considered a pair. It was long ago and in during sixties. Everyone who knew them expected the relationship to explode in a passionate affair, and at the very least marriage. It never happened.

The feelings were there, but Mildred could not bring herself to connect with a man so threatened by her career. She had struggled to complete her education with tenacity that only her childhood friends and family understood. She worked her ass off as a waitress in a Dinky Town cafe for years to pay tuition. She graduated from her University with honors.

Her first job, and the passion of her life, was working for Hennepin County Hospital. She loved it. She knew John Jacobs well at that time. He was a young homicide detective with the Minneapolis Police Department. She'd met him in college. They dated for two years, before they went their separate ways. They met again three years later, when he brought in an extremely ill psychiatric patient, to her ward. The patient's family had just been brutally murdered. The killer was a neighbor who had been threatening the young man for years.

Mildred and John reestablished the college romance immediately. They talked and connected about everything from soup to nuts. Then, John wanted to marry her and made it very plain he thought her career was expendable. They fought, they argued, they cried, but she was adamant. Mildred refused to give up her life in exchange for a relationship, which clearly would diminish her sense of self. John wanted total surrender of her will to his. The connection was broken and Mildred didn't think she would ever recover.

John drank to heal. At 45 he left the Minneapolis Police Department after 25 years, joined AA, and relocated to Anoka County as an investigator. Now, as retirement loomed on the horizon, he realized his incredible dependence on work to fulfill his emotional deficit.

Faced with Dino Manuchi's body in her drainage ditch brought fear to Mildred's heart. With it came a sense of invasion of self. John Jacobs began to take less precedence in her thoughts. She did wonder, though, how he had gotten here so soon.

"Not quite the same old Mildred, John, but I still do react to murder scenes with the same old gut reaction. No matter who it is, it's a terrible waste of human spirit."

"I don't know how you can wax eloquent about this scumbag. Jesus, Mildred, this is the man who almost got you killed. You haven't forgotten that, right?" His pugnacious jaw lifted in the usual fighting stance.

"Damn, John . . . let it go." She reflected on her feelings, "I never thought Manuchi had anything to do with my accident. I still don't. It was a message to the justice system that the mob wasn't going to tolerate some female Psych Nurse knowing too much about one of their own. That was the message. Manuchi didn't have anything to do with it." She sighed. This conversation and ones just like it had transpired for months after the accident.

John had been there for days. As she drifted in and out of the pain and fog of anesthesia and countless IV drips, her awareness of his pain-etched face would permeate her consciousness. Their connection was almost spiritual. He willed her to live and somehow, in all the raging hell of the next three months, he succeeded in transferring the will to her. She fought and came back to months of Physical Therapy and a doctor who called her crazy for wanting to ride a horse.

"Where did you come from so quick?" She asked.

"Out driving, actually. I spend some of my early mornings cruising around Anoka County, Mildred. I'm an old war-horse, who the powers that be want out to pasture. I wake up at 4 AM and can't sleep. What the hell would you do, lie there and weep into your fuckin' pillow?" His sense of outrage was palpable.

"I'm sorry, John." She ventured to touch his arm. He was five years older than her, and the County was pretty insistent that retirement happen at 65. John thought it was crazy and said so. It didn't matter, he would be retiring on time, their time.

His eyes took in the pain registered on her face. "You go up to the house. Get one of your friends up. You need some support. Call Quim or Will." The words were abrupt, but true. "You know I'll have to finish with you later." The words were a statement she acknowledged with a nod.

She scanned the scene. Never again would this be the serene picture Emil created.

# CHAPTER TWO

As Mildred entered the great room of the home she shared with two friends, Alison looked up from the davenport. She balanced a coffee cup in one hand, while pushing her errant glasses up with the other.

"Where in the hell were you?" Her voice rasped. "I get a little concerned when you're up and about this early." She looked Mildred up and down. "You look like you were rode hard and put away wet. Like that horse of yours." She chuckled.

"You'd better stay sitting, Alison. We've got a problem. No, no that's wrong. I've got a problem."

"You're as white as a ghost. What the hell is wrong with you?" Her face began to take on concern. She started to rise, but Mildred motioned her back down.

Mildred chewed on her lip. Since childhood, she had the habit of biting her lower lip when concentrating on something. "There's a body in the drainage ditch. It's someone I knew." Her sigh was heavy and seemed to drain energy from her. She sat motionless and stared at Alison.

"A body?" Alison queried. "I won't ask something so stupid as, you're sure? Whose body?"

"It's a long story, Alison. I was going to be called as a witness in a criminal trial two years ago. Long before you read my ad for housemates." Her voice dropped. "After Emil died I knew I couldn't live in this barn of a house alone. So, a friend of mine, John Jacobs, as a matter of fact, suggested I advertise."

"I remember." Alison picked up the conversation. "It was after your accident. I know Will was concerned about you, too. He told me about you and this place. He was right, too." She indicated the house around them. "This has been respite for me. It's taken a long time to recover from Gordon's death." She leaned back into the cushions.

"Phew." Mildred blew the hair up from her forehead. "Hand me one of those cups." She poured coffee, surprised to realize she was no longer shaking. "Dino was the man I was taking care of at the time of the accident." She blew on her coffee, then continued. "Everyone said he wanted me dead. It's odd. I never believed that to be the truth. I still think there is someone else. It reminds me of Greek mythology. One of those creatures which have a dozen heads. Every time you cut one off, another takes it's place. Except I think there's just one in charge here."

"What are you talking about, Mildred?" Alison tipped her head and stared.

"I think I have been given a nasty and graphic lesson. Unfortunately, fatal for Dino Manuchi. I think I'm being given an example of what I can look forward to eventually."

Alison's color drained to a pasty hue. "You gotta be kidding." He voice slipped into vernacular speech learned in the Chicago streets. "This is a safe place. You told me it was okay. Will assured me this was secluded, and a quiet place for recovery." Her voice harbored doubt.

"It is. Seclusion and safety were the principle reasons for 160 acres of property. Look Alison, I know you're upset. Trust me; no one will bother you here. It's me that's the target. I'm the retired nurse who remains a threat to someone. It's doesn't take a rocket scientist to see Manuchi's body and not get the message. He was displayed, Alison, spread out in that water to mimic my injuries. The difference is, he wasn't meant to survive." Her eyes narrowed. "I wonder. All those strange phone calls with no one there. Jesus, I knew I should have caller ID."

"You think?" Alison inquired. She began to seethe inside. How could this happen at just this time? She knew from bitter experience, she must get a hold on her rage. "You think This Dino was calling you? Why?"

"Why indeed? I think Dino was tired of being the fall-guy. I never thought he was the force behind the mob. He was show. Pure, simple, window-dressing for all of us to look at while the real brains sat in the background and waited."

"You know my sentiments on the mob. Growing up in Chicago was shit! My dad was a two-bit hustler who was selling me to his drunken friends when I was eight years old, for God's sake! He was on the fringe. It's crap!"

Mildred broke in, "look, I didn't mean to imply I think some mobster was nice. But as criminals go, Manuchi was different. And," she added emphatically, "I don't think he wanted me dead."

"What's the argument about?" A slow voice drawled from the doorway. "You two are not exactly quiet early-birds. I heard you all the way to the back of the second floor." She reached for the coffee pot." Hand me one of those cups." She poured deftly, then turned an inquiring eye on each of the two of them.

"A body." Alison answered. "In our drainage ditch. Mildred thinks she knows him."

"What kind of body?" Freddy asked. "You mean like someone had an accident?"

"No accident. This person was placed there. Very deliberately and positioned to give me a message." Mildred had stopped pacing and finally sat across from the two of them. "It's odd. I think about death a lot. Not so much because I'm afraid of it. That year in the hospital, you remember Freddy, you are the one who talked and listened through the hell and depression."

Freddy nodded. "Go on. What's the connection?"

"I've never thought it was over. Somewhere deep inside, I knew the devil would have his due. The time would come, when I'd be the target again. I just don't know how they knew I was thinking about it all again."

"What does that mean, thinking about it? What is IT?" Alison asked.

"I've never been satisfied with that case being dropped. The drug case Manuchi was involved in two years ago. "I was Dino Manuchi's Nurse." She rubbed her fingers together, "he was this close to sharing some information with me the day of the accident." Mildred's face glowed with satisfaction. "Now I know I was right."

"Okay, I'm not following this." Freddy reorganized her legs and placed them on the coffee table. "Start at the beginning. I want to know what's fact and what's fiction. You know me, rational emotive to the core." She settled into the cushions, and waited for an answer.

Alison squirmed and got up to leave. "I've got to get dressed. I don't want to face any more bad news without makeup and some clothes." She peered down at her lounge pajamas. "These are real sweet, but I don't think the occasions is quite right for them." Her mouth twisted wryly.

*   *   *

Alison couldn't wait to get out of the room. She felt like she was practically running. She was barely in her room, when she swept up the phone and dialed. "Will!" she gasped into the receiver. "You've gotta get over here. Something terrible has happened. I can't deal with this." Her voice sounded broken and she stifled a sob. "It's like I can never get away from it." She stopped and listened. His voice could always sooth her.

"Look, Will, this is terrible. We've got a dead body here! It's that guy Mildred was working with two years ago in the Psychiatric Ward. He's dead! Outside in OUR ditch, OUT FRONT! You gotta come." She finally sat down and began to relax. "Okay, ten minutes. Hurry!"

She hung up the phone and stuffed her fists into her eyes to stop the tears. She resented Mildred's problems. She resented her fears. When Mildred would talk about growing up in Covington, Louisiana, so insulated and well-fed with parents who loved her, Alison wanted to puke. Sometimes she wanted to say, "When you were out in the Bayou riding your god-damn horses, I was being screwed by some drunken sod!" Yet, though she was tempted, she kept her own silent counsel. The only person who knew her secret was Father Will.

*     *     *

Freddy leaned back into the cushions. "Okay, now talk, Mildred." She focused on Mildred's face. "You need to express some emotion here. You look like death, and your face is as stony as Mount Rushmore. No gritting teeth and bullying this time. Talk!" She demanded.

"I don't know where to start." She said. It was true. The images of memory were all so pressing, it was almost impossible to find a spot to begin.

"Begin at the beginning. What feels like the beginning for you?" She asked in her polished psychologist manner. "Pretend you're filling me in on the story of your life, the short version. All my clients begin somewhere."

"Well, Freddy, I'm not your client, but it began with the accident. I really do believe I was this close," she snapped her fingers, "to understanding something important. Fred Gorman had found another witness; he was coming up to see me that evening. I remember thinking on the way home, it was great to have this sense of possibility, that maybe the case would soon be over. I liked Dino Manuchi. I still think he was always meant to be the fall-guy. I believe that if he had taken the stand, the case would not have continued. He didn't have the real information necessary to win and put the bad-guys behind bars. Now, the case seems clearer. Whoever is behind the mob, probably thinks I know more than I do. Dino and I did talk a lot. Someone thinks he told me a lot more than he should have. That's my guess. Maybe, they think I even know the name of the top people in the mob. I don't know, but it's the only thing that makes sense." Mildred moved to get more comfortable.

"I'm still cloudy on what possibilities were floating around in my head that day. Maybe it was that it just didn't seem as if the attorneys really had a solid case with Dino. He didn't know enough. Sometimes, I think the case was meant to go ahead. In reality, it would have folded because Dino didn't have the facts needed to win the case. This new witness Fred Gorman had found seemed more likely to be someone with substance," she continued.

"The accident interfered with my memory. I was on Lexington Avenue driving along without a care in the world. At least that's how it felt. One minute, I was floating along like the world had nothing to offer but possibilities. The next minute, this huge shape, a cement truck, loomed out from the left forcing me off the road into the ditch. I don't remember shit after that!"

"What was so important about Fred's news? Let it alone consciously, Mildred. Let it be in the back of your mind. Like Jung was fond of pointing out, we are all part of the collective unconscious. Let the memory come without forcing." Freddy drained her cup. She leaned toward her friend extending it for a refill.

"The odd thing is, this is the first time I can really envision the truck. I knew it was a cement truck. Hah!" she laughed shortly, "doesn't the mob always use cement trucks? But Freddy, I really can see it this time. The memory is clear, it was a blue and grey cement truck. My god! It's real! I remember it!" She grinned in triumph.

"That's the first step. What we have to work out is Fred's news. What was it he had to tell you that was so damn important?"

"Unfortunately, we'll never know the answer to that riddle. He died a month later of a heart attack. That's why the case died. Any new information he had went to the grave with him." Mildred sighed. "The nasty thing is, whoever is behind it, still thinks I know something. That's the frustrating part of it all. I don't know shit about anything, but someone obviously thinks I do. Of course, I do have his files. But," she mused, "I've been through them a number of times. Nothing clicks."

"If they think you know something, trust me kiddo, you do know." Freddy's voice was flat and sure. "Memory is an odd thing. We can go for years with no recollection of anything particular. Then, one day, we smell lilacs or violets or some odd scent, and a torrent of memories will flood into our mind. A whole period of time will be recovered. Our minds are marvelous instruments of knowledge. Someday, we might just figure them out." She added.

"Freddy, you really think this could happen? I could remember something significant about the trial, or witnesses, or something else?"

"Look, Fred was hot on the trail of something or someone. He said he had a significant piece of evidence. He said he had a new witness. He was thorough, he was intelligent, he was a top-notch investigator. What do you think, Mil? The guy had something. What you have to figure out is what!"

"Freddy, I have tried to figure it out, as you so succinctly put it. I have nothing. It was two years ago. Every shred of documentation, every piece of information, every bit of data, it's all just where I put it. In files, on discs, in boxes, all stored awaiting my return. It's not gonna happen. That part of my life is over." She noticed Freddy's look of doubt. "Trust me, it's over. Even the John Jacobs part. He's the same old John as always. Still thinks he was right about everything, Manuchi, the trial, my entire professional life. As he has said so many times, I could scream, 'Mil, if you hadn't been involved in THAT career, this wouldn't have happened'. He still doesn't get it, Psychiatric Nursing and practice IS MY life!" Her voice rose with feeling.

The phone rang. Mildred reached for it and answered before it reached her ear. "Quim! Oh is it good to hear your voice!" Mildred held the phone close to her ear. "He did." She listened intently for a minute. "You bet, both of you come on over. And, yes, I'll accept your offer to stay for a few days."

"Alison must have called Father Will. He called Quimby. He'll be here in about a half hour." Mildred looked toward the stairs. "From what Quim says, Alison is upset."

"Shit, Mildred, when isn't she? Alison is your original fruitcake. She may be one hell of a gothic novelist, but she's about 'a half a bubble off plumb' and you know it. I don't know why you keep defending her. Don't tell me it's sisterly love either. I've seen the way she looks at you. I don't know why you don't send her packing. She's a pain in the ass and I don't trust her."

The two friends had been through this argument a dozen times in the past three months. "Almost from the day you moved in, you've been on my case about Alison. Forget it, Freddy. I'm not going to send her packing, as you so tenderly put it. She's hardly here except for about four months of the year. She travels. She goes on book tours. She's gone so much, I hardly know she's around." Mildred said.

"I don't trust her!" Freddy insisted. "There's something not right. You know how I am about people. I've got her pegged. Underneath all the whimsy and romance novel crap, there's a stainless steel heart. I'm telling you, she's not what she pretends to be."

"How can you not be who you say you are, when you're a famous novelist? Freddy, just drop it, will you?" Mildred coaxed. "I've got John Jacobs coming to question me about everything I ever thought about John Manuchi, much less know, and I gotta say, he didn't deserve to die that way."

"Oh God, Mil, I'm sorry. You've been through a terrible morning and I'm bitching about Alison." She pushed up from the couch. "I'm gonna go fix us some breakfast." She sensed rather than saw Mildred's response. "You are going to have something to eat. I know you don't feel like it, but I'll tell you something, Mildred, I'll spoon feed you if I have to 'cause this day is going to get real long." Her voice drawled the sentence as she reverted to her native New Orleanian accent. "You don't have to eat much, but you have to eat something." She put the coffee pot and cups on a tray and carried them out of the room.

# CHAPTER THREE

Jeffrey Anderson Quimby filled the doorway. His six foot two height belied his gentle disposition. Mildred looked up at him, but just barely. In her stocking feet she was five foot ten, with a pair of low heels, she was six feet tall. "Oh Quim," she stepped into his arms and just stood there. "I'm so glad you're here. Come on in." She motioned him into the hallway. "Will got here a half hour ago. He's with Alison."

"He said he was heading right over," Quim's resonant voice filled the space. "I packed a few things and stopped to pick up some clothes at the cleaners. I'm here for the duration, if you need me." He reassured her.

"I can't tell you how glad I am that you can stay." Her voice wavered, then she went on, "John Jacobs is in charge of the investigation. He suggested I call you. You beat me to it. For once, I was going to take his advice."

"Well, I'm glad you did. You know, Mil, John's never going to change. He looks different than he did in college, but his temperament hasn't changed one iota." Quim kept his arm around her shoulder. "His loss, my gain." He assured her.

"Let me show you where to put your bags." Mildred led him up the stairs into a spacious room facing south. "Right below my room," she stated laughingly. "There's a really large sitting room." She walked to a doorway and opened it. "It's a great place to relax and watch TV or read a book." She indicated the bookshelves with a wave of her hand. "I've never had the opportunity to really give you a tour of this house. I'll rectify that today. I really do appreciate you coming here. For the first time in my life, I really don't know what the hell to do. You know, Quim, death doesn't scare me anymore, but this is bigger than just dying. There's a killer out there somewhere that thinks this is some kind of game. It's sick, that what it is. This person has no thought about the sacrilege of destroying a human life. It's wrong and it's psychopathic. I know that's an outdated psychiatric term, but this person has no conscience. Anyone that's in charge of the kind of drug dealing Manuchi was a front for, is a worthless human being in my opinion. It's one area where I believe in the death penalty." She motioned him into the sitting room. "Sit down for a minute. It's not just that I'm glad to have you here right now. I'm also glad to have you in my life. When we were in college, I never understood why we didn't hit it off better than we did. I think I understand that better now. John interfered with a lot of it. He was so intense." Mildred smiled. "I thought intense men were romantic. Kind of like Heathcliff. You know what I'm talking about, Quim. You tried to tell me then, and I wouldn't listen. I was so young, and I was so in love."

He listened, then leaned back and pulled his pipe from his pocket. He motioned with it, questioning if he could smoke.

"It's okay. I love pipes and cigars. I'm not so glad to see you still smoke both. It's probably not healthy, but then neither is being on someone's hit list." She smiled. "at least my sense of humor is still as active as ever."

"That's been quite evident since we started getting reacquainted. I'm glad you still favor classical music, especially Bach." He tapped his pipe, "I thought I was seeing visions when you popped up out of no-where at Orchestra Hall. Then I knew, for the first time in years, my luck had returned."

"Luck, schmuck!" Mildred leaned against him, "that was no luck, it was pure divine guidance. I had no more planned to attend that concert than I planned a trip to Mars. It was Freddy and her perennial extra ticket. If I didn't know better, I'd think you two planned it. But," she added quickly in response to his look, "she didn't know I was back in town from New Orleans. I called her late that afternoon and surprised her. So," she sighed, "I knew you two hadn't hatched any plot to get us together."

"Well, whatever it was, divine or not, providence or not, I'll never be one damn bit sorry." He reached around her and held her close. His lips touched her ear. He kissed it lightly. She nestled against him. For the first time since she awakened this morning, she felt secure. It was a nice feeling.

\*      \*      \*

Mildred's sense of security did not last very long. At 9 o'clock John Jacobs arrived at the door. Mildred knew it was him, by the sound of the dogs' barking. John always had a positive impact on her dogs. In a word, "besotted" was the only way to describe their loyalty to him. Whenever he came to visit, he had treats for them. Not today. Today he had no idea he would be coming to see Mildred about anything.

"Mil", he said as she answered to door, "we need to talk. Is there a private spot where we can be undisturbed?" He added when he saw Quim.

"Of course," Mildred stated matter-of-factly. She indicated the direction with a wave of her arm. "I'll get us some coffee and something to eat."

"You don't need to bother with any food. Coffee's fine," he said.

"It's no bother. Freddy is making breakfast. She'll bring something in to us. I'll just let her know you're here."

John walked over to the door to the library. He was always impressed, and somewhat overwhelmed, by the number of books Mildred and Emil had collected over the years. Oddly enough, the room didn't indicate either masculine or feminine décor. It was simply a very comfortable room with lots of leather wingback chairs and hassocks.

He settled into his favorite chair. It suited him somehow. Mildred teased him that she really had him in mind when she purchased it. He lit a pipe as he settled back and opened a spiral notebook.

"You still use those notebooks?" Her question had a wry twist to it. John glanced up at her. She had appeared soundlessly while he was lighting his pipe.

"Yeah, I do. For some reason I have a hard time with change."

"Not that I've ever noticed." This time the humor was evident. Time had not changed her smile or her capacity for laughter. "You are as unchanging as the Mississippi".

"Right!" John looked at her intently. "How are you doing?" He emphasized the YOU. "You were pretty upset when you found Dino."

"Upset hardly describes how I felt. But I did manage to calm down some. It helps to have people in the house. If Alison or Freddy hadn't been here it might have been a lot different." Mildred acknowledged his concern. "The thing is, I always knew something like this was going to happen. Dino still represented a threat to the Mob. No matter how you look at it, this is a predictable outcome from the trial."

"The non-trial, you mean." John stated flatly. "The son of a bitch had it coming, Mil. He was in as far as you can get. I don't know why you have such a hard time accepting it. This guy was a dirtbag.!"

"Look John, you aren't going to change my mind about Dino. I know he was a criminal. I never denied that fact. But, I did get to know him and how he thought when he was in the hospital. We talked a great deal. Dino was a man who wanted out. And, you're right! He was as dirty as they get. But, he did want out! The problem is, he knew way too much to be safe for them to take a chance on. The fact that he was going to be a major witness against them did not enhance his likelihood of survival," she paused, "or mine." He talked a lot, but he didn't share any real evidence. Frankly, I don't think he had any real evidence to share. I think he was set-up to share information that was concocted by them. That's the conclusion I was coming to when the accident happened. I think someone knew I was coming to this conclusion, when my accident was arranged. He was going to be their sacrificial lamb."

"Mildred, you have a pompous way of saying, he was a marked man." He motioned for her to sit down across from him. "He marked you, too."

"He knew it, John. As I said, we talked a lot. I probably know more about Dino Manuchi than his wife does. That's why I'm a threat. Someone thinks he told me something he shouldn't have. That's the simple truth. The problem for me is, he didn't. He never said a word about who did what, or when they did it."

"I believe you." He emphasized. "The people behind this incident don't believe it. You're going to need some protection, otherwise you're a sitting duck."

That's always been true, John. They know where I live. I'm not going to go into hiding. I absolutely will not do it. First, disappearing would only convince them I knew something I don't. Secondly, I am not going to leave my home. If I did agree to leave, it puts someone else in charge of my life. I just won't do it!" Mildred shook her head emphatically. "I've also got the dogs. Anubis is a trained K-9. He doesn't let anyone in unless I want them here."

"Mil, he's one dog and he's not immortal. They'll kill him. Pretty simple to kill a dog, even one as smart as Anubis."

"Then I guess, I'll just take my chances. I'm not going, period!"

"There's no reasoning with you, is there?" His question hung in the space between them. "You just simply don't stop to think other people care about you and want you safe." John looked into her eyes.

Mildred reacted immediately, "John, you've always got to act like I'm doing something personal to you. It really isn't like that, you know. I know you care what happens to me. You just never seem to get it, that I am a person who will not run from reality. I've spent my life working with people who have reality problems. I appreciate the fact that I am able to function, even when things get horribly nasty."

"For God's sake, Mill, I'm not finding fault with you living with reality. I'm finding fault with the possibility you aren't long for this reality. They mean to kill you. How much more do you need to know?" his frustration grew rapidly. "I happen to give a shit! I always have. I don't suppose it's going to ever go away. I've learned to live with it. It doesn't mean I have to like it. Understand?"

Mildred nodded in assent. "I tell you what. If you know someone that I can hire to live here and act as guard, I'll do that. You know a lot of retired cops. Isn't there somebody in that crowd who does security work?"

He leaned back and studied her face. "Yeah. I do know someone. I don't know if you'll appreciate him. It's a guy you never liked, Georgie Bonnaunt." He watched her face.

Mildred's distaste was evident. "Jeeze, he's a sleezeball! Isn't there someone else?"

"I'll tell you this, no-one is gonna get past this guy. I know you don't like him. But liking him is not the point, is it? He'll keep you safe. And what's more, you won't even know he's here."

"Believe me, I'll know he's here!" she stated passionately. "He's the one person I could never stand to be around."

There were interrupted by the sound of the door. Freddy brought in a tray with two plates bearing waffles. She set it down on the coffee table in front of John. "Mildred, I fixed you something, too. I know you said you couldn't eat, but I think you better try." She set out the silver and napkins. "There's more coffee, too." She turned to John, "I fried the bacon crisp. I know you like it that way."

Without saying any more she turned and walked out of the room. The door shut softly behind her.

Mildred realized with a pang, she was hungry. "Let's eat this while it's hot. We can talk about Dino afterwards." She picked up a knife and fork.

# CHAPTER FOUR

By the time Mildred and John had finished eating, she had relaxed enough to think more clearly. She did feel better. Freddy was right. Food did make a difference. She turned to John, a smile came to her lips. "That helped."

"She's a great chef." John agreed. "Not that waffles are that hard to manage, but with my culinary skills, this was pure ambrosia." He leaned back. "Mind if I light up again?"

"No, go ahead." She poured them each another cup of coffee. "How do you like this stuff?" she indicated the coffee pot.

"It's great. Why?"

"Brought it back with me from New Orleans. I was there for awhile and got attached to the flavor. It's Community Coffee. Wish they had it here. Anyway, I was there almost a month."

"I know." John answered. He noticed the look she gave him. "I called while you were gone. I do check in once in awhile, you know."

She sighed. "I know you do." She made the statement flatly. Underneath her facial blandness, she was feeling disturbed. No matter how long she went without talking to John, or seeing him, the sense of connection remained.

"Mil, I know you don't like to think about us, but I want to discuss it."

She interrupted him, "John, what's the point of going over the past? It's lost forever. Nothing ever stays the same. You and I just simply can't get past some fundamental stuff. You want to rule the roost, and I say NO! Nothing has changed. We are always going to be the people we are and you and I are like leopards who can't change their spots."

"Yeah. You're right Mil. However, maybe we can rearrange the spots a little."

"What ARE you talking about?" She raised her voice to highlight the question.

"We'll talk about it after I check out what happened this morning. Okay?" he asked.

"Alright," she agreed. "What do you want to know?"

"What time did you get up?" He began to write her answers as soon as she spoke.

"I woke up early. Very early!" She emphasized. "I think something woke me up. But, I don't know what. I had all the windows open. I could hear the horses out in the pasture. It wasn't that sound. I listened for a long time and finally gave up trying to sleep. I got up, dressed, made coffee, and went out to get Maud to go for a ride. That's all. Until I got out to the road, everything seemed as normal as apple pie."

"Did you notice anything unusual?"

"Nothing," she stated as she looked off to the right. "There was nothing different that I noticed. Of course, as I was riding I remembered this is the anniversary of the accident. *That* was disturbing."

"Yeah." He agreed. "That's what woke me up early. I was up at 4 AM too. Except I knew what woke me up. I was thinking about you in the hospital. Happens that sometimes, I just get to thinking and I can't stop."

"You know John, that's the other thing we have never talked about. The accident, I mean. We," she shook her head, "actually not we, more to the point, I", her voice wavered, "have been unwilling to talk about it. You saved my life. I never asked how you managed to be there all the time. Every time I woke up, you were there. How did you do that?"

"Took a leave of absence. Nothing to it, really. I hadn't taken vacation in years. Told 'em I was going to be away, and that was that. If they didn't like it, tough shit!" He drew a deep breath. "You wonder why I hated Manuchi? Well, if it wasn't for that piece of shit, you would've never been in danger. The accident would have never happened, Emil probably wouldn't have died, and we wouldn't be having this conversation this morning. Right?"

"Your logic is impeccable. Still, we had other differences you know." She added.

"I know." He said simply. "Let's get on with this. So, until you got out to the road, nothing seemed out of place?"

"Nothing." She thought back over the morning ride. "It wasn't until we were on the bridge, that I noticed anything. And that was more because of Maud. She got skittish and started acting up. When I looked around, I saw Dino." She felt the familiar lurch of here stomach.

"Okay. Was there anything out of place by the drainage ditch? Anything that just didn't seem right?" He queried.

"Nothing. Believe me, I have thought about virtually nothing else since I found him. You know me, John, I don't miss much. I didn't see a damn thing different, except him." She twirled her coffee around in the cup, and then took a sip. "I think the scene is burned into my mind."

"It was meant to tell you something." John removed the pipe from his mouth. "There will be a post on him. Then I'll know if what I think is true."

"What's that?" Mildred inquired.

"I don't think he died from the injuries. I think he was drowned. When I let myself think logically about it, it makes sense." He looked at her with concern. "You got the point, in reference to his injuries. Even down to which leg was impaled on a steel rod, it mimicked your accident. The similarities to your injuries are too exact to be coincidence. This is clearly a message. The fact is, what would have caused your death initially, was not the wounds, it was death by drowning."

"That was painfully obvious to me." Mildred stared into her coffee cup for several long moments. It was eerily quiet. "For all your dislike of Manuchi, it was a horrible way to die. He had to have been conscious when he was laid in the ditch. Maybe by that time, he was in such pain from his injuries, death in any manner was preferable to living. I just don't know."

John snapped his notebook shut. "I don't think there is anything else you can tell me. There's just no way you could have been responsible for this murder. I've got to get on my way. There's a hell of a lot to do. I have to inform his wife she's a widow. It doesn't appeal to me. She has two kids, too. As a matter of fact, they aren't very old. It's going to be a shock no matter how much his wife knew about his business. I'll call later when I get the chance. You have my cell number. Call if you think of anything." John pulled himself out of the chair with reluctance.

"If I do think of something, I'll call. I have Fred Gorman's files and I'll take a look. There may be something there."

"Right," He started for the door. "Oh yeah. I'll call George right away. He's bored, so I know he'll be available. You'll probably see him by this afternoon. Okay?" he peered at her closely.

Freddy and Quin were in the kitchen. Mildred joined them after she let John out of the front door. "I brought the dishes back," she stated even though it was obvious. "I'll have another cup of coffee, then I can finish getting you settled in your room, Quim."

"Already done!" he answered. "Freddy and I did it while you were with John. I could use a tour of the house, though. This place is enormous. What in the world made Emil build something this big?"

"Long story, Quim. Emil and I were going to use this place as a retreat center. I was going to retire from the hospital and organize workshops. We talked about doing something like this for a long time. Course, I didn't plan on an accident, or on Emil dying. Actually, I may still do something like that. I definitely need an occupation. After the accident I didn't go back to work. It seemed pointless somehow. And then, of course, I was in physical therapy for a year. It wasn't exactly conducive to being a Psychiatric Nurse."

"So you retired?" he asked.

"Yep! I decided to take this opportunity to do some different things. Besides, working with a physical therapist and really doing credit to myself, I had to concentrate on being able to walk again. It was hard work." Mildred explained. "It was months before I could walk with a cane. Then I started working on other stuff, like how I'd ride a horse again. That was tricky."

"I'll bet. I missed most of that year." Quim acknowledged. "About the time we all knew you were going to live, I was sent to England for a year."

"The letters were a godsend, Quim. They were wonderful letters. I still have them in a box."

"You saved them?" he asked. "So did I. I kept them all, too. One thing we're both good at is letter writing. It's a lost art."

"Anyway," Mildred broke in, "I don't suppose either one of us will ever be famous, but they do comprise quite an active correspondence."

"Not to change the subject, but what did John have to say?" he asked.

"Well, he thinks I am the target. Manuchi's body being placed in front of my property is a clear message for me. I knew it as soon as I saw the body. There was no mistaking the fact that his injuries mimicked my accident. The really bizarre thing is, I have no idea why. I suppose the Mob, for lack of a better term, thinks I know something. Dino Manuchi and I talked a lot when he was on the unit. There was no question he wanted to be done with the criminal lifestyle. He knew too much. The fact that he was going to testify against them, did not ensure a healthy and long life. I still wonder though, if he really knew as much as he thought he did. I think he was spoon-fed information that ultimately would have been worthless. My part was testifying about his sanity. I know the Feds were talking about the Witness Protection Program, but he really didn't want to do it. In some ways, he and I were alike. I won't run either. John thinks I'm screwy, but I'm not going anywhere. So," she drew the word out, "we compromised. I told him to arrange for a bodyguard for me."

"What?" Freddy interjected. "A bodyguard! How in the world?"

"Well, it won't be too difficult. This place has a very complex security system. I really haven't used it to the fullest potential. However, it is top of the line security. Emil was a fanatic about safety. Especially since he had several burglaries at the construction company. As a matter of fact, I've never even shown it to John. He has no idea about it."

"Well, I didn't know either," Freddy looked around the room with care. "Is it here?"

"Yes," Mildred replied."

"Knowing you, Mildred, you probably haven't used it." Quim stated with a little smile. "I've never known you to show fear. However, this situation is clearly quite different from anything you have ever experienced."

"That's true. It's also true I haven't used the security system to it's potential. But," she stated, "I do use it."

"When?" Freddy asked. "You haven't mentioned to me I would set off an alarm if I opened the wrong door."

"True. Actually, I haven't worried about the house itself. With three dogs running around, you have the best early warning system possible. Anubis sleeps in my room. Whenever he senses something amiss, he wakes me up. Consequently, I don't use the system in the house. I do have it activated in other places." Mildred stated matter-of-factly.

"Where? You're not going to tell me there are cameras everywhere are you?" Freddy asked, he voice betraying fear. "I don't like the idea of being spied upon."

"Freddy," Mildred shook her head in a negative. "I do not spy on guests in this home. Besides, if you were gonna bump me off, you would have done it years ago, when we used to fight all the time."

"Well," Freddy answered as her temper cooled, "That sure is the truth. Remember that fight we had over Justine Emerson? You were really pissed at me over her."

"Good God, I forgot about that. You really did piss me off. We even had a physical fight over it." Mildred started to laugh, "You remember how it ended?"

"I'm not likely to forget!" Freddy started to join the laughter.

"Is there a joke here I'm too dim to get?" Quim asked the two of them. "I seem to be in the dark about this event."

"You are!" Mildred answered. "You see Freddy lived on the Lake. Lake Ponchatrain. That's where we met."

"Yeah! My parents were trying to give me some culture. I'd been to several private schools, but they weren't happy with the results. So, they sent me to a Catholic High School near New Orleans. They figured what the private schools couldn't achieve, the Nuns at St. Cecelia's could. Oh brother, what a mistake." Freddy was starting to belly laugh.

Mildred had calmed down a bit and was able to a least talk. "Freddy was the most 'out of sight' girl I had ever seen, much less to have as a seat-partner at school. The first thing she did was make a pass at me. Right in school!"

"Yeah! Right behind the Nun's back. Wasn't it Sister George that taught that English class? She was really something. Walked around with a ruler in her hand all the time. And she used it, too!" Freddy had become serious. "Anyway, I reached over and patted Mildred on the butt. She flew out of her desk like a dervish. What a reaction! Then, she turned and looked at me with those blazing eyes of hers and hissed. 'Don't you ever touch my person again!' It was absolutely a stitch. I'd never heard anybody sound so refined," Freddy drew out the word prissily, "she absolutely sounded like some Dame of the Realm in England."

"Well, it was a shock! Here I was, sitting in my English class and this strange, and I mean *straaange* girl next to me, feels me up. What the hell would anybody do? I stood up and let her know I was having none of that, thank you very much!"

"The crazy part was, Sister George was so busy at the board writing out examples of past participles, that she hadn't a clue what was happening behind her back." Freddy said. "The whole class was aware. They were all waiting to see what would happen next."

"What did?" Quim asked.

"Nothing!" Mildred answered him. "Absolutely nothing. Not then, anyway. I told Freddy I would talk with her later and I did."

"Yeah. We met after school. My God, we went out for pizza at the Welcome Inn in Metarie that day. Remember those paper thin crusts? They were the best!" Freddy extolled. "I've never found pizza like that here. Anyway, Mildred didn't write me off. As a matter of fact she was so ignorant about sex, we had a little talk about the 'birds and the bees' that evening."

"You're making it sound like I was an ignorant idiot!" Mildred turned to Quim, "The truth is I didn't know shit about gay or lesbian lifestyles. Freddy here, educated me on the subject. The Nuns didn't teach that in Sex Education and Health Classes."

"I bet not." Quim grinned. "So what was the fight about?' Who was Justine Emerson?"

"She was a fabulous looking girl in the Senior Class. I had a real thing for her. Mildred told me to lay off because Justine had enough troubles as it was. I didn't listen and took her out on a date. It pushed her over the edge."

"I'd warned you she wasn't very stable emotionally."

"Yeah, but you didn't tell me she'd been raped by her step-father! That would've helped a little." Freddy shot back. "As you can see, there is still some emotion about this."

"In the long run, it worked out. Justine ended up in an exclusive Psychiatric Unit and actually did very well. As a matter of fact, it was her situation that got me interested in Psychiatric Nursing."

"What about the fight you two had? What happened?" Quim pressed for an answer.

"We were in Freddy's yard. They lived right on Lake Ponchatrain, like I told you. Anyway, we were literally hitting each other. Her father heard the commotion and came out of the house. When he saw what was happening, he turned on the garden hose and let us have it! It was cold, wet, and certainly a shock. The two of us tumbled off the retaining wall and fell into the lake." Mildred had a faraway look on her face. "Was THAT a shock! It was deep and cold! My God! I thought my heart was gonna stop! But it broke up the fight."

"Yeah! He hauled the two of us out of the lake and into his study. Grilled us about the fight, and then we had quite a talk."

"Your dad was a smart man. Still is pretty sharp for that matter." Mildred added. "He wanted to know what the hell was going on and so we told him."

"Actually he told both of us, he was already aware of my sexual orientation. He had never said anything, because he felt when I was ready I would talk with him about it." Freddy shared. "It's odd, even though my dad was a Psychiatrist, it never occurred to me, that he might have ME figured out. That was a shock!"

"It really cemented our friendship, though. After that, Freddy and I were almost inseparable. We even went on some double dates. Naturally the boys I went out with, were hand-picked, so to speak. There weren't many boys who weren't threatened by a double date with his girl friend, and a Lesbian and her girl friend. It did work out. I went with the same young man for several years in High School. He got to know Freddy pretty well. We still get together in New Orleans once a year."

"So, did Justine recover and come back to school?" Quim still was curious what had happened to her.

"She did. We still see her, too." Freddy answered him. "Justine lives in St. Paul. She owns an exclusive antique shop there. She ended up seeing my dad's female partner, Iris Babcock. She was a Psychologist with their practice. Justine recovered very well. Now she is the Director of a Women's Shelter in Ramsey County. The antique shop is managed by one of the women from the shelter. She employs some of the other women too. Working in the shop provides an opportunity to get job experience and give the women a chance for an income.

Her husband is an attorney in Stillwater. He's on the Board of the shelter, too. They have 5 children, countless animals, the least of which is a three-legged weasel."

"Sounds like someone I know." Quim looked at Mildred. "You always have an odd assortment of animals here, too."

"My own private animal shelter, is that what you're getting at?" Mildred laughed. "It is true, I take in a lot of waifs of the animal kingdom, but I do find homes for them." She added.

"She takes in human waifs, too." Freddy said pointedly. "Like Alison Lippencott. Now that woman is a case in point. She is weird! I don't care if she is a famous novelist. I don't trust her one inch. She's creepy, weepy, and a drip!"

"Freddy, you just don't like her. She's only been here for 8 months. Four of those she was on book tours and traveling to where ever she goes, to get subject matter for those romances she writes." Mildred was almost out of breath after her protest. "You don't even know anything about her. I did get references before I agreed to rent to her."

"I don't care! She's still a creep. And I can't stand" Freddy drew out the words, "her swooning maiden shit. God almighty, if she's that worried about herself, she should live in a security apartment or something. She certainly doesn't strike me as the country sort of person."

"Well that's true. She doesn't." Mildred said. "What she told me she needed was a quiet place to write. She certainly has that. She hardly ever comes downstairs until late afternoon. She eats breakfast and goes up there to write. You can hardly tell she's here. She does a lot of her research for historical data from the internet."

"You mean hysterical data. Don't you?" Freddy interrupted. "There's always a maiden in distress, hand clasped to her heaving bosoms, and lot's of fainting and swooning. But, they always get their man. You know," Freddy added, "I don't know any men who really like the clinging, fear filled, swooning-maidens she describes. Yes, Quim, I do know some men. In fact, I have quite a number of male friends." Freddy responded to the unspoken question on his face. "I like men. Just because I'm a lesbian, doesn't mean I hate the male gender. I'm probably more comfortable with men than most women are. After all, we have a lot in common." She said and grinned at him.

*    *    *

George Bonnaunt arrived at 2 o'clock in the afternoon. He looked the same as ever. Mildred let him in and showed him where to stash his gear. He looked around the room with ease. They were standing by the central control for the security system.

"Private entrance and all, huh?" George queried. "This is really a good set-up."

"Emil wanted it to be state of the art. He put a lot of thought into this. He was a believer in protection. Mildred sighed, "I haven't used it much. Didn't seem to be much need. With Freddy and Alison here, it seemed more of a burden, than anything."

"Speaking of Alison and Freddy, who are they? How well do you know them? George put the questions to her in a matter-of-fact manner. "Could be you have a nest of vipers here. Whad-ja think?"

"I've known Freddy since high school. Alison came with some pretty impressive references. She's practically a household word. Everyone reads Alison Lippencott novels. There's always a fight for them at the library when they first come out. She's usually on the New York Times Best Seller list for months. So I guess, in answer to your question, Alison certainly is who she appears to be." Mildred peered at him over her glasses.

"Can't be too careful," he mused. He then waved his hand at the wall of monitors. "These cover the entire house and grounds?"

"Yes," Mildred answered. "There are monitors in all the major rooms. I don't have them in the bedrooms, but there is one in every sitting room on the second and third floors."

"Hopefully when your guests are in their rooms, they're sleeping peacefully, and not planning something nefarious." George looked at her, "how'd you decide to hire me anyway? You and I have never liked each other much. So it surprises me some." He sat down at the main control monitor. "John must be touting my expertise."

"He recommends you highly. Basically says he doesn't trust anyone else to do the job." Mildred ventured. "We don't have a lot in common, George, but I'm not a fool. I need someone to provide safety. It isn't just for myself. The other two women are staying here and," she added, "my daughter is coming with her two children next week. I have to do something!"

"Isn't there some way to keep the kids away?" he asked. "Now watching over adults is one thing, but having two kids here is something else. Iwouldn't recommend it."

Mildred interrupted, "There isn't much choice. Renee, my daughter is having surgery on Monday. She can't put it off, and she cannot be at home alone with two active children. Freddy's going to take care of the children, while I take care of my daughter. She paused, and then added, "Perhaps I can talk Freddy into taking the children on a trip. That would get them out of here. Still, if my family is in danger, too, then it's probably better they are here."

"In theory, Mildred, in theory. Not to change the subject, but what are you going to tell your guests about me?" he asked.

"I've already told them, I was going to have a bodyguard. I also let them know about the security system. What I don't care to go into is how extensive the system is. You need to know. I will do anything, within reason, to be cooperative with your directives. But I do want you to know, I do not intend to stop living because some individual wishes me harm."

George leaned back in the chair and looked up at her. He appeared pensive, and then spoke, "Mildred, do you have any idea what a piece of cake it would be to take you out? Now I'm not even considering someone coming on your property. What I see is, a guy with a long range rifle and scope. Mildred Smythe is history! BAM!"

"I am aware of the possibilities, George. I've thought about this a lot. I've known for some time, that the danger was real." Mildred paused, then continued, "if you can get this system functioning at the optimum level, I think we can at least feel safe in the house."

"I've got a crew. They can not only spell me at the monitors, but they can walk the grounds. How many acres have you got here?"

"One hundred and sixty," she answered. "At least 60 percent is wooded. Near the fence lines, we left the brush thick to provide more privacy. It's awful thick, too. Black raspberry bushes and lot's of underbrush."

"That's good! What about access to the property? Any other gates besides the main one? You haven't got a field road coming in the back, do you?"

"I think by now it's pretty well grown over. We'll have to check. Once we were done with the construction and landscaping, we closed that road down and put in Alfalfa for the horses. All of the property line is fenced, and the fields are too soft to drive through. A person could walk in, but they'd be on the monitor if they did. That field is the only open expanse we have. However, the foreman lives in a house on the opposite side of the property. His gate has access to County Road 74. He drives through the woods on the bridal path I use for the horses. It's rough in spots, but it works."

"So in actuality, you do have another way in here?" George inquired.

"When you put it that way, yes." She answered succinctly. Mildred watched the monitors for a while. "Do you really think someone has been coming around here and watching us?"

"Well, it seems like your daily habits are known to someone, so I assume there is a breach in the security somewhere. The thing is, you really haven't been using this system the way it was intended. So there's no telling what the scoop is. I'll have everything up to snuff by the end of the day. Then we'll be able to appraise the situation." He looked up at her. "Let me get a feel for everything here. I'll be able to let you know by this evening. I can fill you and Jacobs in at the same time. He's coming by, right?"

"To my knowledge, yes. He said it could be late, but then what's new?" Mildred added with a faint smile. "John has a habit of being cognizant of his own time, no one else's."

# CHAPTER FIVE

During the afternoon, Mildred took a nap. She realized how exhausted she felt after Alison came down with her friend, Father Will. It seemed as if Alison couldn't stop talking. Will encouraged her to take a tranquilizer when he realized she was close to losing emotional control. By then, Mildred had a headache and just wanted to have peace and quiet.

"I'm heading up to take a nap. I'm not going to be worth two cents if I don't take care of myself." Mildred said to Father Will. Alison had curled up on the large sofa in the Great Room. Quim and Freddy were off in the kitchen creating something interesting for dinner that evening.

As she climbed the stairs, Mildred paused and looked around the three story hallway. There was a walk-way on the second and third floors of the house. On each floor you could walk the circle around the central staircase. At the back of the house on each floor was a central sitting area like an informal living room. When she and Emil had planned this place, it had been their intent to use it as a retreat center. The actual bedrooms, on the second floor were not large, but they were conformably furnished. There were six in all with a shared bathroom between each.

Mildred had her room on the third floor. This floor plan was different in that there were only four bedrooms. Mildred's was quite large and shared a sitting room with one of the other bedrooms. Her bath was spacious and contained a spa tub, separate shower room, and a private toilet and bidet area.

From her room there was a private entrance to a library area. This was a large room with many windows facing east and south. On the north wall of the room there was a large fireplace. It was situated centrally in the large expanse of wall space. Books were housed everywhere on built-in shelving. A large, down filled couch and two large easy chairs were dominant. Good reading lamps were placed strategically by each chair and the couch. It had been designed as a sanctuary for Mildred and Emil when the proposed retreat center became a reality.

In the end, however, it did not fulfill that purpose. Mildred used this room as her private place when she was recovering from the accident. The house had a small elevator, which was rarely used, except when she couldn't climb stairs. If the retreat center ever became a reality, it would be used for guests who were physically handicapped. The house was close to eight thousand square feet.

Mildred's rooms were on the south side of the structure facing the small pond and a wooded garden area. From the vantage point of her rooms she could also see the patio and pool area, and in the distance, the bridged driveway where the Murder Squad was still very much involved in their investigation.

She laid her head on the pillow and was instantly asleep.

*    *    *

The ringing phone awoke her an hour later. She lifted the receiver and held it to her ear. "Yes?" She drawled into the phone.

"Hi Mom, it's me, Renee. I wanted to check and see what time you wanted me and the kids to arrive. We can come over this evening, or wait until tomorrow morning. The kid's can hardly stand the wait."

"Either would be fine." Mildred paused, "Renee, there's something I have to tell you." Her voice hesitated briefly. "There was an incident at the front of the property today. A man's body was found out there. Well, actually I found a man's body out there, when I was out riding Maud this morning."

"An accident?" Renee's voice queried.

"No," Mildred spoke reluctantly. "It was no accident." She sat up on the edge of the bed to clear her head. "I knew who it was."

"Mom, just tell me," Renee drew out the word mom. "You have a habit of trying to put the best front on things. This sounds like one of those times. Just give."

Mildred could picture her daughter. Renee was the last arrival of the triplets. She weighed the least at birth. Since then, however, she pushed through the ranks of the other two, and had never looked back. She was the attorney for Smythe Construction Company. The other two daughters were the President and Vice-President. All three of Emil and Mildred's daughters had gone into the family business.

When they were growing up, the kids idolized Emil. He took them everywhere. Ultimately, they went to work with him.

"Mom," Renee's voice broke through Mildred's reverie. "We'd better come there in the morning. It sounds like today has been hellish. Who's there with you? Besides that idiot Alison?" Renee's dislike of the writer was barely masked during her visits. "She is probably all heaving chest and whimpering faints."

Mildred's chuckle rose from her belly. "Renee, enough. Alison is having a difficult time alright. But Will is here, and Quim arrived to stay as long as I need him."

"Great! I haven't seen Uncle Quim for such a long time. Not since he came back from England. God, it's been over a year since he came back and I've been so busy, I've hardly had a chance to visit you, much less see him."

"Well, my dear, you'll get lot's of opportunity in the coming week. But, I should tell you, before you bring the kids out here, the person was someone I knew."

"Who?" Renee's voice lifted in pitch. "Not someone I know, was it?"

"No, the man was Dino Manuchi." Mildred's voice was soft as she communicated the information. "He was the man in the ditch. I really don't know if it's wise to come out here with the kids or not. John made me hire a security person and bodyguard."

Renee's voice interrupted. "Bodyguard! What for? Mom!" Her voice once again rolled her mother's name over her tongue, making three syllables out of it, "what is it you aren't telling me?" She demanded.

"Well, this is the man I was going to testify about three years ago. In the trial that was dropped," she added cryptically. "Anyway, this was the man."

"You bet I'm coming over there!" Renee emphasized emphatically. "No one is going to threaten my mother and get away with it. The kids and I are coming tonight! We're going to room up there with you." She added with assertion.

"I don't know if bringing the kids is wise." Mildred said. She heard Renee's drawn breath. "Okay! There's room up here. You'll have to share though, Quim is staying in one of the bedrooms. You and the kids can have the rooms on the East side of the house."

"Fine," Renee responded, "I'll be there in an hour. We're all packed and ready to go, so all I have to do is lock up the house. The cat's coming with us, I hope that's okay? I didn't really ask if she could come."

"It's fine. She'll stay up here anyway." Mildred murmured.

"Well, I'm not so sure, this cat has started to wander a lot more. For an animal who was scared of her shadow three months ago, she's made a remarkable recovery." The cat in question, had been rescued by Renee and Mildred from the animal shelter. She had been burned in a fire that had destroyed the barn she was born in, with three other kittens. She was the only one who had burns, the other cats had escaped without injury.

"If she wanders, she'll meet the dogs, that's all." Mildred assured. "I'd better get up and go on downstairs. No telling what's been happening since I came up here for a nap."

"Okay. I'll see you within an hour." Renee said before she hung up the phone.

Mildred stopped in the bathroom before she went down. She ran a brush through her hair and changed clothes. She put on a pair of old jeans and a flannel shirt. Comfort clothes. The kind she grew up with in a sleepy Louisiana town.

Her father had been a farmer. He raised cattle and sugar cane. One of the things Mildred vividly remembered was always feeling poor. They never seemed to have any money. Every time her father got a dime in his pocket, he bought land. Between taxes, cattle feed, and upkeep on the sugarcane farm, there was barely enough to get by on. She and her mother raised a garden, had chickens, and pigs. Chores and homework were what Mildred remembered from her childhood. She was very smart and loved to read. Many nights she was up reading in her bedroom until the wee hours of the morning.

When it came time for High School, her dad wanted her to study in the city. That was how she arrived at St. Cecelia's Catholic Academy for Young Ladies. They had no money for tuition, but her father had a connection with the school. He supplied their beef, poultry, and cane syrup. He also owned a piece of property the Church wanted to buy in rural Louisiana. He traded for his daughter's education. In the fifties, anything was possible. The nun's enjoyed filet migon, and Mildred had room, board, and tuition.

She and Freddy were inseparable after their first notorious meeting. It was Freddy who came to the University of Minnesota for her psychology degree. After being in practice for five years, she returned to the U, and got her MD. Freddy was not only a renowned Psychologist, she was no damn slouch as a Psychiatrist, either.

# CHAPTER SIX

Mildred had a housekeeper and cook, but that did not deter Freddy from taking over the kitchen. Francis, who guarded her kitchen fiercely, didn't bat an eye when Freddy marched in and took over. Francis laughed and stated," I've been meaning to go to the city and visit my sister. She's been bugging me since our Mama came up here to visit. Now, I'm gone!" With that statement she flounced out of the kitchen to pack her bags. Ten minutes later she waggled her fingers at Freddy and added, "you know you are the only person I'd trust my kitchen to, now don't you, girlfriend?"

Freddy acknowledged her assertion and went back to her baking.

The evening began with dinner. Freddy had set up the formal dining room. It was clear to her that there were going to be a lot of people dropping in and out. She didn't want the traffic to distract people from their food. One thing about Freddy, she demanded allegiance to eating, when she prepared the menu. In that, she was very different from Francis. Francis could care less, she just thought people were pig-headed who didn't appreciate her cooking. "If they didn't wanna eat, fine! There's more for the rest of us." She would just laugh as she served up warmed-over-dinner for lunch the next day. Generally, there was quite a group in her kitchen.

Freddy had set up the dining room for nine. Although the day was hot, she was baking what she referred to as, Succulent Pig Roast, Oven Browned Potatoes, and Steamed Asparagus. Dessert was plain old Rhubarb Pie. Freddy loved Rhubarb with a passion only a southerner could muster. The stuff wouldn't grow in Louisiana, so naturally she coveted it and ate it every chance she could.

Mildred was holed up with Renee and the children in the library. She wanted a chance to talk with the kids before they started running over the place like two wildcats.

Erica kept interrupting, "but I just want to go and see what's going on . . ." she insisted.

"NO, that's absolutely what you can't do!" Mildred insisted. "It is not a game. The man was killed and left out there. I do not want you going anywhere near that drainage ditch. Do you hear me?"

Oh, Grandma, you are so stubborn." Erica's voice insisted. "I said I won't go right out there by them, I just want to get near enough to see."

"You heard what Grandma said. You are not to go anywhere near the road. You saw how busy the sheriff was out there. There's deputies all over the place. They have the area secured."

"Well, if it's secure, we aren't going to be able to cause any problems." Hunter insisted, chiming in with his sister. As far as he was concerned, anywhere that Erica led, he would follow. Unlike most of his friends, who didn't like girls, he liked his sister. "I'll take care of her, she won't get hurt."

"It's not a matter of getting hurt. The sheriff's men are checking all the grounds near the driveway. Anything out of place could be important. That's why children would be a problem." Mildred said matter-of-factly. "No, you aren't in danger, but you might accidentally disturb something and destroy important evidence. So, I expect you will follow the rules. The pool is open, you can ride the horses, you can do almost anything, but go anywhere near those deputies. Understand?" Mildred looked both of them in the eye.

"Yes, Grandma, we understand." They both nodded solemnly. They did understand.

Renee looked at her two children. "You had best be telling the truth. 'Cause you know you'll both be sent to your Auntie's house if you don't behave."

"Yes, ma'am, we know." Their eyes regarded hers thoughtfully.

"Alright, that's settled. Now why don't you two kids run and see what your Aunt Freddy's got for you in the kitchen."

"Mom, it'll ruin their supper." Renee said.

"Phooey, it never bothered your appetite when you were their age. They eat everything that isn't nailed down in that kitchen. Let 'em be." Mildred's eyes followed them as they left the room. "We need to talk about this situation. John Jacobs will be by for supper, too. He wants to talk with me after forensics is done with the area out there."

"Mom, what does John think about this?" Renee asked simply.

"He thinks someone is giving me a death message. He thinks," she reiterated what he had said that morning, "that I am in grave danger. He insisted I hire a security man and body-guard. I've done that. George Bonnaunt got here this afternoon. He's all settled in, on the lower level. He looked over the security system your dad put in and thinks it will do the job. I don't know how our house mates are going to feel about being under surveillance, but there's no way around it. I think John's right, and with you and the children here, I don't want to take any chances."

"Oh, Mom," Renee sighed, "I just don't want anything to happen to you. It was so bad when you were in the hospital and I didn't think you'd live. Thank God for John. He never lost hope or faith in you surviving. You know Mom, he's in love with you."

Mildred glanced at her daughter. Renee was so earnest. Of the three sisters she was far and away, the most serious one. She was also the one who has faith in the under-dog. "I know you like John. We've talked about this before. He gets so intense."

"That's right, he is intense. He's in love with you. He has been for years. I'll tell you Mom, you have more in common with John than you ever did with Dad. Now there was a mismatch made in Heaven. You and Dad got along fine, but you were both absorbed in your businesses. Dad breathed construction and you embodied nursing. It was like living with two Mount Olympus Gods. I'm like you, I'm out to save the world. Dad, on the other hand, wanted to build the perfect homes. He did, too. This place is a monument to his genius. He built it so you could fulfill your dreams. But he also built something that speaks to the beauty of wood, rock, and glass. I guess he figured if people came here to contemplate the spiritual nature of their chosen vocations, they needed their environment to be serene."

"He did that alright." Mildred agreed.

"Mom, you aren't going to marry Quim, are you?" She peered at Mildred edgily.

"What in the world . . ."

"I know, I know, it's none of my business." Renee's words tumbled out of her mouth. "I just have to tell you, though, I think it would be a very bad idea."

"I'm curious why?" Mildred inquired.

"Because he's such a futz!" The words burst in a torrent, "he's fussy, prissy, everything just so, and to top it off, he doesn't like kids."

"Come on, Renee, how can you say that? He's always been wonderful to all of you girls, and he certainly loves your children."

"No, Mom. He tolerates my children. Kids know when someone likes them. Now, John likes them. He loves them, even. He comes to visit me and the kids a lot. After you started to get better, he used to come to the house and take me and the kids out for hot dogs, to ball games, he even took us all to the symphony one afternoon. Said it was good "culturally for the children" He's actually a gas to be with!" Renee's eye twinkled with delight. "He even took the kids camping last summer when you were gone to Mexico."

"You never mentioned it." Mildred studied her daughter's face. "How come?"

"I just figured you'd think he was buttering me up to get on your good side. Sometimes I don't think you really know people at all. Being a Psychiatric Nurse and all, you shouldn't be so gullible with people." She watched Mildred's response.

"What do you mean?" Her mother asked, "You've never said anything like this before."

"Well I'll tell you, Mom. No one was threatening to kill you before you got involved with Dino Manuchi. Now I don't entirely agree with John about him, but I do agree you're in great danger. The people you can really trust around here are Francis, Freddy, and the crew. That's all!"

"Renee!" Mildred reacted, "I'm surprised at you. Quim maybe a futz, as you so succinctly put it, but he is certainly harmless. I've known him a long time, Renee. He was a good friend in college and he's still a good friend."

"Okay. I guess as long as he's a friend, it's okay. But if this guy starts making noises about marriage, you might as well know, none of us would be impressed with him as a stepfather." Renee got up from the chair. She looked uncomfortable. "Maybe I shouldn't have been quite so frank about it." She sighed. "It's hard to know what to say to your mother who's 62 and certainly is able to make up her own mind if she wants to get married again. I'm going to go help Freddy in the kitchen. We'll talk later, okay?"

"Fine," Mildred tried to keep a biting edge out of her voice. Its one thing for your children to be independent, quite another, she realized, when they assessed your friends differently than you.

*    *    *

The dining room table was beautiful. Freddy had outdone herself with the place settings and the silver. No one was dressed formally, except the table. It shone, sparkled, and glittered with crystal, silver, and china. Fresh flowers graced each place setting and the napkins were stiffly upright in molded position.

"Freddy taught us how to fold formal napkins, Grandma." Hunter stated as he bowed his head for Grace.

"I see that," replied Mildred. She glanced around the table. Everyone was here; even John had arrived in time for the Pork Roast Sublime, as Freddy referred to it. "Let's pray." She said simply.

After Grace was said, the food was passed with amazing speed. Soon everyone was talking to everyone else. John had arrived just as the food was placed on the table. This caused a number of comments on the detective qualities of his stomach. Freddy had invited George Bonnaunt up from his isolated place in the lower level of the house. The candles spread gentle light. It flickered and glowed, touching silver and glassware. The setting was so genteel; it was hard to believe a murder had occurred that morning.

Mildred began to comment on this train of thought, when Freddy interrupted her, "I know what you're thinking. Just forget it for the time being. After dinner is soon enough to begin dealing with reality again. Consider this a time of fortification and taking on energy. I am a great believer that we can handle anything, we just have to prepare ourselves for it." "Since when did you get so philosophical?" inquired Quim. "I don't recall you being so spiritual when we were in college."

"Quim, you haven't talked with me about anything deeper than the rhubarb pie we're having for dessert. Ever! I have been a student of The Spiritual Path since I finished my BS at the U. To give you credit, you did go on to good old Harvard for your graduate work, and missed my conversion. I went down to visit a friend in Madison one weekend. There's a Buddhist Center there just outside the city. I met several very interesting people and began to study. Of course I realized early on, the contemplative life was not for me. I did have a great desire to study psychology. So this took most of my energy. I did, however, begin to practice Yoga exercises. During my practice I began to attend seminars and retreats based in the Buddhist philosophy. I got interested. Actually, it inspired me to return to college and get my MD." Freddy glanced around the table. "Good grief! My life story isn't so interesting that I'm the only one talking."

"Oh, Aunt Freddy," Renee, "I think it's very interesting. We should look at doing what Mom has always wanted to do here, offer some retreats and seminars. You could be the star of the show!"

"That's not the point of the Buddhist Way." Freddy answered, "It's actually quite a simple life that's espoused."

"I know. I still think it would be a great idea to begin doing some of the things my mother and dad had in mind. This place is too big for family living. It was designed to be a center for contemplation and retreat. I was kidding you about being the star of the show. But, you do know more about it than anyone here."

"She's right." stated Mildred. "We really should talk about this idea. I know you don't have the time to do retreats, but you do know people who do. I think we could spark a great deal of interest in the Twin Cities with spiritual retreats so close to the city. A person could easily get here for weekends without a lot of traveling."

"How many people could attend?" The question surprised Mildred, as it came from George Bonnaunt. "I haven't had the chance to really look over the building, but it looks like you could accommodate quite a few people."

Mildred thought about the question. She and Emil had considered what size the groups should be to have the best interaction between attendees. They actually had done quite a lot of thinking and discussing on the topic. "We thought the small groups should not exceed ten people. This would give the intimacy for really in-depth discussion. The larger groups, twenty or more, would be more geared for day seminars. A taste, so to speak, of the topic. Then if someone wanted more detailed study, they would be encouraged to attend either weekend or week long retreats."

George nodded. "It sounds like the two of you really looked into how to set up programs."

"I did. I was considering retirement right before the accident. After the trial, I was going to put in my resignation. I'd set up the Psychiatric Units and I had spent ten years there. That's enough time. I wanted to do some more creative things with people. Help them to study who they are, and hopefully discover themselves, spiritually and emotionally. I think we all need time for reflection and retreat. Life isn't just about making money and getting things. Although most of the world thinks that way, it isn't necessarily the best way to live." Mildred's face glowed as she spoke. "I think the greatest adventure a person can go on, is the discovery of the inner-self."

"Well put!" Quim's boisterous voice boom, "I agree. If you don't know who you are, you'll never be a success." He beamed around the table.

"Hear! Hear!" Alison's voice joined his. "I think it's a marvelous idea. Certainly beats creeping around here worrying about dead bodies in a ditch."

John pushed his chair back from the table, "excuse me for a minute." He got up and left the room.

Mildred's eyes followed him, then studied the people at the table, one by one. "I am inspired by the discussion of retreats and seminars. This has been a very pleasant discussion. Now, I think, it's back to reality for me. John and I will be in the library. Now, Erica and Hunter remember what I told you about staying out of the way."

"They can come with me," George's voice boomed. "They know the property and I have to walk the parameter. I might as well have some old hands to help me. They certainly know your back yard." His eyes queried Mildred's.

"They certainly do," She answered. Her attitude about George thawing a touch, "actually, Hunter helped set fence posts just last summer, so he knows where everything is." Mildred assured him.

"Great, well kids, you interested?"

"Oh boy!" Hunter responded. "You bet! Do we get to do surveillance too?" His excitement was palpable.

"Well, let's just say I need your expert advice." He smiled at him. "Let's go!" His glance took in both children.

Erica placed her napkin next to her plate. She looked solemnly at Mildred, as she rose from her chair. "You just be sure and take care of yourself, Mamaw, I don't want to worry about you."

"Honey, you know I'll take care of myself. Nothing's going to happen to me. I still plan on dancing the jig at your wedding. So you go on, now. I'll be fine." She reassured.

After they left, it seemed like everyone spoke at once. Alison laughed at something said by Father Will. He had been silent much of the meal, now he joined in the conversation.

"Alison and I were talking about a trip we took to Chicago a few weeks ago. It was pretty interesting. We went to the old neighborhood.

Things have changed a lot since we left there. Lots of Asian and Mexican people in that area now. The place looks better, too."

"Yeah! The store my foster parents owned is now a shop for Asian foods. Really something. If you wanted to buy it, they had it. I've never seen anything quite like it."

"Sure you have, back when we were in Saigon. Gordon was in charge of Stores for the Army. I was stationed there as a Chaplain," he explained to the group, "and Alison was visiting her husband. It was back before things got too hot and nobody visited."

"It's odd! Now people are vacationing there." Alison said softly. "Back then, only the Military and the very brave went to Vietnam. I'd like to go back sometime."

"We used to go to the open markets. That's what the store in the old neighborhood reminded me of, the street markets in Saigon. Odd thing is, they stocked almost the same things."

"How long have you two known each other?" Quim asked.

"We met when we were kids. Will was living on the streets and I had just run away from home. My dad was a fringe member of the mob. I was being abused and I didn't like it. Even as a kid, I understood I didn't have to put up with the shit my dad was trying to dish out. He was selling me, plain and simple."

Freddy gasped. "My God! Alison. I didn't know that! Jeez, you've been through a lot of shit!"

"Yeah." Alison's voice reverted to her Chicago slang. It was never far away from her tongue. She had taught herself to sound more refined, but when she started talking about the old neighborhood and her childhood, her origins were unmistakable.

"How did you get started writing?" Quim asked.

"I kept a journal, even as a kid. I always liked make-believe. Probably 'cause my life was such as piece of shit in reality. I did write about the world as I saw it. Pretty strong stuff, my journals were not easy reading."

"Do you read them once in awhile?" Freddy was curious.

"Naw! I threw 'em out years ago. Don't want that stuff hanging around for somebody to read. Anyway, what's the point, it's not healthy to dig around in all that old stuff. When it's over, it's over, I like to think!" Alison emphasized.

"Boy, I wish that were the case for some of my clients." Freddy answered. "I have any number of people that wish they could let the past go and die a peaceful death. These people can't stop thinking about it."

"Well, you just have to make up your mind and do it," Insisted Alison. "It helps for me to write. Lots of my plots, 'hey that rhymes'. Anyway, a lot of my plotting follows some of the situations I had to deal with as a teenager in the streets of Chicago. But these stories always have a positive ending. Unlike some of the reality I grew up with."

"But you got out of there. How? What saved you?" Quim's voice was curious.

"Maybe I can answer that question." Father Will interjected. "Alison and I met each other. I was a thief and she was being abused. We were both smart kids. We knew there was another life outside of the streets, but we had to figure how to out get of there. Both of us had dropped out of school and were doing what we could to survive."

"Yeah! My foster father, whew! He was a bookmaker. Of course the reason he rescued me was 'cause I was a cute little girl, and he 'liked' little girls. What he didn't realize was I was smart. I was smarter than him, smarter than his soon to be dead wife, and smarter than most of the creeps he associated with every day." Alison spoke as if she were reading one of her stories. "It went on for three years. Like I said, my stepmother died, so the old man had me to himself. I was seventeen by then, no judge was going to put him in jail, and I realized I wasn't actually too bad off. I lived in a clean house, had enough food to eat. And I was the best dressed kid on the streets. So, I shut my mouth and put up with it. Besides, by then Will and I were getting ready to take the GEDs."

"An Episcopal Priest I had met was helping us. That was the beginning of my path into the church." Will shared. "That Priest was the first person, besides Alison, that was ever kind to me. He was my friend until he died."

"We passed the GEDs with flying colors. I applied for college. I guess I should back up a little. My stepfather died suddenly. One day he was there, the next he wasn't. What I didn't know is the creep was a multi-millionaire. He was a closet miser. He had a will and left the whole kaboodle to me. Storefront and all, was mine to do with as I wished. Like a fairy-tale come true, except for the incest part. Well, I'm smart enough to know I should shut up and take the money. I did. Will and I applied for Northwestern University and got accepted."

"We were both Summa Cum Laude graduates. We both got accepted into the University of Chicago. Then I decided to go into the ministry and we parted company for awhile. That's when Alison met Gordon. He was a graduate student in one of her classes."

"No wonder you write fiction. Your life reads like a Horatio Alger novel. Who else would survive all that and then write romance novels?"

"I gotta tell you, not many people." Alison agreed.

*     *     *

John was waiting for Mildred in the library. He was ensconced in the wing back chair he favored. A pipe was clamped in his teeth. On the coffee table in front of him was a small spiral notebook. It was the same brand, the same size he used in college. Mildred couldn't help but smile at the picture of disgruntled contentment in front of her. John was struggling to keep from being seduced by the deep comfort of the plump cushions. He looked like a man torn between two loves; one a commitment of honor, the other a commitment of the heart. She wondered which would win.

"Good, I'm glad you're here. I won't keep you long, Mil, but I have to go over your statement from this morning." He settled back in the chair with the notebook on the broad arm. He flipped it open with practiced ease to the last dog-eared pages.

"Okay, let's start from the time you woke up this morning. You said you heard noises in the field."

"Horses, John, I said I heard the nickering of the horses and the sound usually puts me back to sleep." Mildred longed for the feel of soft and cool sheets wrapped around her. She longed for sleep that would erase the events of the morning and take her back to yesterday. Last night she had been so tired, so worn out from the unnatural heat of this May. She had been exhausted from being in Minneapolis all day at a meeting for the Women's Shelter. She had slept from the moment her head had hit the pillow.

The nicker of the horses had awakened her. The faint slam of a car door surfaced in her memory. "John, I think the reason the horses were restless wasn't just the heat. I think they heard something. I just barely can remember what sounded like a car door shutting."

"What time?" He body leaned forward pressing for the information. "Did you look at the clock? Was it light yet? Anything that will give a fix on the time he was put there."

"I can't say I looked at the clock, John. However, it was way before sunrise. I didn't fall back to sleep as soundly, and then I finally got up and got dressed. I was out in the stable getting Maud saddled by 6 AM. We puttered in the exercise ring for awhile, before we set out to pick up the morning paper. The paper usually gets here around 6:30, so there was no point in heading out there too early." Mildred sipped her coffee.

John leaned back in his chair and studied her. "I can't believe this." He sighed. "Honest to God, if gray hair comes from worry and concern, I should be snow white by now. Mildred, I've been telling you for a year to be careful. I have always thought it was just a matter of time before some two-bit criminal was gonna come out here and blow you away. It's like they just kinda put you on ice, so to speak. They know where you are, they know who your family is, they know your friends. Jeez, Mildred, these people are gonna kill you." His frustration was rising by the second, "but you just keep on going along like nothin' in the world is gonna touch ya."

"John, we have been through this a thousand times. I will not live my life in a prison. Even if it's a beautiful one like this house. I want to be able to come and go, I want to be able to shop, and go to movies, and live like other people."

"You aren't quite like other people. You are only alive by some miraculous medicine and hard work. I do not want to lose you again." He emphasized by slapping his notebook on the table. "Mildred, can we just come to some understanding here? Could you please listen to what I have to propose?

"What?" Mildred knew John was upset, but she had not quite understood the depth of his concern until this moment. "Alright. What is it you want me to do? I'll do it, if for no other reason than Renee and the kids are here. I will follow your instructions to the absolute letter." Her face bore the resolute appearance of a person who has accepted the inevitable.

"For starters, you are not to go anywhere without George along with you. I don't care where it is. When you go out in the field, to the stable, to the pool, anytime you step foot outside of this building, I want him or one of his men, with you. Got that?" He demanded.

"I also want you to limit your social contact for the next . . . at least few weeks."

"Now wait a minute, John. I've got some obligations I can't just walk away from with a snap of the finger. There are two very important meetings involving the Shelter Programs. I have got to be there for those. I'm the chair of the committee. These are two times when George is going to learn more about battered women than he ever dreamt."

"It'll be good for him." John countered. "I want you to list all the events you can't miss. Cancel everything else. I want to know what the schedule is starting with tomorrow morning. I don't want anything to change, or you to deviate from the plan at all. Got that?"

Mildred smiled. She knew exactly what John was driving at. From the time she was a child, she had a habit of straying from the organized, to the adventurous. She was the bane of her school teachers from the time she was old enough to walk, talk, and attend school. Her parents could have wall-papered the house with notes sent home from teachers during grammar school. It only seemed to exacerbate with age. Emil had despaired about these habits. Her three daughters just rolled their eyes and went on about their business when Mildred went off on a tangent. At this point, Mildred felt she was doing much better with this penchant for change. The accident had curtailed her adventurous spirit somewhat, but had not diminished it.

She didn't quite know when she realized John was quiet. She glanced at him and what shocked to see the naked look of concern on his face. Her hand went involuntarily to her mouth. "John, don't look at me like that. It scares me!"

He looked startled. "I'm tired, Mildred. Maybe they're right. Maybe it's time I retire." His heavy eyebrows drew together in thoughtful contemplation. "Maybe, I'm just getting too damn old and crabby to pull it off anymore. God knows, I think the Murder Squad would love to rid of me."

"John, you're right! You're tired, you've been up since before I woke up this morning, and it's late. Tell me honestly, is there any more you can do this evening? I mean really. All the forensic evidence has been gathered, labeled, and sent to the lab. The troops are going to canvas the neighborhood for any possible sighting of something weird. All the people you need to talk to have been seen. So, what's keeping you from going home and getting a good nights sleep?"

He looked at her. The haunted brooding returned to his eyes. "The truth is, Mildred, I'm scared to death if I leave you, something will happen and I'll lose the best friend I ever had. I could never forgive myself if they got to you. This has nothing to do with being a cop. This has to do with the fact that I have cared about you since the first time I ever laid eyes on you back in Minneapolis." He pushed his hair back off his forehead and smoothed it down." I know you broke up with me because I was so damned intense. It's true. I have the same problem with that as you have with your damned, adventurous spirit. The fact is, though, the two of us have made it to our sixties. I have learned a couple things. One of them is, I'll be damned if I'll lose our friendship, such as it is, by letting myself get carried away again."

"You're not going to lose our friendship, John. We both need to work on our intense natures. It's just the way we are. Just like you can't change the color of your eyes, you can't change your basic personality."

"Well, you've got the namby-pamby hanging around again."

"Quim?" Mildred inquired. "Namby-Pamby? Where do you pull these archaic names from, John?" She snickered. "You're the second person tonight to point out Quim's personality traits."

"Who else? Not Freddy? She likes him! I can't believe she'd find fault with the paragon of virtue." He zinged his sentiments at her. "He is so futsy! Always so proper. How in the hell can you stand to be around this guy, much less have him stay here? When I suggested you call him, I didn't mean for him to move in. Be careful, Mildred. This guy thinks you're gonna marry him."

"Marry!" What are you talking about, John? Quim hasn't even been on a real date with me. What in the world would make you think he's planning marriage?"

"Trust me, Mil, I've been around the block a couple of times. I maybe get a little cranky sometimes, get moody, you know how I am. I'm still observant. When I retire, the best homicide detective in this county is going off the payroll. I know people and how they think. I know what they're thinking, before they know what they're gonna think. So it isn't hard for me to know what Jeff Quimby Anderson is up to here."

She raised a hand in protest. "You cannot be serious. Quim hasn't said a word to me about wanting to . . . ." She hesitated. "Well, he has said a couple of things about how lucky he was to run into me at Orchestra Hall." She mused.

"I just know people. This is a guy who has never married. He has lived in apartments all his life. He's had really good jobs and great pay, but he's still a 'working stiff', so to speak. He's thinking about retirement, he's thinking maybe it's time he took a good look at the future and how he's gonna live. He's thinking, maybe Mildred doesn't look too bad at 62 years old. Especially since she still has interest in a construction company and she owns 160 acres of prime real estate in East Bethel."

"That sounds so mercenary. You make him out to be a soldier of fortune, or something." Mildred interjected.

"I'll tell you Mildred, there are a few things you don't know about Quim. A lot of years have passed since we were in college. I was older than you two, went to school on the GI Bill. Quim was a guy creating a persona. He did not grow up in tweeds, with daddy smoking stogies and drinking high-class brandy after dinner at night. His dad was a steel—worker in Indiana and mom was a waitress. Tell me something. Has he ever suggested to you that you meet his mother?" John asked her.

"No, why?" Mildred answered with a question.

"Cause his momma lives here in Minneapolis now. He moved her here about five years ago from Chicago area. He has her placed in a very nice nursing home. Nothing fancy, but a good one. He never visits her."

"How in the world do you know that?" Mildred asked. "Where's his father? Is he still around?"

"Naw! He was involved in an industrial accident and died. There was a fairly good settlement for mom. That's when Quim moved her here to the Twin Cities." He paused before he spoke again. "It really is a great nursing home. They don't let her get lonely. If the guests don't have visitors, the nursing home has a fleet of volunteers who come in on a regular basis. They kind of adopt the residents who don't have anybody."

"How did you find out about this?" Mildred wanted to know.

"In my investigation two years ago." He watched her face as he spoke. "When someone is a victim of attempted murder, lots of people get investigated. Quim was one of your friends. He hadn't seen you for awhile, but you corresponded on a regular basis."

"You investigated Quim?" She demanded. "Who else?"

"Oh, let's see. Freddy, Justine, employees of the construction company, I could go on, but most of the rest were just grabbing at straws."

"My god! I had no idea. Why would you think any one of these people would have wanted to kill me?"

"Didn't know for sure. It was obvious the reason was probably connected to Manuchi, but we still had to check out people you were close to and could gain by your death. Even Emil was checked out. Now that wasn't my idea. Emil would never have done anything to hurt you, that I know."

"I'm thankful for that!" She commented with a touch of sarcasm. "How could you be so sure about Emil?"

"All those fishing trips. You can't spend that kind of time with a guy and not begin to understand how he thinks. Now Emil was a go-getter.

He really was a more cut-throat business man than you realized, Mil, but he was as straight as a person could be. This man breathed honesty. That's why he was so successful. He was an outstanding architect and builder. But, he was also a person of great integrity. He didn't cut corners, he didn't try to con people into something they couldn't afford or didn't want, he didn't push. He listened to his clients and then gave them the best building he could construct for them." John had obviously thought about Emil quite a bit. "We got to be pretty damn good friends. He knew how I felt about you. He also knew I'd never interfere with your marriage."

Mildred looked shocked, "well of course not." She paused thoughtfully, "so where did your investigation lead you? You obviously cleared my friends. Right?"

"Yeah! Everybody checked out, even Quim."

"So where is his mother?" she inquired. "How old is she? He still isn't visiting her?"

"Nope! Got to give the guy the credit he deserves. He does work hard. And, he did spend close to 15 months in Britain at Oxford. But filial duties do not seem to be part of his plan. He's a good professor and writer, not too great as a son."

"He is a great writer. His travel articles are everywhere. I see him in National Geographic on a regular basis." She smoothed her blouse with her hand and looked at him thoughtfully. "But that doesn't make him a great son, is that what you're implying? So where do you go from here? What are we gonna do, John?

"Just remember, Mildred, some advice my mother gave to me. Look at how your friends treat their mothers. That's how they'll treat their wives some day." John watched her face. "My mother was pretty smart. She was good with people, too."

Mildred laughed. At first it was just the touch of a smile, and then it broadened. His remark about being 'good with people, too," implied his mother was as good with people as he was. The John Jacobs, Mildred knew was intense, pushy, a regular ferret as he went after information. The very thought of him as 'good with people' sent her howling within half a minute. "You can't be serious!" burst from her lips. "John, you have alienated more people with your interrogation techniques, than anyone I know." She gasped between snorts of laughter.

"Well, what I meant was, I'm an excellent investigator. Mil, you don't have to . . ." he protested as she continued to laugh.

"Oh, John, surely you realize how ridiculous it sounded. 'My mother was good with people, too.' I know what you're driving at, but it just struck me so funny." She wiped a tear from her eye.

He started to laugh, too. It might have been because he was so tired, it might have been the release of tension, or it just might have been the sight of Mildred holding her sides and shaking with laughter. He kept trying to stop, but then he would picture how serious he looked when he made his comment to Mildred. Each time they began to feel a lessening of the mirth, they would look at one another, and start in again.

Mildred thought it might have gone on all night, when the door opened and Freddy's voice inquired," are you two okay?" This brought on another round, but they were able to finally regain some control, and offered a muffled, "Yeah, we're okay."

"I've gotta go home and get some sleep. I must be punchy. Just keep in mind you've gotta follow the security rules and things will go fine."

"By the way, you mentioned something about leopards and spots. What were you talking about?" Mildred asked as she walked him to the front door.

""We'll talk another time. I've got an idea for a partnership, you and me. No, Mildred, don't get that look," he answered the unspoken comment, "I'm not talking marriage here. We'll get to it. Promise, Okay?" his voiced lifted with the question.

"Alright. I'll talk with you tomorrow." She said to his retreating back. She closed the door.

# CHAPTER SEVEN

Mildred rode the small elevator to the third floor. As the door slid open, she heard the sound of voices in the sitting area. Freddy and Quim were there, as well as Renee. The children had gone to bed. Renee had insisted after their trek around the property, a shower and bedtime was in order.

Hunter had squawked about it, but Erica was stoic and accepting. Both of them had fallen asleep as soon as they hit their beds.

The discussion was lively. Mildred wasn't sure she was up to this. Her neck was stiff with tension and she wanted nothing more than a warm Jacuzzi and the comfort of her bed. "I hope you aren't planning to camp out here." She stated, "I'm not fit for anything but my bath and my bed."

"We were just coming up with a general plan of action. Dividing up the duties, so to speak." Quim said as he emptied his pipe in the ashtray. He gently bumped the bowl to encourage any additional tobacco to come loose. "We decided that no one should go off on their own. So we've come up with a plan to guarantee togetherness." He smiled at Mildred.

"God help us," Mildred rejoined, "I know your famous plans, Freddy. Never let this woman organize your vacation plans, or you won't have any scheduled time for naps, side-trips, or sleep at night." She shared this information with the other two participants. "I am not going to have you set up my day for me, guys. So forget it! I am also not going to sit here and discuss this hare-brained idea til midnight, or some god-awful hour. I am going to bed. If you want to organize a time to make plans for tomorrow morning, that's fine. I'll be up at 5 AM."

"Are you joking?" Freddy's voice lifted in pitch. "Surely you are not serious?"

"Oh, but I am." Mildred assured with a grin. "I get up quite early, as you well know. If you want to have a chance to discuss the guidelines for security here, you'd better plan to get up early. George is going to want to set some basic rules. His partner is also going to be here then," she thought for a moment. "His name is Joel Beaumont. He sounds like an interesting guy. George didn't tell me much about him, but apparently he was a DJ in one of the nightclubs. The guy is a genius with sound equipment. He and George apparently met on one of George's jobs. He was impressed with Joel's skills and encouraged him to come into the security business. I guess the guy thought it was a good idea. Anyway, he's George's partner, so he must be damned good.

"That George is an interesting fella," Quim said tentatively. "I'm not sure he's the kind of person I could develop any rapport with or not." He was now sucking vigorously on the pipe stem. "Damn things! Half the time they don't draw right and the other half of the time, you run out of your favorite tobacco." He grinned at the group and went after the pipe bowl with a cleaning tool.

Mildred looked at her daughter. "Renee, you need to get some sleep. So do I. I'll be down in the kitchen at 6 AM. If the rest of you want to meet there, fine. Otherwise, I'll fill you in on what George thinks we need to do. I know Alison won't be up at that hour. She is in bed, right?" Her voice lifted with the question. "She looked exhausted at dinner. Will said he was going to visit with her for awhile and then see to it that she got settled in for the night. I suspect he meant, he'd make sure he got some medications in her to settle her nerves."

"The woman's . . . ." Freddy saw the look on Mildred's face, "got some problems."

"That's as kind a statement as I have heard you make all evening," Quim shared. "We've been having a meeting of the 'rescue fair damsels and change them into well-functioning women' committee this evening. Alison was the agenda item."

"She blew me away with her monologue about her childhood. I'm glad the kids were gone with George when she talked about it." Renee stated.

"I don't think she would have brought it up, if they had been there. She's not totally out-there," Freddy admitted. "Actually, she's a hell of a smart woman. You're right about that, Mildred. God, I feel like I'm sitting in a college dorm, raking someone over the coals. 'Get over it!' I'm telling myself. I've got an attitude about her all right. I do need to take a look at that." Freddy rose from the overstuffed couch she was sitting on, "I'm going to bed. If you're serious about 6 AM, I need to get my beauty rest." She touched Quim's sleeve, "Come on, Quimby, you big bear. It's time for Goldilocks to go to bed. Escort me to the sleep chamber, and then you go to bed, too." She ordered him.

The two of them walked down the stairs to the second floor. Mildred rose and walked slowly to her bedroom. Renee was right behind her and followed her in. "Just a sec', mom," she said. "Do you think it's a good idea to have me and the kids here? We could go to Lisa Jane's in White Bear."

"I think you are as safe here as you would be there, probably safer. If someone really wanted to get at me through the children, they would have an easier time of it away from here. Your dad was very thoughtful about this security system. The entire property is set up for observation. George told me it's one of the best systems he's ever encountered in the 'private sector', as he put it."

"I had no idea dad was so conscious of that kind of thing," Renee answered. "He never talked about being worried about burglary and theft."

"The break-in at the company four years ago got him worried about it. You know how he was about his designs. There are plans here in his office that the three of you have never seen. He was started on a new concept for a project in Colorado when he died. The plans are in a drawer down there. I just haven't thought about them. I suppose the three of you should take them to the company and look them over. The client hired a different architect when Emil died. I haven't heard from him since then."

"Well," Renee gave Mildred a hug, "I just wanted to see what you thought. I agree, it's better for us to stay here with you. Just promise me you will be careful. I'm worried about you. I know how you get an idea and then race off to check it out. You just can't keep doing that right now. John's really worried about you. That's why I wanted to talk to you alone. He thinks whoever is behind Manuchi's murder, doesn't mean to let you get away again. I just don't understand it! There must be something you know, that you don't remember. What did you and Dino talk about when he was in the hospital?"

"Honest to God, Renee, I don't remember anything significant. There was nothing, NADA," she emphasized emphatically. "We simply never had any conversation that in any way could be construed to be something important! It just didn't happen!" Mildred's frustration was evident.

"That's what's so maddening. It isn't something I forgot because of the accident. There was nothing to forget."

"Okay, mom, I believe you. Let's hope that we can somehow communicate the truth to whoever is behind his death. I don't want to lose my mother, too. It was hell when we didn't know if you'd live or die. I don't ever want go through anything like that again. I mean, think about it! Why would someone in the mob want to kill someone who isn't involved in their business? It doesn't make sense." Renee expounded.

Mildred sighed deeply. "I know, Renee. I agree. I do know this, too, I am not going to stop my life and my commitments because of it. If I do that, then I've let someone else take charge of my life and my choices. I'd rather be dead, than do that to myself. Look, it's late, you go get some sleep. Nothing is going to happen tonight." She gave her daughter a hug and escorted her to the door. "I'll see you in the morning."

Mildred was right. The night passed quietly.

# CHAPTER EIGHT

Mildred awoke in the morning with a cat on her chest. He was kneading his paws into her quilt and making demands for breakfast.

"Honestly, Pyewacket, isn't anyone else awake yet? Whoo! You have sharp needles, cut it out!" She urged the cat over to the side of the bed with a firm hand.

She sat up in the bed and looked out the window. There was fog in the low fields near Settler's Pond. It engulfed one end of the horses' pasture. Horse's silhouettes appeared like muted corks bobbing on the surface of a cottony lake. It was an eerie kind of comfort, but the fog added to Mildred's sense of security.

She got up and went into the bathroom. The cat, aggravated at being excluded, protested loudly and slipped his claws under the door. "Shush!" her voice was heard, "I'll be out right away. You are not going to melt away like a starving waif."

The sound of water running in the sink seemed to satisfy him. He sat back on his haunches and waited. When she appeared, Mildred had slipped into a jogging suit and a pair of thick socks. The cat, ever compliant when food was in the very near future, followed her out of the room, down the stairs, and into the kitchen. When he had been given his morning rations, Mildred focused on preparing a large urn of coffee.

While the coffee perked, she stepped out of the kitchen into a covered screen porch. It was an informal living area with wicker couches, chairs, rockers, and a wicker dining table that easily seated ten.

Mildred sat in one of the rockers facing the woods. She remembered when she and Emil would sit out here for hours after dinner. The day would drift slowly into the evening, and then into the night. Sometimes they would watch the inky blackness until a parade of stars had marched across the sky. That was the year before Mildred's accident.

She thought of that year as one of the happiest of her life. It was the first time she and Emil spent significant amounts of time together. It was before Dino Manuchi was incarcerated on her psychiatric unit. It was before the drug trial.

Now, with the morning light beginning to seep across the maple floor of the porch, she realized how much she loved living in this house. She acknowledged how the beautiful planes of wood, rock and glass seemed to envelop her in the security and warmth of her departed husband's presence. After all the tragedy and loss, it felt as if he was still here, protecting her.

"It's so odd," she remarked audibly.

"What's odd?" Freddy's sleepy voice drifted to her from the kitchen doorway.

"Oh!" Mildred turned, startled, "I really didn't think you'd get up this early."

"I can be quite the early-bird if I have to," Freddy answered. "But I do need coffee. Is it ready yet?"

"Should be." Mildred walked past her in the doorway. She checked the urn. The red light was on indicating the brewing was completed. Mildred poured two steaming cups, adding a dollop of cream to her cup. "Let's go back out on the porch." She led the way.

"What was so odd?" Freddy reverted to her original question.

"I was just thinking how comfortable I have always felt in this house. It's almost like it's alive somehow." She looked at Freddy from under lowered lids, "I know it sounds childish, magical even. But, it is a special place to me. Maybe it's because Emil took such pains to create a place where I would feel it was mine. That is what he did. We really had some interesting ideas for this farm."

"Like what?" Freddy inquired curiously, "I mean . . . ." She paused for words, "I always knew you wanted to have retreats here, but it sounds like there was more to it than just that. Having retreats, I mean. What else were the two of you thinking about besides education or spiritual seminars?"

"We toyed with the idea of having a place where elderly people could live together. There's a lot of acreage here. We thought about construction of four bedroom homes, single-story, handicapped accessible, for the elderly. Places where folks with little income besides Social Security could live together and pool their resources. The sticking point would be finding compatible elderly to share these homes."

Mildred sat back in her chair. "Actually I do have two homes like that now. They're located in the city. The houses are nothing special. They're set up like foster homes for the elderly. I have a live in manager in each of them. The people who live there are physically and mentally stable. There are no residents who have dementia or anything that causes mental impairment. It was an experiment to see if it would work. And, it does seem to be working. Emil and I bought two big old houses in Minneapolis and did some rehab on them before I had the accident."

"How many people are living there?" Freddy asked.

"Each house has seven residents. It operates like a family setting. Every one pitches in and does the chores. Stuff like dishes, cleaning, grass cutting, meals, preparing the household budget. There haven't been any serious problems. Once in awhile the residents get to arguing among themselves. Then the manager helps to solve the conflict".

"Almost like communes . . . ." Freddy mused. "The idea's not bad, you know. There are an awful lot of older people who don't have any family, who end up living by themselves. It's not always by choice that they're alone." She looked at Mildred closely, "are you still thinking of doing this out here?"

"Actually, yes." Mildred answered. "I was going to talk with my daughters about it. They manage the Construction Company now. Emil had several designs for groups of homes, in a cul-de-sac. We were thinking of using the twenty acres that front on E. Bethel Blvd. The stickler is how many people would be living there and how would the county, state, and federal agencies feel about a retirement community out here."

"Bingo!" Freddy said cocking her finger like the universal sign for a small handgun, and pulling the trigger. "When you have to involve the government, it's always a hassle." Freddy was sitting in one of the wicker chairs by the window. "Lots of paperwork and detail planning. Gee, are you going to need an experienced psychologist?"

"I hadn't thought about it, Freddy." Mildred sipped her coffee.

"Ah, a chance for future planning. I'm at that age, you know. Now I suppose we need to talk about what's going on around here. It would be nice if we could ignore it, but that's not gonna happen."

"I haven't thought about much else." Mildred assured. "It really helped to get a good nights sleep. I didn't think I would, but I did."

"It's like the worst has happened, and you're still here. There isn't much you can do to control someone else. So," Freddy reflected reasonably, "what we have to do is to look at how we want to handle the situation. What are the important things, and what are the priorities for doing them."

A movement at the kitchen doorway caught their attention. Alison and Quim stood there. Alison looked more relaxed than she had when she went to bed the previous evening. Mildred surmised she had taken something for sleep and it had worked.

"Planning the day's events?" Quim inquired, "I have a couple of appointments in town that I really shouldn't put off. I'll leave right after rush-hour and be back here by 2 or 2:30 this afternoon. I hope that will work all right. Or," he turned toward Mildred, "do you need for me to be here? I can cancel if I have to, I just need to know soon, so I can make the calls."

"I have a luncheon engagement," Alison chimed in, "I could drive in with you and then I wouldn't have to go by myself. I'm meeting a friend, but I think it would be okay if you dropped me at her place. She could drive us to the restaurant where we're having a meeting with my agent and my attorney."

"I could do that." Quim answered amiably. "John sort of implied we should travel in twos or more, if we could."

Mildred spoke to both of them, "now look, I think it is important for us to continue to live our lives. I have no intention of changing my everyday life and my commitments. That would feed right into what this person wants. I will not live in fear and I will not let someone else control my behavior." She emphasized her feelings, "after being as close to death as I have been, there are no secret places I'm afraid of anymore. So, my advice to you is this! Go and do what you have to do. Besides, I don't think anyone else is the target. I think it is clearly me alone who is in danger."

"What about the kids? You don't think they're at risk?" Alison asked with wide eyes. "I should think you would worry about them, even if you're not concerned about yourself." Her eyes bored accusingly into Mildred's.

"No, I don't think so. For one thing, I have never spoken to my grand-children about Dino Manuchi. What would have been the point? They don't have a clue about his hospitalization or who he was. I have never been aware the mob takes out children. I suppose it could happen accidentally when they've been after someone else. But," she answered Alison matter-of-factly, "unless they're dealing with a hard-core adolescent who's been working the streets, kids are usually not on hit lists."

"I suppose you're right. You probably know more than I do about it." She answered in agreement.

"I don't know, Mildred. I think Alison's right. This is no place for the kids. You should send them somewhere else while this is going on. They could get hurt! Then what? You'd never forgive yourself"

Mildred felt a chill down her spine. What if the children were in danger? She realized what Quim was saying was true. She'd could never forgive herself if something happened to them.

Freddy was out of her chair and at Mildred's side. "Look, you two, cut her some slack! Mildred's been through a lot of shit since yesterday morning. If you want my opinion, I don't think the kids are in danger from the killer. First, Mildred's clearly the target. Second, I think attempts would have been made at their own home. For God's sake, people know where Renee lives. These kids would have been targets long before this. If somebody really wanted to get to Mildred through the kids, it would have happened a long time ago. Think about it. Now for crying out loud, give it a rest, dammit!" Freddy practically screamed at Alison. "You keep your melodramas in your damn books."

Mildred put a hand on Freddy's arm. "Take it easy, Freddy. I don't think Alison meant to get everybody all worked up."

"I didn't," she agreed swiftly, "I just don't want anybody to get hurt. I've seen enough hurt and pain in my life to last forever. I just want it to stop!"

Quim put an arm around her and glared at Freddy. "Sometimes, you just piss me off." He led Alison to the table, "let me get you some coffee. We all need to calm down and act rational. Isn't that your stock in trade?" he directed at Freddy.

"Okay, I was a little hasty, I apologize." She said to Alison. "I do have a tendency to be a bit overprotective of Mildred."

"I'm a little short-tempered myself." Quim interjected. "I surely don't want anything to happen to you either, Mildred. I have a vested interest in your continued health and long life."

Freddy looked at him, "Quim, do I detect a romantic interest here? Am I the John Alden to your Miles Standish?"

He blushed. "Pfh! I'm just concerned, that's all. You're one of my oldest friends. I surely don't want to see anything happen to you." Quim continued as smoothly as he could.

Freddy looked at him closely. Then she got up from her seat next to Mildred. "Well, since you're up Sir Galahad, I'll leave you to protect the ladies and I'll go and fix us up some breakfast. How's that sound?" She asked the group.

"You have my vote of confidence," Quim said. "If you need assistance I would be most happy to help." He offered.

"I'm more apt to be creative by myself." Freddy answered quickly. She went into the kitchen and closed the door behind her.

# CHAPTER NINE

Freddy outdid herself for breakfast. She made Omelets to order. Renee and the children must have smelled bacon and ham sizzling in the frying pan. All of them showed up eagerly looking for breakfast.

Renee pushed aside Freddy's insistence she could do it by herself, and organized the kids for the job of setting the table on the porch. While this task was in process, no one was able to converse without raising their voices. They argued which tablecloth to use and then, which glasses matched the pottery dishes. The banter was good natured and soon they were all laughing as Erica filled them in on the evening's activities.

"I know we walked through Poison Ivy. I took a shower and really scrubbed myself after I put our clothes in the washer. I think bleach and strong soap will get out the oils. I can't guarantee Hunter did the same. He never washes his hands right!" She said.

"I do, too!" Hunter yelled at her. "I did a good job. I told mom and she checked me out." He stuck his tongue out at her.

George and Joel arrived from the lower level and added to the confusion. George confirmed the Poison Ivy patch to Mildred. "We'll have to get some weed killer out there. It's right on the fence line, east of the field road to the house on County Rd. 74. I'm going to close off that access for the time being. We don't want anyone using that road. It'll make security a lot easier."

"I told him where Grandpa kept the fence panels in the barn. We're gonna work on it today." Hunter shared proudly. "I'm gonna help with security. He said I could."

George looked at Mildred. "We need to sit down this morning and go over the plans Joel and I worked out. It'll be helpful if all of you let us know what your schedules are for the next week. I am going to put one of my men at the front of the driveway, by the bridge. That way we can have some control over who comes and goes, at least by vehicle."

"Alison and I are going into Minneapolis this morning. She and I both have meetings, but we should be able to get home by 2:30 or so. I have some business appointments I really don't want to miss. Alison is meeting with her friend for lunch. We'll come back together when we're done."

"Sounds like a plan," George agreed. "What about you, Mildred, do you have to go anywhere today?"

"No, I think I need to sit down with you and decide how we're going to arrange everything. John should probably be involved in whatever we decide. If we don't involve him, he'll find a problem with it, sure as shooting." She said to George.

"He's pretty much left it up to me. Says security isn't his business. But, you're right, I want him to know exactly what I have in mind before we get too much planned."

Alison got up from the table, "I'm going to get ready. Quim, When do you want to leave?" She directed at him.

"If we could be out of here by 9 o'clock I would be happy. My appointments are at 10:30 and 1 o'clock. I should be set to come back by 2:30 or so. Is that going to give you enough time with your luncheon?" He inquired of her.

"Sure. We're going to discuss some preliminary business. Ashley has written a book. It's really quite extraordinarily good. I am introducing her to my agent. I invited my attorney, just in case."

"Just in case?" Freddy asked.

"Just in case Ashley has impressed my agent. If that happens, she'll need an attorney to sign the contracts. It pays to do these things right." She stated. "I'd better get ready, you know how long it takes me, and Quim is on a time line." She left the room.

The children cleared the table after their mother made the suggestion they help. Renee and Freddy loaded the dishwasher and cleaned up the kitchen and porch. George and Mildred sat on the porch and watched the horses.

"I've pretty much got the system checked out," George assured her. "Joel's going to camp out here with me, to keep an eye on the cameras. The rest of the surveillance can be done by placing a person at the main drive around the clock. We'll need a couple of people to releave us once in awhile, down in the security room. I can't look at a screen all the time."

He leaned back in the chair and stretched. "Your late husband did a helluva job when he had this system installed. We can literally watch the entire grounds from the control room. I am amazed how many cameras are out there. They cover all the significant places on the entire grounds."

"What about inside? I know Emil wanted to have security without invading people's privacy in their bedrooms."

"Nice of him!" George chuckled. "However, there's a system that monitors each room. If someone decides to exit the house from their bedroom window, they're gonna be on candid camera."

"What about listening?" She inquired.

"No sweat. Let's hope your guests aren't planning a coup. There is not a place in this house that I don't have access to, via monitoring equipment of one kind or another. It's state of the art." He grinned at her. "By the way, hope you don't mind me putting the grandson to work. Keep him busy, keep him outta mischief."

"It's a great idea. I just don't want him to be a pest. Renee has to be admitted to the hospital this evening. Her surgery is scheduled for tomorrow morning." She told him. "Both the kids are old enough to do a lot of things on their own. I never have any problems taking care of them, they're so self sufficient. I didn't plan on the circumstances, however."

"No one plans on murder." He answered her. "I've gotta call John. I don't suppose it matters when he comes over, does it?"

"No, I'm here all day. One of Renee's sisters is taking her to the hospital, so I don't have to leave for anything else. Tomorrow, of course, I plan to be at the hospital for a good part of the day. Renee is scheduled first thing in the morning. I've got to be there by 6:45 AM."

"Who'll be with the kids tomorrow?" George asked her.

"Francis will be here. She's coming back this afternoon. Freddy can't keep her out of her kitchen longer than a couple of meals. Francis has worked for me for the past twenty-five years. She was at Bald Eagle with Emil and I in our old house. She practically raised my children. I had a nanny before Francis came to us. Triplets are a handful, you know, and they were quite rambunctious."

"It's hard to picture you with triplets. I always think of you as the no-nonsense nurse, not as a mother with three kids running around under her feet."

"Well, George, it taught me one thing." She laughed, "I learned how to balance my time and juggle my obligations. Perfect training for administering a Psychiatric Hospital."

# CHAPTER TEN

Alison was excited. She hadn't seen Ashley for several months. Not since she had returned from the Grecian Islands. It had taken her by surprise to learn her friend had written a book. What was even more surprising, it was a Gothic Romance. She couldn't wait to read it.

Her finger lingered on the doorbell. What if it didn't go well? What if Ashley wasn't satisfied? What if she thought Alison could do more for her to help her get published?" He thoughts were interrupted, by the door flying open.

Ashley was there, arms opened wide to hug her friend. "I saw you coming up the walk. I'm so excited! I can hardly wait to get to lunch. Do you think there's a possibility he may like my book? Oh, Alison, I'm so thrilled you are doing this for me. I just can't thank you enough." Her happiness gushed over Alison in a flood.

"I'm happy to be able to help." Alison assured. "Are you ready? I thought we could do a little shopping while we're downtown. I avoid the place, but once I'm here, I usually enjoy going through the shops."

"I'll just grab my purse and the manuscript. It'll be safe in the car, won't it?" She inquired.

"Well, you've got a back-up copy right?" Alison asked.

"Absolutely. You'll never guess what it's filed under, so I'll tell you. 'Spirits!' Neat password, huh? Specters, haunting, ghosts, that kind of thing. I think it's kinda cool."

Alison smiled at her friend. They had been bosom buddies since the University of Chicago years. Ashley had been her maid of honor when she married Gordon. Will had been the best man. In college they had shared an apartment and sometimes dated the same men. Neither one of them had seriously contemplated getting married. Alison was shocked by her feelings when she met Gordon. She simply had to marry him.

"There are lots of ghosts in our past." Alison said laughingly. "I cannot imagine what it would be like without you there."

"Me neither, you've been my greatest fan." Ashley confided. "Well, I'm set, let's get going."

"Here's to success!" Alison quipped.

*　　*　　*

Two hours later they swanked into the darkened restaurant at the Whitcomb Hotel. It was conservative, elegant, and very expensive. Heavy linens and fine silver were carefully placed on mahogany dining tables. Chairs were delicate Chippendale. The draped windows overlooked the Mississippi River. At noon their delicate folds were pulled back discretely offering a dramatic view of the river.

Tables supported pools of subdued light emanating from flickering candles. They were escorted to a table occupied by two men. Both men rose. Each gave Alison a perfunctory kiss on the cheek and shook hands with Ashley, as they were introduced to her.

"I've taken the liberty of ordering you each a glass of wine." Alison's attorney Milton Bonnaventure offered. "I've placed you ladies together. Alison you're here, next to me."

She allowed herself to be seated. The four of them engaged in conversation about social things. To herself, Alison thought they sounded like four people who had nothing better to do than waste time, money, and energy, for no purpose. She knew that wasn't true, however it all felt so futile.

"Alison tells us you've written a book." Ronnie McDougal said to Ashley. "She's encouraged me to read it. Says you're quite talented and I couldn't go wrong taking you on as a client."

"I appreciate you're being willing to read it. It's hard to get an agent. They always want you to have a published book in your background. The publishers suggest you use an agent to submit your manuscripts. It's hard." Ashley stated matter-of-factly. "You can't seem to get an agent without being published and you can't seem to get published without an agent. It's kind of a vicious circle."

"Well, we'll see. If your manuscript is as good as Alison thinks it is, more than likely, I'll be interested in it. The wine was served to each of them. Alison had begun a conversation across the table to her attorney. Ashley was in conversation with the agent. Alison poured water from a crystal pitcher into their water glasses. Then as she began to interact with the attorney once again, she spoke, "this is silly. Ashley, you take my chair and I'll take yours. That way we won't be talking across the table and interfering with each other's conversations. What do you think?"

"Sure Ashley said," She rose and reached for her glass. "Hell, we don't need to change glasses; we haven't had any wine yet." She changed seats. Alison moved to the seat on her left, and Ashley moved to the right. She picked up her conversation with Ronnie." I think it's time for a toast though. I'm confident you're going to like my book and I feel like my writing career is about to take off for parts unknown." She raised her wine glass.

Everyone picked up their glasses and joined her, "Here's to success and happiness!" Ashley said.

"And here's to the future and all it will bring," added Ronnie. "I'd like another successful author."

They touched glasses and drank. Ashley drained her glass and sat down abruptly. At first it wasn't evident what was wrong. Then it became painfully clear. She was collapsing into her chair. She was dying in front of their eyes. Alison leaned toward her. Her body felt wooden. Her head felt light. A faint scent of bitter almonds reached her nostrils. Then she fell.

The Maitre De appeared from the shadows. "Madam! Is something wrong?" Even as the words spilled from his mouth, he knew what was wrong. He signaled for the second-in-command to call the police. He was an experienced restaurateur. He knew exactly what would happen next.

# CHAPTER ELEVEN

*"For in and out, above, about, below,*
*"Tis nothing but a magic shadow show.*
*Played in a box whose candle is the sun,*
*Round which we phantom figures come and go."*
*Omar Khayyam*

Mildred stopped for lunch at midday. She and Freddy were just dipping into bowls of Tomato Soup and Crackers, when John Jacobs materialized in the doorway. "Got some left for a starving man?" He inquired of them.

"Sure enough." Freddy answered. "Just help yourself. Soup's on the stove, everything else is on the counter. There's salad in the frig." She waved in his direction. "George should be surfacing pretty soon. He and Hunter are out in the woods, mending fences."

"I won't even bite on that statement. Hunter's home from school?" John asked.

"Renee took them out of school today. She was going in the hospital by 3 o'clock this afternoon, so she wanted to get the kids over here last evening."

"What's she having done?" John asked.

"A biopsy early in the morning. The doctor wants some major tests, too. That's why she's going in this afternoon. They're gonna do a couple of scans and get her prepped for surgery."

"Are you planning on going with her?

"No, her sister Virginia is going to stay with her. I've spent enough time in hospitals. They didn't even ask me." Mildred replied dryly.

"I wonder why?" Freddy interjected. "Say," she asked John, "have you discovered anything new about Dino Manuchi?"

"Forensics got a partial footprint. Considering he was drowned in the ditch, there wasn't any evidence of a major struggle. The grass was trampled in a straight path to the ditch. It must have been short and sweet. It's amazing to me there's not more to be found. Two people carried him, but there isn't much there for us to use. He must have been almost dead, when he was brought there."

"Any tissue exam yet?" Mildred inquired.

"Full Postmortum later today. Busy schedule this morning. The doc couldn't squeeze it in. She's a busy lady," he intoned.

The phone rang. Mildred got up to answer it. She handed it to John Jacobs. "It's for you. Sounds important."

"Lieutenant Jacobs here!" He listened intently, then his face lost color. "When?" The inquiry was curt. "I'll be there." He hung up the phone.

"Mil!"

"John, what's wrong?" her face changed from laughter to concerned. "What was that about?"

"Sit down, both of you. That was a friend of mine in Minneapolis. Homicide Division. You know him, Mil, Lieutenant Harold Hershey."

"Yes, I remember him. Hershey Bar . . ." She replied. "What's going on?"

"There's been another murder. Alison's friend was poisoned. Alison had to be taken to the hospital because she collapsed at the scene. She's in the Emergency Room at Hennipen County." He shared with them. "Hershey says they'll question her there and then see that she gets home. It probably won't be until this evening sometime. Quim's there, too."

It seemed almost psychic. The phone rang at just that moment. It was Quim. John took the call and assured him the two women were fine. The deep baritone of his voice could be heard across the room. John began nodding his head side to side. "No, Quim, not right now." He paused in the conversation. "No. You can discuss it later when you get to the house with Alison." He was emphatic in his refusal. Finally he hung up.

"Whew! That guy is pushy! Did you know that, Mil? When he gets an idea, it's like a pit bull with a bone, he doesn't let go."

"I have noticed that tendency," Freddy chimed in. "What did he want?" She paused, smote her forehead with her palm and added, "of course. He wanted to talk to Mildred and share all the gory details, right?"

"Freddy, you're in the wrong profession." John agreed. "He was determined to talk with you, Mil. I'm going to meet with Hershey in an hour. I would have a hard time believing there's not some connection with the Manuchi murder. The problem is, those two people didn't even know each other. Manuchi didn't know Alison, either. Hershey thinks she was the intended victim. That's part of the hysteria that caused the trip to the Emergency Room."

"Alison is a nervous wreck. This is not going to assure her that the world in which she lives, is safe. I think," Freddy mulled studiously, "that this gal Ashley is her best friend. It seems to me, she said they met at the University of Chicago in the late 50s. They've been close ever since then."

"Well, I've got to go. Hershey said I could be there when they question Alison. Her request," he answered to Freddy's raised eyebrows. "She seems to think she was the intended victim, too. So she and Hershey agree on at least one point."

"I can't see any connection," Mildred mused. Her face was pale. The fine lines around her eyes had deepened. "Alison has been out of the country more than she's been in it. She travels eight months of the year. She just got back from the Greek Islands, for Pete's sake."

"I'll let you know." John told the both of them. "Fill George in on what's going on here. He . . . ." John's sentence was interrupted by George and Hunter entering the room.

"John, I was going to call you." George said. "Place is secure. I have someone at the front, and the back entrance is fenced. Good security coverage with camera and laser. I don't think anyone will trespass without us picking it up."

"Good! That relieves my mind. There's been another murder." He told George. "Mildred will tell you about it, I've gotta go." He gave Mildred a hug in passing. "You take care of yourself and do whatever this man tells you to do. Got it?" He knew how stubborn she could be.

"John, believe me, I'm not going anywhere without someone with me. How long do you think it will be before you finish?"

"Depends on how the interview with Alison and her cohorts goes. All of the patrons at the tables around them were questioned and their names and addresses obtained. The customers at the Whitcomb are pretty high class. Nobody there seemed to know the victim. They knew who Alison was by name recognition, that's it!"

"Jeez! I can hardly believe this is happening." Freddy said. "Alison's a writer. Why would anybody want to kill her?" She blushed and looked at Mildred. "You know what I mean. She could drive you nuts, but that doesn't mean someone would kill her for that. There's no way this could be coincidence, is there?"

"Anything is possible," John said, "I'll be in touch later." He was gone.

"Grandma, who got killed?" Hunter asked. "It isn't that lady, who lives here, is it?"

His question hung in the air, as he looked from one to the other of them.

"No, honey, it wasn't her. She's fine. Her friend was killed though. Lieutenant Jacobs has to go ask her some questions. Then she'll come home. Don't you worry about it."

Mildred put her arms around her grandson and cast a worried glance at George and Freddy. "Where's Anubis?"

"I'm assigning him to the kids. We've been working with him this morning. He went on rounds with us. That's where Erica is now, with the dog."

George had trained Anubis. One of his business endeavors was training guard dogs. John had insisted Mildred get a dog after her accident. That was when Mildred had met George the first time and had taken an instant dislike to the man. It was hard for her to believe she was now paying him to protect her life.

Freddy was the first one to move. She commented, "I'll just finish getting this kitchen clean. Francis won't appreciate a mess when she gets back. Why don't the rest of you do whatever?" She waved them off with her hand.

# CHAPTER TWELVE

*"Oh what a tangled web we weave,*
*When first we practice to deceive"*
William Shakespeare

Mildred went up to her room and dressed. She had decided she did have a couple of errands to run. She knew George would have a fit, but then that was his job. Fifteen minutes later she went to the porch where Freddy was sitting with the newspaper. Francis was back listening to the gory details.

"Freddy, I want you to come with me. I have a couple of things I need to do. I promised John I wouldn't go any where alone, so I'm asking you to be my partner."

"Where are we going, grandma?" Erica's voice came from the corner of the porch. She and Anubis were sitting there quietly watching Hunter and George load fence posts on the small tractor. "I'm bored just sitting around here. Aunt Virginia is here, she and mom are leaving in about a half hour. There's nothing to do."

Mildred looked at Freddy, "What do you think? You suppose we could take Erica with us? I need to take a run over to the women's shelter. There's some paper work I can do there and I want to talk with a couple of people. Loose ends, you might say."

"I don't know why it would hurt? Seems the focus is in Minneapolis right now. It's probably a good time to go."

"Let's do it then." Mildred spoke to Francis, "let George know we'll be back within an hour and a half. It's only fifteen minutes to the shelter. I thought on the way back, I'd stop at Soderquist's for the groceries you need."

"I can get those, Mildred, you don't need to bother with that, too."

"No problem. I don't want to stop living and doing the everyday things. I've said that to John and I'll say it to George, if he has objections. Besides, he and Hunter are occupied with the fence. I'll let his security person at the driveway know where I'm going and when I'll be back."

"All right, here's the list." Francis handed her the paper. "I'll get started on dinner. How many are going to be here? I thought I'd make barbecued ribs?"

"Oh boy!" Freddy chimed in, "I think roughly it's ten or so. Make enough so there are leftovers. That way we'll be safe and if anything is left, I'll have something for a midnight snack, if I get hungry." She grinned.

"Snacks?" Mildred hooted. "You keep talking about this diet you're on, but you keep eating all this stuff."

"A girl's gotta keep her strength up," Freddy countered. She motioned to Erica, "Come on, Erica, let's get this grandma going before she changes her mind and leaves us here."

The three of them left the room and walked to the garage. Mildred decided to drive the van. It was the least conspicuous of the three cars. She definitely didn't want to take Freddy's car. It was flame red and definitely sporty. Besides, she had files to bring home and groceries to load in the back. They got in and Mildred drove down the long driveway.

She hadn't been out to the road since finding Manuchi's body. Mildred didn't know what she expected to see. When she got to the bridge and stopped to talk to the security guard, she felt let-down somehow. There was yellow ribbon around the area where the police had been investigating, but other than that, nothing seemed changed.

It seemed to her, Manuchi's death had made no impact except trampled grass and a yellow ribbon, which even as she watched, tore loose from it's mooring and flapped in the wind. It seemed like a poor epitaph for a man's life.

Freddy reached over and touched her arm. Erica's voice came from the back seat. "Grandma, don't feel bad. You know he's with the angels now. That's what you've always told me, so you've got to believe he's okay." Her voice was firm and steady.

"Ms. Smythe, Mr. Bonnaunt didn't tell me you were going anywhere. Does he know you're leaving?"

"He was busy out in the barn. My grandson is with him. We're only going to be gone about an hour and a half. I have some papers I have to pick up at the women's shelter and I have some calls to make. We'll stop at the grocery store on the way home. It really is okay. We'll be fine."

"I don't know about this. Let me call him . . ." He quickly punched some numbers. After a lag, he spoke into the phone.

"Tell him we are going!" Mildred stated emphatically. "I will not be a prisoner in my own home. We're going to be fine!" She gunned the engine.

"He's not happy, wants you to wait 'til he gets here." He started to walk toward the car.

Mildred slipped the engine in gear and pulled forward and over the bridge. "Tell him we'll be back when I said we would. She drove expertly onto East Bethel Blvd. Within a few minutes she made a turn onto Klondyke and headed for Highway 65.

"He's gonna be mad, grandma." Erica said. "I thought you told Lt. Jacobs you weren't going anywhere. He's gonna be mad, too."

"Listen, Squeak," Mildred used her pet name for Erica, "By the time he finds out about it, we'll be back to the house." She drove rapidly on the gravel road.

Mildred was correct. The traffic was not bad and they arrived at the shelter in just thirteen minutes. As she walked in the door, her eyes focused on the newspapers lying on a table in the hall.

The reception area was cramped. This was mainly because few persons ever sat there for long and visitors were discouraged. Most of the people who came and went were police officers, county social workers, and attorneys.

Freddy sucked in her breath, "Whoa . . . Look at what it says, 'MURDER IN ANOKA COUNTY'. A prominent citizen was discovered by local resident Thursday morning. Ms. Mildred Smythe was out for an early morning ride on her horse and discovered the body of Mr. Dino Manuchi, a prominent businessman from Anoka. At this time, the county sheriff's office is denying any evidence of a motive for the killing. Mr. Manuchi was the owner of a string of restaurants in local communities."

"That's enough." Mildred said. She used her key to let them into the office area. One of the volunteers was sitting at a desk.

"Mrs. Smythe." The woman looked startled. "We didn't expect to see you . . . I mean; we thought you wouldn't want to come in today." She seemed embarrassed. "Jennifer canceled the meeting for this morning. I . . ."

"It's okay. I'm not going to stay. And it's good the meeting was canceled. I just came by to pick up the files I've been working on." Mildred assured her. "I wanted to make sure everything was all right here. I'm going to make a couple of phone calls from Jennifer's office." She walked past the volunteer. "I won't be long. Freddy, why don't you and Erica go into the family room. I'll come and get you when I'm done."

Freddy agreed and she and Erica went through an archway into a sunny and spacious room. A number of mothers and children were there. A small television was turned on to 'Barney and Friends', and a group of mothers were sitting around a table talking and sipping coffee. One of them greeted Freddy, "Hi, Dr. Beaudreaux. We didn't think you'd come in today. Hi, Erica." She added.

"We're not staying. I will be in tomorrow. I have a few appointments and I don't plan on canceling them." She assured. "It's hard to get people together for family sessions unless I come in on Saturdays. I don't want to put these off for a week. We can't hold up placement in secure housing because I can't get here."

"I don't know if I'd be wanting to work after what you guys have been through," someone else said. "We read the paper this morning. It was all over the local news last night. All the local channels had it. You must have had reporters everywhere."

"They didn't come to the house. The police wouldn't let them through the barricade. So we really didn't see much. But, you're right. It hasn't been easy." Freddy agreed.

"Mrs. Manuchi must be having a terrible time. She's such a nice lady. I worked in one of their restaurants once. She came in and did the books. I thought I'd heard she was on the board for the shelter, but I've never seen her here." The mother named Sandy added.

"She is on the board." Freddy said, "I think Mildred is going to call and offer any help she may need."

"We'd like to do something for her. It's got to be a terrible thing to have your husband killed like that. The news said he had terrible injuries and then he was drowned. Is that true?" One of them asked.

"It's true. I didn't see him, but Mildred did. She's pretty upset about it. She liked Mr. Manuchi a lot."

"Well she had that terrible accident two years ago." Sandy added. "I remember that because it was when I first moved out here with my boyfriend. I was afraid to drive on Lexington Avenue for a long time after the accident. It was weird. They never found the driver of the truck that ran her off the road, did they?"

"No." Freddy's answer was curt. "They didn't!" She turned to Erica. "I'll be right back. I'm going to see how long your grandmother is going to be."

Erica sat down with the women. One of them brought her a bottle of Coca Cola. "How are you doing?" Geri asked. "You were here with Mildred last week, weren't you? My little girl said you played scrabble with her. That was real nice of you. She has a hard time talking with other kids. So that was a big help."

"I like to play with the kids. Lots of 'em are my age, so we get along and can talk about stuff," she said. "The ones that are younger are fun, too. I like to baby-sit, so it's no problem to come here and play with the kids."

"That's real nice of you honey. Lots of folks would like to pretend we don't exist."

"Not me and my grandma. She's a crusader. That's what my grandma's friends say. They worry about her, though. She gets tired." Erica shared.

"I know she does. But she still comes here and helps us a lot. She does fund raising and spends a lot of time talking to companies who might sponsor our programs." Sandy had taken a chair next to Erica. "You tell your grandma, anyway we can help, we will. There's lots of women she's helped." She finished saying before she rose. "I've got to go. I'm in charge of the babies in the nursery. I watch 'em for the mothers who have to go to court." She left the room.

Freddy and Mildred walked in, "I spoke to her for just a few minutes. We're going to get together after the funeral," Mildred said.

"Erica, we're ready to go," Freddy told her. "C'mon, let's get to the grocery store and get back home, before George has a total fit."

"Who'd you speak to, grandma?" Erica asked as they headed out the door.

Mildred remained quiet, but Freddy answered, "She talked to Mr. Manuchi's widow. Your grandma knows her, so she wanted to call her and offer her condolences."

"Couldn't she do that from home?" Erica quizzed. "Why did we have to come all the way down here?"

"I had some papers I needed to pick up, hon. Now," she said to Erica, "let's go do the shopping and get back to the house." She led the way to the car.

Driving to Soderquist's was uneventful. Francis had called the butcher and ordered the ribs for barbecue. After a stop at the meat counter and a short conversation with the butcher, Mildred just had to pick up vegetables for salad and more milk. "Is he ever a conversationalist!" She stated to Freddy and Erica.

"Sounded like he's real concerned about Francis, if you ask me." Freddy replied'

"I don't know how she does it, but everyone she meets seems to fall in love with her. It's like fatal attraction. Last fall, I had the nursery bring more perennial plants to expand the flower beds. Before I knew it, Francis was out there with the coffee pot and her usual array of goodies. By the end of the day, everyone was on a first name basis. This spring, the manager didn't ask me how I was, he asked about Francis."

Freddy laughed. "Listen, Mildred, you know the army moves on its' stomach. So, apparently, do nursery workers. The power of food is deadly. What have I been telling you all these years? You know what she's doing right now?"

"No," Mildred looked at Freddy, "I don't! What?"

"Putting in the kitchen garden. That's what the trip to town was really about. She's putting in a soul garden."

"What is that?" Mildred asked, then she hesitated. "Got to be greens. Lot's of greens. What else, let's see. Okra, beans of all sorts, tomatoes, green peppers, other peppers, lots of 'em. I guess I know the usual stuff. If she could grow her own rice, she would."

The three of them put the groceries in the back of the van. "Well, that's it. No more excuses, it's time to go back home." Mildred said wistfully. "Why is it, I'm perfectly content to stay home days at a time. But now, that I've been more or less ordered to stay home, I want to run all over the place. Doesn't make sense."

"Sure it does. You don't want anybody telling you what to do. It's as simple as that." Freddy said matter-of-factly. "No one wants to feel their control is taken away. It's human nature." She took in a deep breath.

Mildred interrupted, "Freddy, I don't need psychology lecture number 28. I think I get the picture. Let's just get back to the house, I'm exhausted. I'm going to try and get a short nap."

The drive home was quiet. It was quiet in the kitchen when they brought in the groceries. No one was in sight. Mildred and Freddy put the food away. Freddy shrugged, "this is almost too quiet, where are they?"

As if in answer, Francis appeared at the door to the porch. She had an empty basket in her hands. She saw their look and answered. "Now you know that's a growing boy. He needs his meals right on time. I just took them a few things. Out there working on them fences all day. That boy's gonna be bone tired." She shook her head.

"Francis, Hunter is having the time of his life. If you keep feeding him like that, his mother is going to have to put him on a diet." Freddy laughed as she talked.

"Well Miss! He's not the only one should be worried 'bout his waist line. Seems to me a couple of grownups around here, could use a little weight loss." She eyed Freddy significantly.

"Now, Francis," Freddy answered, "you know what I've told you. I have to keep my strength up or I get crabby. That's not good for my clients."

"Listen here Missy," Francis was warming to the old argument, "You jus' need to start listenin' to me. I know what I'm talking about. You jus' cut out some fats and you'll sure take off them extra pounds."

Mildred watched the two of them. Then she quietly turned, and she and Erica left the room.

# CHAPTER THIRTEEN

Erica awoke before Mildred. The heavy, sweet scent of barbecue sauce hung in the air. She breathed deep and rolled to a sitting position. She had slept on a daybed beneath the window. The temperature today was lower than yesterday, so she had covered with a light quilt.

She went over to Mildred's bed. She noticed her grandmother's eyes were open. "How long have you been awake, grandma?" She asked.

"Oh, not long," Mildred said sleepily. She sniffed. "Smells like Francis has outdone herself. We'd better get down there or there won't be anything left."

The two of them brushed teeth and hair and headed down the stairs. They could hear Hunter in the kitchen. He sounded hungry and tired. He hadn't taken a nap. "Oh dear," Mildred murmured. "He really should have come upstairs for a nap, too. Now he's going to be a handful."

However, when Mildred walked into the kitchen, Hunter was already seated at a table, a plate of ribs in front of him. "This young man needs to eat and bathe, and then go to bed." Francis decreed. "I'll see to it while ya'll are eatin'." She assured.

"Oh, Francis, you don't have to do that." Mildred said.

"I'm tired. Ya'll can clear the dishes and load that dishwasher. I've had a long day. My sister wore me out in town. Then come home to this goings' on, is more than a body can bear. I'm going up to bed after I get this boy taken care of. He don' mind, do you boy?" She ruffled his hair as he ate.

Hunter's only answer was a shake of the head. His disposition was improving as he ate. He had a piece of strawberry shortcake next to his plate. "Dessert looks pretty good, too." Erica stated. "Is that what we all get? Or is it just for Hunter 'cause he did fence posts?"

"No, young lady, it's not just for him. There's plenty to go around. Are those hands washed for dinner?" She inspected Erica's hands.

"Of course," Erica protested. "I always wash my hands." She huffed into the dining room and took her place at the table. Everyone else was already there, except Alison and Quim, who weren't back yet.

Virginia was at the table though. She filled them in on the afternoon spent at the hospital with Renee. "I'll be there with her in the morning, mom. You've got enough. Her tests so far seem to be negative. The exploratory surgery will rule out the rest of his concerns. It doesn't look as if there's a malignancy."

Mildred sighed in relief. "I knew I was concerned, I just wouldn't let myself think how worried I was." She said. She sat down at her place and picked up a large checkered napkin. After tying it around her neck, she asked for the platter of ribs. "I have to cover up or I have barbecue sauce all over everything."

George passed the ribs to her. He was a sticky looking mess. "I guess I should have covered up a little better," He laughed and wiped his mouth on the napkin. "I'll have to take another shower before I can call it a night."

Mildred looked around the table. Besides George, there were now two other security men. Joel was not there. George introduced the men to everyone. He then told everyone what the men would be doing. "This is a big place. However, there really isn't anywhere anyone could hide on the property, where they can't be detected. So, in essence, there really isn't a problem. The field road is now impassible. Joel and I put in fencing and a locked gate. No one's coming through there. By the way, he needs a plate of ribs. He's in the security control room. Maybe someone could fix a plate and I'll take it down to him."

Freddy agreed. There was nothing heard for a few minutes except the sound of eating. Finally, when it seemed as though a spell had been cast on them, Erica spoke up, "when do you think they'll get home?"

"They?" Mildred puzzled. "Oh," she let out an exasperated sigh, "Quim and Alison. I must be losing it. I didn't know who you were talking about for a minute there." She thought for a moment, "I don't suppose they'll be real late. They'll probably eat before they come home. Quim will never last without a meal. He gets crabby if a meal is too late. Very grouchy, as a matter of fact. Probably got a blood sugar problem.

He's gonna have to watch it." Mildred stopped talking and listened. "That's a car."

As if they knew they were being discussed, Alison and Quim appeared in the doorway. Although he looked somewhat ruffled, he voiced only one concern, "is there any left?"

"Lots!" Freddy answered him. "When Francis makes ribs, we make sure there is enough. Sit down and dig in."

He didn't need to be asked twice. He sat quickly and soon serving plates were lining up near his chair. "This potato salad is wonderful. What the hell does she do to the potato to make it taste this good?" He asked everyone in general.

Mildred laughed. "If you can talk Francis out of her secret recipes, you could make it as an international spy. She doesn't tell anyone anything."

"I've tried," Freddy added, "to get her to share, but no way is she gonna part with any of those sacred measurements. It's the same old ingredients, but it's how she spices stuff. There is something just a little different, that you can't put your finger on. It drives me nuts not to be able to get it. I've tried." She wound down. After a short silence, Freddy asked, "how did it go?"

"What?" Alison asked. "How did what go? You mean like the police grilling me like a common criminal? You'd think I killed her, the way they acted! I thought it would help to have Lt. Jacobs there. It didn't make any difference. They asked me all kinds of questions and then told me not to leave town. I'm pissed. My best friend dies like that, and they question me like I'm some kind of murderess. What the hell! I thought the police were supposed to go after the criminals, but they don't. They harass people like me."

Quim agreed. "They were a little rough on her, I thought."

"What do you mean?" Mildred asked. "The police have to ask questions. They need to know what happened. It's very repetitive questioning. They keep looking for something someone missed or doesn't remember without prodding."

"Well, I think they did a lot of prodding." Alison huffed. "I told them they should question that waiter who served the wine. I had never seen him before. But no," she dragged out the word no, "they had to keep harping on me. I'm just very glad my attorney and agent were there. They were able to say I never touched that glass of wine. Holy shit! If they hadn't been there, I'd probably be sitting in jail right now, and not here eating dinner."

"We would have bailed you out, sweetie." Freddy rolled her eyes at Alison. She was attempting to mollify her somewhat, to no avail. "Look, you didn't end up in jail. You were warned not to leave town. You are a suspect in a murder case. Just think how much good data you are gaining for a plot. If all else fails, write a book."

"Oh my God! Where's the book?" Alison jumped up.

"What book?" Mildred asked.

"Ashley's! I left it in the car." She was really upset. "I promised her I'd have my agent and publisher read it. Oh God, I hope it's still there."

"Well who would take it?" Quim asked her. "It's not as if anyone else knew about the book. It's probably still in the car. We'll find it tomorrow."

"No, those cops are the ones who caused all this confusion with all their questions. I want them to look now." She got up from the table, "I'm going to call that Lt. Hershey and tell him he'd better find it. They're the ones who escorted me right to the hospital and wouldn't let me drive my car."

"Alison, you weren't in any shape to be driving a car. You fainted dead away. What were they supposed to do. Splash water on your face and ask you to follow them to the hospital?" Quim's voice was steady and consoling. He gave Mildred's face a searching look.

She interpreted the look correctly. "Will said he would get here as soon as he could. He has a parishioner in the hospital who's dying. He didn't feel he could leave right at that time. But he said to tell you he would come as soon as he could."

"It might be tomorrow though." Freddy added. "I talked to him, too. He said to tell you to remember all the stuff you've dealt with when you guys were kids. He said you could deal with anything after that. I'm not sure what he meant, but I figured you would know."

Alison looked at her. "Yeah!" She seemed lost in thought.

George got to his feet. "We've got to get someone to relieve Joel and myself. Give reports and all that, so you'll have to excuse us." He pushed back his chair and stepped back from the table. "Ms. Lippencott have more faith in the police." He directed at her. "They're pretty damn good at their jobs. They'll find the killer, believe me."

The other two men stood and pushed back their chairs. Mildred smiled at them, "do you want to take anything to munch on down there. There's plenty of food."

"Nah! We'll take breaks and just come up to the kitchen if we need anything. Thanks anyway." George answered. The three of them got up from the table. George hesitated, "maybe I will stop in the kitchen and fix Joel a plate of food. It could be a while before he gets a chance to come over here." He headed in the direction of the kitchen. The other two men followed him.

Freddy stood up and began to clear the table. Mildred got up to help. Quim helped Alison to her feet, "I'll walk Alison up to her room. She's exhausted from all this." He gave Mildred a look that pleaded, "Please bear with me here. I'm doing all I can to cope with the situation. Alison says she has some medication, so we'll get that and I'll get her settled in. I won't be long," he assured.

"In a pig's right eye," Freddy added when they were out of earshot. "Man, is he deluded, or what?"

"He has not had the experience with her, that you and I have," Mildred answered, as she stacked plates. "Let's get this table cleared and then we can go in the library and talk."

"I'll help," Erica chimed in, "I'll bring the leftovers in and put them on the counter. You'll have to put the food away. I don't know where anything goes."

Hunter and Francis were gone when they entered the kitchen. Their plates had been rinsed and set in the sink. Everything was spotless. Francis had cleaned up from the meal preparation while Hunter was eating.

Mildred and Erica brought in the dirty dishes from the dining room. Freddy loaded the oversize dishwasher. In ten minutes they were done. "We didn't have dessert. Why don't I put on the coffee and we'll have dessert in the library after Quim comes down from consoling Alison."

"Don't be nasty, Freddy. She really has had a shock. If something like that happened to you, I don't know what I'd do. But I think I'd be ready to commit murder. I cannot conceive what it's like to have your oldest and dearest friend drop dead of poisoning right in front of your eyes. I know this, if it had been you, I'd be one helluva basket case!"

They warmly embraced.

"Are you two going to stand there all night hugging each other. I could use some help here!" Erica's voice peeped into their consciousness.

She had large tray with pottery dessert bowls, a bowl of strawberries, whipped cream, silverware and coffee cups. "I put a cup on for me, too. There should be enough settings for everyone. I don't think Alison is coming back downstairs, but I put one on for Mr. Anderson, Father Will, and Lt. Jacobs, if he comes."

"Erica, this is great." Freddy picked up the tray, "You open the door and I'll carry it through to the other room."

The coffee maker had finished percolating, Mildred put the coffee in an insulated pot and followed behind the other two.

# CHAPTER FOURTEEN

The small group settled in the library. This room and the four-season porch were used more than any other rooms on the first floor. It went without saying, the kitchen was popular, too, but the kitchen was the domain of Mildred's housekeeper and cook, Francis. Francis ruled her kingdom and the kingdom began in the kitchen. She had worked with Mildred for more years than she wanted to acknowledge.

Mildred had met Francis in Louisiana. She had been battered severely by her live-in boyfriend. Pregnant with a second child, she had sought help from an agency that Mildred was affiliated with during college break. Mildred had helped Francis evade the persistent boyfriend by moving her and her child to her own parents' farm. Francis had flourished there and Mildred's parents were loved having her there. However, when Mildred had married Emil, Francis came north to live with them.

When Emil and Mildred had first discussed the possibility of establishing a retreat center, Francis was included in the planning. Now, with the plans on hold, Francis was using the time as an opportunity to study haute cuisine. Her reasoning was simple. When the retreat center finally opened, she would be qualified to serve not only excellent meals, but would also be a chef.

As the group settled in with their shortcake, Francis was the topic of conversation. "I can't believe she can make something so simple taste so damn good!" Freddy mumbled between bites. "What in the hell does she do to this stuff?"

"Francis doesn't do, she creates." Mildred answered her. "She's always been a wonderful cook. My mother said she had never met anyone who could make buttermilk biscuits like Francis. She has 'the touch' with a capitol T."

"Honest to God, Mil, she could make a fortune with a restaurant."

The three of them were happily ensconced in the wing chairs. Erica was sipping her coffee, heavily laced with milk and sugar. "This is so good." She was perched on the edge of her chair. "My mother doesn't think I should drink coffee, but I love it so much."

"A little bit of it never hurts. My grandfather used to give it to me when I was a little girl. My mother didn't like it, either. So he would be real careful around her. We never mentioned his illicit sharing of his morning coffee with me out on the back porch. He loved it with lots of cream and sugar. So that's how I drank it, too." Mildred reminisced. "Your mother used to drink it as a little girl, too."

"Say, how is she doing?" Freddy asked. "She called, but you two didn't talk very long."

"She was done with the all the tests. She said they'll do the surgery in the morning. She's scheduled at 7:30. Virginia's going to be there. She'll call as soon as Renee is out of surgery. The doctor thinks the biopsy will be benign. They won't know for sure though, until they can do the pathology exam. I just hope this will solve the problems she's been having."

"I do, too." Freddy added. "It's too bad all this is happening now. Worrying about Renee, on top of dealing with Dino Manuchi's death, is difficult to say the least."

"I think she'll be fine. Otherwise, I'd be camped out at the hospital. You're right though, it is stressful. I have a headache that won't go away. I know it's tension.

The phone rang and Mildred reached for it. "Hello," she paused. "John, where are you?" she listened, then spoke, "what?" She exclaimed. "What happened?"

Freddy leaned forward in her chair.

"Okay, I'll wait. We'll see you then."

"What's up? Is he on the way here?" Freddy asked, putting her coffee down.

"He said he'll be here in about a half an hour." She looked disturbed.

"What's wrong? What did he tell you? You're as pale as a ghost." Freddy expressed concern. "Mildred!" she pronounced her name drawing out the syllables "What's going on, tell me."

"There was another body found." She turned her pale face to Freddy. "The wine waiter. They found his body in an alley just a block from the restaurant. He wouldn't tell me anymore on the phone."

"The wine waiter. What's he got to do with it?" Freddy thought for a minute. "Oh, sure! That makes sense." She was thinking out loud."

"What makes sense?" Inquired a voice from the doorway. Quim stood there looking solemn and tired.

"John just called. They found the body of the wine waiter in an alley a block from the Whitcomb Hotel."

"The guy who disappeared?" Quim asked. He came into the room and sank with an exhausted sigh on the sofa. "They were looking for him this afternoon. Seems he disappeared about the same time Ashley died." His voice sounded dull and flat. "The police wanted to question him. He was the only person, in all likelihood, who could have tampered with the wine glass."

"Well, does that solve who did it or not?" Freddy asked. "He's the only person who could have tampered with the wine. He's the only one who disappears after the murder!" she added smugly.

"I don't know that it means he killed her." Mildred chimed in. She handed Quim a cup of coffee and indicated the shortcake with her hand. She served him a piece, when he answered in the affirmative. "Here you are." She handed the dish to him.

"It could mean he knew something." Mildred directed her statement to Freddy. "He may have seen someone put something in the glass. We just don't know. That seems most likely to me. I think he saw something."

"Grandma," Erica piped up, "this is scary. Does this mean someone could come out here and kill us?" Her voice shook. "Is someone going to really try to kill you?"

"Erica, honey, no-one is going to hurt us. That's why we have George and Joel here. No one is going to get past the security guard at the driveway. The police are patrolling the road all the time. We're safe here. That's why Lt. Jacobs doesn't want me to leave. He can't protect me as well away from the house." Mildred reassured her granddaughter.

"You're sure?" Erica's voice sounded little.

"I'm very sure." She was reassured again. "There are a lot of people here who won't let anything happen to us."

Erica snuggled back into the chair. "Okay," she said and quietly sipped her coffee.

"Mil, did John say when he would get here?" Quim asked.

"He's on his way. He said about a half an hour." She answered his question. "I don't know how much he'll be able to tell us about what is going on, but I sure hope we can be told something."

"Well, your buddies, the police, are pretty efficient at questioning. I feel like I was at the table at the Whitcomb." He served himself some shortcake and strawberries. "It's pretty intense. Gives me a whole new perspective on John's personality."

"Really?" Freddy asked. "How so?"

"I've always thought of him as a cop, but I never really knew what that meant in terms of interface with the public. Personally, I would find that kind of work distasteful. Hammering away at people, trying to break down their defenses. It's just not me."

"Oh," Freddy's voice rose incrementally. "How would you define your personality exactly?"

"You're fishing, Freddy dear, but I'll tell you anyway." He cleared his throat, setting the bowl of strawberry shortcake on the table. "I'm more of an intellectual type. Academia, Library Science, Teaching. I should have gone into teaching at the University level. Always had some regrets about that, but what can one do? It's a life well lived, so far, and I can't go back and change what has been."

What has been, Freddy thought to herself, is a man who did not get the woman he wanted, so he's waiting patiently for the chance to reappear. If you can't make money, marry it. "You've never married either, how come?" She asked innocently.

"Never found quite the right person, I guess." He cast a veiled glance at Mildred. "Besides, I traveled so much. It would have been hard on the little woman, had there been one."

"Little woman?" Erica's voice surfaced. "Mr. Anderson, that's archaic!"

"Touché!" Freddy added, her voice becoming indignant. "That's just how you men get. Little woman, indeed!" She sputtered.

Mildred laughed. "You've gotten the two feminists on your case, Quim. I suggest all of you change the subject. I don't want a roaring debate over the plight of the feminist movement tonight. I've got enough on my mind."

"Don't lose heart, Mil," Freddy intoned, "just remember Quim and I make beautiful music together in the kitchen."

"Ah, yes, my dear," he agreed, "that we do. I love to create elegant dishes with Freddy. She has a superb sense of what works together. Foods, I mean. I don't know how you do with people." He looked thoughtful, "but my dear it was simply too divine that you brought Mildred to Orchestra Hall that evening. I guess if I think about your matchmaking ability in the personal sense, you do well." He looked smug as he smiled at Mildred.

"Quim, I didn't have a clue you would be there. So don't get any ideas that I planned to run into you." Freddy defended. "I do not match make! It doesn't work. I have found during my professional career, some of the most incongruous people seem to make wonderful marriage partners. I think the ability to succeed is not in the match, but in the communication between the people involved. If you discuss problems and issues as they arise, you put out the incendiary potential of future emotional stockpiles." Freddy elucidated.

"What in the hell did you just say?" Quim asked. "It sounds like professional therapy-speak."

"It was," Freddy laughed. "What I really said was this, don't tell your partner what the trouble is and you'll be in divorce court in a whiz . . . ."

"Well put." Mildred said. She got up from her chair. "I thought I heard a car engine. John is here. Erica," she directed at the child, "I think it's time for you to go up and get ready for bed. You can read for awhile, but I don't think this conversation is for your ears."

Erica protested. "But grandma, I'm old enough to stay up for awhile. I won't get in the way. I want to hear what's going on. I promise I'll keep quiet. You won't even know I'm here." She insisted.

"No, come on," Mildred was firm. "This time you need to go upstairs." She went to the foot of the stairs and kissed her granddaughter goodnight. "I'll be up in a couple of hours. No-one will bother you, I promise." She watched the young girl climb the stairs.

"Okay, goodnight," Erica's words floated behind her in the darkened hallway.

# CHAPTER FIFTEEN

John settled in his chair. Mildred had asked if he wanted some supper. He didn't, so she served him shortcake and a cup of coffee. All of them watched him eat. After a few bites, John raised his head and said, "So, can't a man eat in peace?"

Freddy snorted, "Right! You come in from a murder scene. We're all waiting to hear the latest installment, and you sit and eat shortcake. Yeah, you're right. A man can't eat in peace when the rest of us are dying to know what the hell is going on. So, talk! You can eat later." She ordered firmly.

"Well," John replied. "You are out of luck. I can't talk about the Minneapolis case. It's not my case to discuss. I really can't tell you any more than you already know. They did identify the waiter. He was a casual at the Whitcomb. He had regular hours at one of the Manuchi Restaurants."

"Well, that's information!" Freddy exclaimed. "If you're not supposed . . ."

John interrupted, "I can tell you the superficial facts. His name's gonna be in the Minneapolis Star and Pioneer Press tomorrow morning. His names no secret. He had identification on him. His relatives have been notified."

"So what can you tell us?" Quim asked belligerently "I can tell you I'm not impressed with how the police treat people they are questioning. Poor Alison was feeling like she'd been through a shredder."

"Most people do, Quimby, most people do," John agreed. "It's not for the pleasure of social interaction, that the police question people. Usually something pretty nasty has occurred and the cops are trying to sort out the truth. That's the way the bad guys end up in jail." He looked at Freddy, "and just to keep it on the up and up, Freddy, that goes for the bad gals, too." He grinned at her.

"I don't see anything funny about this. I'm concerned about how Alison was treated. She was trying to be helpful. She said the questions sounded like you and Lt. Hershey thought she killed Ashley."

"Ninety percent of the time, someone close to a person does the killing. Miss Lippencott was there on the scene. She's a long time friend of the victim. Of course they're gonna question her carefully. They questioned her attorney and her agent, too."

He assured Quim. "Being a cop in a murder investigation is tough stuff. We don't usually know the people involved in the crime. So, we have to ask a lot of questions. Some of them get real personal."

"Well, it just felt so invasive." Quim muttered. "It even sounded like you were asking if they had a sexual relationship. Really!" he exploded. "That didn't seem called for."

John peered at Quim over his glasses. "Now, tell me professor, are you going to loosen up here a little bit. I didn't stop by here to get blasted for doing my goddamn job. So either you sit back and listen or you can excuse yourself. I came over here to talk with Mildred primarily. The rest of you, as interested as you are, aren't necessary. You weren't witnesses and you weren't on the scene of either crime. So cool it or leave. Am I clear?" John asked him.

"Damn it, I'm not trying to be obstreperous, but I do believe in good manners."

"I can tell you've never seen too many murder scenes. If you had, you'd plant your fuckin' manners on the back burner. You didn't see Mr. Manuchi yesterday morning. Mildred did. Upset her a lot. Why don't you ask her how she feels about questioning murder suspects?" John looked at Mildred.

Mildred was pale but she spoke up, "Quim, Ashley probably didn't look too good after she was poisoned. Death by cyanide is not pleasant. I didn't see her, but I did see Dino Manuchi. There is no question in my mind, Dino was placed in my drainage ditch to tell me I would be one of the next victims. It was also patently clear, my death would not be pleasant either. That's why John is being so blunt. He knows us personally. That makes catching the killer significant. He doesn't want one of us to be murdered."

Quim blanched under his mustache. "I've never seen anyone whose been murdered. I guess you're right. It's just I can't believe anyone would think Alison would kill anybody."

"Am I being defended behind my back?" Alison entered the room. She had a bottle of brandy and a glass in her hands. "I stopped at the pantry and picked up a little nourishment." She brandished the bottle. "Can I sit by you, professor? You seem to be my only knight these days."

Quim smiled wryly at her words. He liked puns. Her statement brought to mind his favorite poet, Omar Khayyam. Some of Khayyam's words 'checkered board of nights and days,' from one of his poems began to play in Quim's thoughts, as 'knights and daze'. He knew he was tired.

Alison said, "Will called me. He can't come this evening. I don't know why it is, when I am most needy, my friends don't have time for me. But," she added, "I have all of you." She waved her hand to indicate the entire group. "I just couldn't stand being cooped up in my rooms any longer. So, I came down here. Besides, Will wouldn't be able to do anything, anyway."

"I'm glad you came down. You've had a terrible experience. Believe me, Alison, I know how you feel. Finding Dino Manuchi dead was something I will never forget. At least he didn't die before my eyes. You must feel terrible." Mildred said.

"You'll never know, Mildred," Alison's eyes were glittering. "I've known that woman all of my adult life. I really don't know how I'm going to stand living without her. We've been through so much together. I just can't tell you how awful it is." Her voice shook.

"I'm so very sorry, Alison," Mildred comforted. "I can only imagine how I would feel if something happened to my oldest and dearest friend." Her glance took in Freddy. "You're right. It would be the nightmare of my life."

"It's just that death is so final," Alison sobbed, "I'll never be able to see her again. I just can't imagine how life is going to be. We were so close."

Quim moved closer to her and put a consoling arm around her shoulders. For the time being, at least, she let him comfort her. He pulled a snowy handkerchief out of his pocket and handed it to her. For just a second, her eyes twinkled in their tears. Only Quim would have a fresh hanky to loan to a lady in distress. The ironic humor of it was not lost on her.

"So, Lt. Jacobs, has anything been clarified?" Alison's voice quivered. Will the person who did this be brought to justice?"

"I think so." John cleared his throat. "Murderers are not necessarily smart. Many crimes of this nature are not well thought out in advance. In Manuchi's case, we're reasonably sure his death was planned. Certainly the injuries did not occur out on the road. We're hoping that the forensic examination will give us some clues as to what transpired in the hours before his death."

"How can that be helpful? Quim inquired. "All you have is the body. You don't know where he was killed, who killed him, none of that. So what can he tell you after he's dead? I'm really curious," he added when he saw John's face. "You do these things all the time, but I know absolutely nothing about forensic medicine."

"Pathology exams can tell us a great deal." John told them. "It's not just a matter of what was eaten at the last meal anymore. Nowadays the doctor can detect foreign substances, like carpet fibers or fuzz from a blanket, on the clothes of the deceased. If they were transported by car and stashed in the truck, fibers from that carpet could be detected. If the murderer lost a hair in the scuffle and was on the body, DNA testing could be used to hopefully identify the killer. It's really awesome, that's just a couple of the superficial things that can be identified. Blood, urine, semen from the killer can be convicting evidence. It just depends on what you have."

"Good lord. It's distasteful!" Quim said quietly, "I've never given it a thought before this."

"Killing someone is distasteful!" John stated flatly. "It's as old as humanity, unfortunately. Seems like human beings value a lot of things before human life. Money and power are high on the list. I'll never get used to it and I'm ready to retire."

Freddy chimed in, "I'm continually amazed myself. When I used to be in private practice, I thought the world was pretty bland. I basically worked with the worried well. Since Mildred got me involved with the Women's Shelter, my cocoon of well-being burst like a ripe tomato."

"That's for sure!" Mildred said. "Your first week there put you into shock. I still can't believe how you didn't know these kinds of problems existed in our society. Battering is definitely a power thing. You've been involved in marriage counseling for years. Lots of battering in marriage. But then, Freddy, you have always been kind of optimistic about people."

"Oh, there were some cases where the woman didn't seem to be getting any better with counseling. But the suggestion of marital separation was not well received by the couple. I'd have the sense there were things missing, pieces of the marriage puzzle that weren't shared with me. One of the women died suddenly in a car accident with her husband. He survived, but just barely. The odd thing was, he married again and within a year that couple was in counseling. The wife listing the same kinds of complaints the first wife expressed. I began to fear for her life and didn't quite know why. Then he died suddenly. One of the injuries from the accident resurfaced and he died. I had the strangest feeling his dead wife reached out of her grave and grabbed him before he could hurt another woman. Odd, don't you think?" She looked at the group.

"Maybe not as odd as you'd think." John acknowledged her question. "We see lot's of examples of 'til death do us part' in my business. This is not just a man's issue either. Even though not nearly as many men are battered or abused, there are some. In general these guys don't talk about it, 'cause they know other people won't understand. Usually they're men who wouldn't dream of striking a woman, even if they were in danger of losing their life. In some cases, that's what happens. Still, the vast majority of battering is against women."

"My god, I had no idea." Quim interjected. "Have I been living in a dream world?"

"I don't know, have you?" Freddy asked. "You're the only one who knows the answer to that question. To some extent we all live in a dream world. There's the reality of the mundane everyday place. Then, in a parallel way, there's the idealistic image we have of what we wish for in our lives. The everyday place is where we go to work, we clean our house, we grocery shop, that kind of stuff. The dream is what we hope for, aspire to accomplish, our fantasies fleshed out in desire. Some people actually believe these two worlds are one. Like the bride who sees her husband as a marvelous prince charming, but to the rest of the world he's a money grubbing stock-broker or something. Her friends can't understand what she sees in him. She doesn't get it, when they tell her he is bull-shitting her. But in the scheme of things, this delusion isn't too tragic. Usually after she lives with the guy for a while, she sees him realistically. Then she decides if the reality and her image can co-exist. If they can't, she leaves."

"If he lets her, that's when the problem can arise," Mildred added.

"Yes," agreed John and Freddy.

"So where are we at, John?" Quim asked. "Is there going to be a solution to the killing? Do you know why Dino Manuchi was killed?"

"In a word, NO." John stated. "However, due to the injuries, the location of the body, the fact that Mildred knew him from a professional interaction, and the fact that his injuries mimicked hers from the accident, I think his death is a message for Mildred."

"So, you think her life is in danger?" Alison asked.

"Yes," he answered simply. "I think she was meant to die two years ago in that accident. Why? None of us has been able to determine the reason for the attempt on her life. But," he paused reflectively, then resumed, "the one thing that stands out in everyone's mind is this. It's believed Dino gave Mildred some information when he was locked up in the Psych Hospital before his trial. She spent time with him, ergo, he told her something."

But, he didn't!" Mildred insisted. "My memory of our interactions is not faulty. The man didn't tell me anything that could even faintly be construed as important to the trial. I hate to say this, but he was as bland as milk toast."

"Criminal milk toast!" John inserted. "I still have a very strong opinion about him, Mil. Association with that guy almost got you killed."

"Association with Mildred may have gotten him killed," Alison quipped. She was leaning forward on the sofa. "Maybe it's the other way round, Lt. Jacobs. Maybe Mildred caused his death."

"That hardly makes any sense. She's the one who was victimized in that car accident. That was definitely an attempt to kill her. It was miraculous that she survived it." He stated intensely. "Believe me, it is truly a miracle she's here with us."

"Well then, there must be some explanation. Was Mr. Manuchi in trouble? I've heard of his restaurants. Pretty high class dining, from what I've surmised. Certainly the income from those places should have generated enough income for the man and his family to live on comfortably."

"It did. They had two sons, both in college, both are studying law. To all intents and purposes they are brilliant and will probably be very successful as attorneys. Their mother is involved in a lot of social concerns. One of them is the local Woman's Shelter. That's where Mildred met her after recovering from the accident." John clarified.

"Oh, John, I talked with her today. She's really having a very hard time of it. The boys have come home from school, but she still is feeling overwhelmed. They've been making all the plans and decisions about the funeral. It's on Monday. She just wants a Memorial Service. He couldn't have an open casket anyway. She doesn't think they need to wait for his body to be released by the coroner. It makes sense to me."

"You talked to her?" John asked.

"Yes, Freddy, Erica, and I took a drive to the shelter to pick up my paperwork. I called her from there." She answered blandly.

His face was red. "You left the house?" It was clear, and evident, John was not happy about her disclosure. "I thought I told you to stay put. I said I didn't want you going anywhere alone. I said you were not safe. I said you need to keep a low profile. I pointed out it seemed clear someone means to kill you. After all this, you left the house and went for a drive?"

"Yes, John," She answered firmly, "I did leave. I also have told you I will not be a prisoner in my own home, no matter how spacious and beautiful. I told you I would rather be dead than to have someone else in control of my life and my decisions. I have a life! I will not be intimidated by some asshole who wants to see me dead. I simply will not give some person the satisfaction of seeing me afraid. I have faced death. I have lived through severe injury. I have lived 62 years. I will not, absolutely not allow anyone to dictate my life terms to me. It's settled John, I took your advice and hired security. The farm is safe and well patrolled. We are safe here, of that I am sure. Otherwise I would move Erica to one of her Aunts' houses. But if you think I am going to stop living and making my own decisions, you are full of shit!"

Quim clapped. "Bravo! Well said! I can't say that I don't agree with her, John. You've known Mildred almost as long as I have. Have you even known her to back down from an issue or a situation? My god. The only thing that is different about Mildred now, is that she is more Mildred than she ever was before now."

"I'd like it to stay that way." John answered emphatically. "Look, what the hell do I have to do? Quit my job and baby-sit you full time to protect you from yourself? What? What is it with you? I understand the attitude you have. Trust me. I don't believe this situation is going to continue indefinitely. We will solve it. I just happen to want you alive and kicking at the end of the investigation."

"That's my goal, too." Mildred answered coolly. "Look, I am not going to get myself killed. I have run my errand, I will stick around and not leave without an armed security person. However, remember Reagan? Our former President, that Reagan? He was shot with the best security men in the business in attendance. So if you really think a bodyguard will stop someone from killing me, think again. As George says, a good hunting rifle with a scope, 'Boom Mildred, You're Dead!' That's what he says, John."

"Okay! I give up! You win. Do what you have to do. I'll do what I have to do. I can put you in protective custody."

Mildred blanched white. "You wouldn't do that! My god! I'll tell you this, John," her voice grew steely cold, as did her eyes, "if you so much as attempt to do this, I will never, ever have anything to do with you again." She rose abruptly and left the room.

It was deathly quiet after she left. Every last one of the group were rendered speechless. Finally, Quim cleared his voice, "I say old man, I think she meant that."

"I think she did." John answered quietly.

# CHAPTER SIXTEEN

Mildred left the room in a fury. If this was blinding rage, then she was experiencing her first bout with it. Nothing had ever touched off this kind of emotion. In one sense, it fascinated her. She could not believe the intensity of her internal emotions. But in the larger sense, she was frightened. More frightened than she had ever been before tonight.

The urge to run until she couldn't run anymore was powerful. She wanted to fling open the door and run out into the night. She wanted to scream and rage and vent until there was not a word of protest left in her mind.

Instead she walked out to the wide porch at the back of the house and sat on one of the chairs. She didn't hear or notice John as he entered the room.

"I'm sorry." His apology was simple. "I'll go if you want me to."

Her immediate reaction was to stiffen and consider his suggestion. She knew this was the moment of definition in their relationship. Never had she expected to have to make a decision about John and herself under this kind of circumstance. Yet, it didn't surprise her. He was a cop and would always think like a cop. She, on the other hand, reacted intuitively and valued her ability to go with gut feelings. Their conflict of will had always been at the base of their interpersonal issues. Never had this been so evident as now.

She knew if she sent him away, he would never be back. It would be irrevocable and like Humpty-Dumpty would never be repaired.

With a start, Mildred realized she loved John. If he was gone from her life, she would die of loneliness for him. It was the simple truth. Slowly, she turned to face him in the darkened porch.

"I love you, John," her honesty surprised her. What ever she had thought she was going to say, was usurped by the intensity of her feelings for him. "I couldn't bear it if you went away. So don't."

"Oh, Mil." He put his arm around her and held her close to him. "I think I'd die if something happened to you."

"We need to go back with the others." She rose from the chair. "When all this is over, we need to talk about this. Obviously, it can't be ignored."

He led the way out of the room and back to the library. Three faces were focused on their entrance. Freddy had put the shortcake and coffee away in the kitchen. In their places, on the low table, stood a bottle of scotch, glasses, and ice in a bucket.

"I'm pouring, what would you like?"

"I've got the brandy." Alison held up the bottle. "If you want some, that is. I think I'm the only one who drinks it in this group."

"You are," Freddy said, "a minority for sure. Each to their own taste, I say. So what's your pleasure, Mil, scotch?"

"Yes, a double with ice."

"I'll have Diet Coke," added John. He reached for the glasses as Freddy finished pouring the scotch and handed him the coke. He handed Mildred her drink. "To solutions," he raised his glass in Mildred's direction.

"Hear! Hear!" agreed Alison, as she took a deep swallow from her brimming glass. She then placed it on the table. "I need to talk a little. I thought I would go crazy up there in my room. Will couldn't come and he's the only one who has ever understood. But I just can't stand it, so I had to come down here with all of you. I'm so scared!" Her voice quivered with emotion. "I know it's selfish, but that could have been me today. I loved Ashley. We were so close. I feel like such a shit because in the end, I'm glad it wasn't me. That's so terrible to feel that way!" Her sobs filled the air.

"Alison," Freddy said calmly, "it's normal to feel that way. Look, if someone had been pointing a gun at Ashley, in all probability, you would have instinctively stepped in front of her to stop her from being shot. That's how intensely you cared about her. But in this case, you had no warning. She drank the wine and died immediately. To be thankful it wasn't yourself is a normal reaction. If you couldn't save her, at least you survived. What you're feeling is survivor guilt."

"I've heard of that," agreed Quim. "Sure, lots of full term GIs, who survived Vietnam, felt that way. They came home and their buddies didn't. They felt guilty because they lived and the others died. We all know our personal faults. What can happen is we falsely assume the guys who lost their lives didn't deserve to die, because we don't know their personal faults. All we know is how good they appeared to be. Ergo, we the sinners should be the ones who died and they, who certainly didn't have faults like us, should have come home."

"In a nutshell!" Freddy agreed. "This happens to survivors of plane wrecks, car accidents, fires, you name it. Hence the name survivor guilt"

"Oh, god!" sighed Alison. "I hope I don't go on feeling this way. I do know this," she turned to John, "you guys had better find that killer before I do, otherwise I'll kill him myself." He angry words bit into the air.

"Let the police handle it, Ms. Lippencott. They do know what they're doing." John assured her. "You could get hurt trying to find a killer."

"Well, Ashley didn't deserve to die like that. She was a good person. She was so proud of writing that book. I'll have to see what the manuscript is like. I had no idea Ashley had any interest in writing her own book. It's thrilling in a way. It will be like talking to her again." Alison's color had returned somewhat. "An author's style tells you a lot about them. When you're creating characters, it's a projection of your own personality into each one of them. In a way, it's kind of scary."

"Right!" Freddy chimed in, "it's like taking a Rorschach exam, or a TAT!"

"What the hell is that?" Quim asked.

"Thematic Apperception Test. You are shown pictures and you tell a simple story about what you see. They're both called perception tests. That's because the person taking the test is projecting what they perceive the picture or ink blots mean."

"Scary . . . ." Quim volunteered. "Remind me to never let you test me. I don't think I want anyone getting into my mind."

"Well, Quim, I hate to tell you this," Freddy grinned at him, "some minds are easier to crack into than others."

"Like safes, I suppose?" Quim joked back at her.

"Yeah, something like that," she answered. "Seriously though, psychological testing can tell you a lot about a person. We use them as tools to assist in making a diagnosis for treatment."

"That's what I meant when I said, a book can tell you about the author." Alison stated. "I don't mean you really know that person, but you do get an idea of their broad range of personality. For example, there are types of people I just can't stand. When I find a personality I am projecting is one of those types, I have to be careful or they are always cast in a negative light. I don't know how else to explain it."

"I know what you mean," Freddy answered. She stopped to take a sip of her scotch. "That's kind of the down side of my business. There are definitely types I don't want to work with, but sometimes I can't be choosy."

"Being a cop, you meet all kinds of people." John added to the discussion. "I recognize types, too. You begin to notice characteristics of either criminals or victims. For example, when I meet a couple, in fairly short order, I know whether or not the wife or girlfriend is battered. Even without the bruises, I know the symptoms in the relationship. It's the kind of thing you wish you didn't see after a while. My job has brought me together with some of the most evil people you could ever meet. It is not for the faint of heart. Lots of cops end up drinking to cope with what they deal with every day. Me, I do AA. Found out the booze doesn't solve a damn thing, but gives you more problems than you ever bargained for."

"So, what the hell is going to happen? Is Mildred here, going to be a captive in her own house?" Quim put the question to John.

"No, I won't do that. However, we do have to have someone go with her when she leaves the grounds. I'm just encouraging some down time on the property." His concern for her was reflected in his glance. "I have made a decision to leave the department. My birthday is next month, but I'm leaving within two weeks. This case has done a lot to make me look at what I want to do for the rest of my life. I'm tired of murders, corpses, perpetrators, crime, you name it, I'm tired of dealing with batterers, people who hate cops." He looked at Mildred, "I want some time to spend with my friends."

Freddy looked at him closely. "You're serious. I never in my wildest thought you'd leave willingly. I thought the department was your whole life. What's changed?"

"I have been thinking about teaching." He replied.

"Teaching!" Freddy's voice rose in disbelief. "John . . . ." Her tone was almost musical as it raised in question. "I can't picture this. Teach how? What?"

"Seminars, workshops, demonstrations on how to use equipment One of the reasons I have been so reluctant to leave and retire is because I think I have a vast knowledge base of procedure and operational strategy that would be lost. I've been talking to department chiefs all over Minnesota. These are people I've gotten to know through common investigations. Many of them want me to start a consultant business. So, I've been thinking of setting up educational workshops for police officers. It's that simple."

"I think it's a great idea, John." Mildred said. "Is this what you eluded to earlier today? Or was it yesterday? I can't remember who said what, when."

"Yeah. I figured with all this turmoil going on, it wasn't the time." He answered.

"Actually, it would take my mind off the worst of it." Mildred told him. "There's nothing quite like a project to take one's mind off morbid thinking."

"Still, the fact remains, Mildred, your life is in eminent danger." John interjected. "I don't want you to lose track of the reality here."

"Believe me, John, I won't" she answered. "I won't."

"Where were we, before we got sidetracked?" Quim asked. He leaned back on the sofa and lit his pipe. The scent of his Cavindish Blend filled the space around the low table. With the pipe in his mouth and the silvery sideburns, which framed his face, Quim looked every inch the professor that he was.

Quim's year in Britain had been spent on a sabbatical leave. He was at Oxford studying literature. Currently he was the head of the English Department at the University. Like his friends, Quim's vocation had brought him into intense interactions with people. It didn't pay to be a professor who was reclusive. At this point in his career, he had also been published many times. Much of his writings were non-fiction. However, in the past two years, he had published several volumes of poetry, which received creditable reviews.

Mildred knew that Quim had recently broken off a decade long relationship with one of his former graduate students. When she and Freddy had run into him at Orchestra Hall in Minneapolis, he had seemed lifeless and despondent. It had not taken the two women long to decipher the reason for his feelings.

Since then, Mildred had made sure to include Quim in a lot of the social activities and fund-raisers for the women's shelter. In a matter of a few months, his demeanor had changed dramatically. He was once again the debonair professor from the University of Minnesota.

As if he knew she was thinking about him, he raised his eyes and looked into hers. He saw a change there. Mildred didn't have the stressed appearance she had previously. Mildred and John had not been absent from the room very long, but Quim knew in his guts, something significant and irrevocable in their relationship had occurred. John no longer looked haunted and Mildred seemed to glow. If he knew anything about human nature, he knew he didn't have a chance with Mildred emotionally. She had simply eluded him and his feelings for her.

He sighed and asked, "is this educational project going to be a joint venture?"

"Yes." Mildred answered emphatically. "We haven't begin even begun the preliminary planning, but it will be a joint venture. I think what we'll do is form a partnership. I certainly have the physical setting for putting on educational seminars. We have a separate building that could house up to twenty people. If there are less than ten attending, we could use this house and the bedrooms upstairs to accommodate them."

"The house is certainly big enough." Alison commented. "Where would my room be? Certainly, I couldn't be on the same floor as a bunch of people attending a workshop. I'd never get any writing done with that kind of distraction."

"I'd move you and Freddy to the third floor with me. There's plenty of room up there. In fact, I'm not so sure that wouldn't be a good idea under any circumstances." Mildred added.

"All those steps," Alison muttered, "would be the death of me."

"Just imagine you're using the stair-stepper at the exercise center." Freddy quipped, then turned to Mildred. "Where do I fit into the partnership?"

"I can answer that," John said. "Psychology is always a factor in every crime. Sometimes it isn't so easy to identify, especially if the crime seems to be a random occurrence. But when you have serial killings, or burglaries with similar mode of operation, then you can take a close look at the psychological factors. Yes, Freddy, we can certainly use your services."

"I guess a gothic romance writer is out." Alison offered. "Of course, I travel so much you couldn't count on me as a secretary, much less an investigator." She saw the look of doubt that crossed Freddy's face. "You don't know much about investigation, do you Freddy? For your information, research for novels is investigation. And I can tell you, if I have some historical facts wrong, my readers will let me know in no uncertain terms. They know it's fiction, but the history had better be correct."

"She's right." John interjected. "Ninety percent of investigation is making calls, doing interviews, checking records over and over again, doing a lot of sitting around in some stationary place to observe people come and go from some other stationary place. It does get quite tedious. Nowadays there's a lot of computer search work, too. This does make things easier, but it's still a lot of grunt work."

"You make your job sound like it's a grind." Freddy said.

"I wouldn't go so far as to say that about it, but it does get to be very repetitive. Essentially you are nosing around to find information someone else doesn't want you to find. Simple." John added.

"I've got to go to bed." Alison said suddenly. "I would just like to forget what is happening for awhile. I hope I can sleep." She got up abruptly from her chair and swayed slightly. "I'm a little unsteady." She took some faltering steps.

"I'll help you get upstairs. No sense in you falling and adding more problems to the list." Quim rose from the sofa next to where Alison had been sitting.

"Just don't take any more pills," Freddy admonished. "If you have problems with sleep, you let me know. For the time being, I don't think you need to add any more to the mix you have on board."

"I won't," Alison said sulkily. She let Quim take her arm and help her out of the room. He shut the door behind them.

# CHAPTER SEVENTEEN

Mildred, John, and Freddy fell back in their chairs. Mildred was the first to speak. "I hope she doesn't take anything. I do worry about her emotional stability."

"She's a difficult person to decipher. I'm never quite sure who the real Alison Lippencott is. Just about the time she seems defined, she displays another facet of her personality." Freddy said.

"Well, it's like she said, a writer projects many personalities. I suppose that's what makes her seem so odd at times. I've got to say this, she's not everybody's cup of tea." John added thoughtfully. "I would have a real hard time spending a lot of time with her."

"Her childhood in Chicago was a nightmare." Freddy shared with the two of them. "I read one of those bios about her. It wasn't real in-depth, but it did talk about how her parents died in a fire. The authorities thought it was gang related, but never got the arsonist. Real crappy thing to happen."

"What little she's said, it sounds like her dad was real abusive. And, if anything she said last night was true, he was selling her to his friends." Mildred added. "God . . . . imagine how she must have felt. Then she gets taken in by a local businessman and his wife, and the same thing happens." She paused. "Well, not exactly the same, but this guy starts having sex with her. She couldn't have been very old. Then, after his wife dies, he really starts in. Jeez, where do these sleazy people come from? Are they born or are they made?"

Mildred inquired of Freddy.

"You're asking mois?" Freddy pointed to her chest. "How would I know? I'm just a psychiatrist, not a miracle worker. I don't know the answer for everything."

"I thought psychiatry had a niche for every type of person." John added.

"Not quite." Freddy said, "The DSM-IV covers a lot. However, sexually deviant personalities are not necessarily mentally ill, they're usually sociopathic personalities. Those folks don't respond to medications. They just plain don't give a damn about anyone else. It isn't a medical illness, it's a criminal activity."

"Yeah, I've dealt with enough of those creeps," John quipped. "Some of them are at Moose Lake, locked up for life."

"You think Alison's dad was deviant?" Mildred asked Freddy.

"I'd say so. From what she said last night, and what little she shared about her foster parents, I'd say she was a childhood victim of severe sexual abuse."

"She sure has overcome a lot to succeed as a writer. Just imagine how it must have been for her, growing up and not having anyplace to turn to for help. Ashley was probably the first girlfriend she ever had. She quit high school, so she must not have had any opportunity to make friends until she went to college. My god!" Mildred said with a grimace, "she really didn't have any childhood. How tragic."

It was such a contrast to Mildred's childhood. As the only child of a farmer and his wife who lived in the countryside of rural Louisiana, she had been cherished and loved. Though they did not have much money, her parents were lavish in their affection. Mildred's gaze swept around the library. When she was growing up, she had dreamt of having books, lots of books. Her dad couldn't afford to buy any for her, because everything he earned went for food, grain for animals, and taxes on the property. She loved the public library. She would go there and indulge her love of literature, by bringing home as many books as she could check out at one time. When she was little, it was only three books a week. It was disappointing, because she usually had them read within two days. Then she had to wait until the following Monday to get some more. The highlight of her young life, was when the librarian made the executive decision to let her check out the number of books adults could take, ten a week. She had acquired glasses for her near-sightedness in Sixth Grade. She wondered if it was from reading so much. During the years of Seventh and Eighth Grade, Mildred was in bibliophile heaven. She read as often as she could. Her world soared with Mythology and Fantasy. Her nose was stuck permanently in a book.

When she and Emil built this house, she designed a library for her book collection. She knew she had as many mysteries as the local branch of the Anoka County Library System. She loved old books, new books, and mysteries. She had acquired several valuable first editions of Mark Twain's books. One was a gift she received as a child, from a Louisiana neighbor, the other she found at a garage sale in St. Paul. She was comfortable in this room. On cold winter evenings, the fireplace would crackle with blazing logs. Mildred would curl up on the sofa and read for hours, consuming herbal tea for nourishment. The books that lined the walls were old friends. She would read and re-read books. Like every dedicated reader, she discovered new things and ideas, plots and sub-plots every time she re-read a book. Now, on this May evening so fraught with tension, the atmosphere of the room gave her strength and courage. This was the core of her universe. This place, this property was her spiritual center.

"Mildred!" John persisted. "Are you listening?" Concern filled his eyes. "Boy, you were sure out there. I was saying that this might be a good opportunity to talk with George and Joel. I'm not sure if Quim is going to rejoin us or not, but we could do some strategy and planning."

"Oh," Mildred sighed, "you're right. I was just feeling more at ease than I have felt since yesterday morning. I can hardly grasp that in the course of one and a half days, there have been three murders. What time is it, anyway?" She inquired.

"Just nine-thirty. Wonder if George really went to bed?" John asked. "I know him. No matter how exhausted he gets, he still stays up all hours. I'll go down and see if he's still up. Be back in a few minutes."

When he left the room, Anubis and Sea Shell went with him. Sea Shell was a tortoise shell cat. Like every one of Mildred's animals, she worshiped John. She also figured he was worth a treat as they passed through the kitchen.

"What magical power does that guy have?" Freddy asked Mildred. "These animals go nuts every time he comes around here. I thought Anubis was a guard dog. He's just as enamored as the rest of the bunch."

"I don't know. They just know he loves them. Unconditional love or something. It's just John's nature. I think sometimes, he gets along better with animals than he does with people. Animals don't commit crimes." Mildred mused.

"Right." Freddy laughed. "Then explain to me why your cats are always stealing things from me."

"Food is different. If it's edible, they aren't responsible. You'd think no-one ever got fed around here. It was just like that at home. My dad always had a crew of yard and house animals following him everywhere. The hope of food was their primal instinct." Mildred said.

"Well, your dad!" Freddy went on, "was the biggest soft touch in the world. It was a joke. You know, it's funny, but John kind of reminds me of him."

"John? You're kidding. I . . ." Mildred protested.

Freddy cut her off, "Mil, listen, your dad was pretty traditional. Remember what a hard time he gave you when you talked about college. What finally persuaded him to support it, was the fact that you were going to study nursing. He figured that would help you when it came time to raise babies. His idea of a career was to stay at home, be a good wife, and raise a passel of children. He also wanted you to marry someone who could carry on the family farm."

"Good thing he's still alive, then." Mildred said, "'cause I have no plans on farming in Louisiana."

"I wouldn't bet the farm on it." She laughed." Why is it, every time you get a chance to go home and visit, you're off like a shot! Don't tell me you don't like that place. You've got Louisiana dirt in your veins. Just a matter of time, sweetie, and you'll go home to roost"

"Freddy, you are so full of it! Sure, I love going home, but my parents are getting on, and I want to spend time with them."

"So tell me, Ms. Denial, when we were down there, why you and your daddy spent all that time going over the family finances and records. He now owns a sizable amount of property, and it's all free and clear. You are the only child, and there's a land-boom in Louisiana. Trust me Toots, you may be a Psych Nurse, but you are sure as heck, going to be a wealthier one than you are already."

"Actually, we talked about leaving the large acreage to the state as a wildlife sanctuary. It's too beautiful to destroy with housing tracts and mini-malls." Mildred told her. "Daddy is going to talk with the Louisiana DNR about it."

"You know, Mil, what's so much fun being from the south? People call their parents mama and daddy until they die at a hundred and one. It's like we're perennial children, no matter our age. It's really comforting, when you think about it. We have conversations about our parents and refer to them as 'your daddy' and 'your mama' like we're little kids. That doesn't seem to happen here in the north. Why is that, do you suppose?"

"Cold weather and the north wind, I guess." Mildred mused.

"Seriously, why is it?" Freddy persisted. "There's something so charming talking to southern people about their ancestors. It's like they have more regard for them or something."

"I don't agree with you. For a lot of reasons, and some of them not so good, family bloodlines have been examined under a microscope. That doesn't happen in the same way, up north. You've met some of the neighbors around here. Most of them, whose families have been here for any amount of time, are Scandinavian. Look at how many of them have told us the histories of their family immigration to Minnesota? We've even heard ghost stores that are enough to keep you awake a few nights." Mildred said.

"I don't know, it just doesn't seem the same." She replied, then mused, "maybe you're right though, I tend to look at things from a southern viewpoint. We're raised with a constant awareness of who your daddy and your mama were. Who their parents were and how they were connected to so and so, that we've known for years. It does get kind of complicated."

Freddy paused in her conversation. The sound of footsteps was heard in the kitchen. Male voices reached their ears.

"I hear John. Sounds like George and Joel were still awake." As Mildred spoke, the men entered the room.

"Having a strategy meeting without the lead security division, I hear," George laughed. Trailing behind him was Anubis and the two other dogs. "I've brought the troops."

"I see that. I hope you realize Francis doesn't let the outside dogs indoors." Freddy was fending off the young dogs and their happy tongues. "I'm not going to need a shower, at this rate." She turned to the terriers. "You two need to behave. If you're going to be in the house, you have to be good dogs." She admonished.

"Good luck," Mildred said to her.

"It's not luck, it's training. Dog, Sit!" George commanded. The two young animals immediately took positions at Freddy's knee.

"How do you do that?" Freddy asked. "I've been trying to get these pups to behave since I moved in here."

"They have to know you mean business. I've watched you, Freddy. You set great boundaries with people, but you don't with the animals.

Believe me, if you want an animal to be well behaved, you have got to train it. This means consistent, firm, reinforced commands. You can't lie down on the job." George continued.

"I know, or you go to the dogs." Freddy laughed.

"You remember," He laughed.

"How could I forget, it's so hokey." She assured him. "If you want to train a dog, you can't get down on his level. You have to be the alpha dog symbolically. Yes, I remember."

"I'll have the dogs sit by me. Here!" He commanded. The two young animals immediately left Freddy's side and went to George. "Sit!" They did. "Now, you see, it's really quite simple." He picked up his can of Diet Coke and leaned back in the chair.

"Don't we wish we could have this same effect on people." Joel offered. He had taken a place in the background. He was an observer, more than a participant in the planning. Joel was by nature a reticent person. His ability to pay attention to detail was astronomical. George couldn't believe it when he first ran into Joel. The guy never missed anything. It was almost uncanny. Sometimes, George told him, it was downright scary.

So, Joel watched and took notes of the meeting.

At just that moment, Quim entered the room. "Ah, the gathering of the troops, I hope I'm welcome." He looked to John for direction. "I've got Alison all tucked up in her bed. I think she's set for the night," he assured.

"Sit down, Quim. You've met George here, but have you met Joel?" John asked him.

"No, I haven't. Good to meet you." He walked around the sofa to shake Joel's hand. "I'm impressed, it seems like Mildred is in capable hands." He then sat down in his vacated wing chair.

"It's getting late," John said. "Why don't we just discuss the status of security here and then call it a night."

"Sounds like a plan," George agreed. "Joel and I have gotten the entire perimeter of the property secure. We fenced off the field road and have activated the security system for the fence line. If someone climbs over, under, or through, we'll know it. There are virtually no areas that have not been checked. The surveillance issue is taken care of at this point. No one will get in here without having their presence known."

"Good." John answered. He pulled his pipe out of his jacket pocket. As he struck a match to the tobacco, he addressed the group. "At this point we know that the killer is still at large. We know that Mildred has been a target. Now, it seems as though Alison has also been targeted as a victim. One of the things the department will do is study the possible connections between the three murders. On the surface, there does not seem to be a connection. Alison did not even know Mildred when Manuchi was in the hospital. There doesn't seem to be any way she could have knowledge of any information he may have shared with someone."

Quim interrupted, "you seem to be making the assumption that Manuchi did indeed share some vital piece of information with Mildred."

"We are not really left with any other possible conclusion. Mildred has led, to all intents and purposes, a pretty blameless life. There were no previous attempts on her life, nor were there any threats of any kind. At least none I'm aware of," he glanced in Mildred's direction.

She indicated he was correct by a shake of her head. He continued, "So we are left with the conclusion that he told her something."

"Well, I have wracked my brain trying to remember any possible thing he could have said to me that would be significant. There was nothing. We did a lot of talking about women's issues. He was quite a supporter of equal opportunity for women. He joked about it at times. Said it really took a woman to run things properly. When I asked him what he was talking about, he would laugh and tell me to talk with his wife and mother. Having met his wife, I know who the strong partner in the restaurant business was. There was no question, she was the real power behind King Dino's throne." Mildred added with a smile. "I've gotten to know her pretty well. She is a dynamic individual. That restaurant chain is quite successful. They were even talking about the possibility of a national expansion."

"His wife didn't mention that to me," John said. "On the other hand, I don't suppose it would have seemed like there could be a connection between his death and expansion of the business."

"There probably isn't." Mildred said. "His death was so savage. The person who killed him, hated him. There was a viciousness to the injuries that indicates a lot of feeling. It was intense, personal, and vicious. It was also meant to intimidate me. What's happened though, is I don't feel intimidated, I feel enraged. I'm with Alison, if the killer pops up in my sights, I'd kill him." She finished.

"And, it wouldn't solve a damn thing. Then you'd go to jail and I'd have no business partner." John stated. "I'm just going to have to keep an eye on you. Believe me, Mildred, we're going to get the person who has committed these crimes. It's just a matter of time.

John turned to George, "so everything's secure here, then?"

"Yeah," came the reply. "A cockroach couldn't squeak through the lines. Trust me." George assured. "One of us will stay awake all night. With the security at the front of the driveway and the system activated, you're all safe."

"Well, I'm exhausted." Mildred said, "I don't know about the rest of you, but I need sleep. Thanks George, it was a good idea to have you here. I believe I will sleep like a baby." She rose from the chair. "If you need to continue feel free. I've got to get some shuteye."

"We're almost done. George and I will finish our business and then I'm leaving," John added. He rose and gave Mildred a hug. "You go on up and get to bed. I'll be back first thing in the morning. Okay?"

"Okay." She agreed. She left the room.

"Well, what do you think Freddy, shall we leave these gentlemen to their discussion and absent ourselves?"

"Seems like a plan." Freddy agreed. "Here, help me clear this table and load the dishwasher. Then, I'll see how tired I am."

The two of them picked up the glasses and bottles, leaving the three men in the library. They shut the door as they left.

# CHAPTER EIGHTEEN

Freddy stood by the wide porch windows. She had opened them wide to the night sky. The porch was designed for four seasons. In the summer, the windows could be opened to allow the flow of air through the entire room. In winter, thermal storm windows kept the room quite snug. But now, in the warm spring air, the scent of Lily of the Valley and Lilacs filled the room with their rich scent. Freddy breathed the perfumed air deep into her lungs. More than anything she missed the scent of Jasmine and Wisteria in the spring. Her childhood home stood on the shore of Lake Ponchatrain. Her favorite months in Louisiana were May and October. It seemed as if this was when the temperature and climate were the most habitable. Although she loved her home state at any time, she did admit August could become quite uncomfortable. People up north would ask how she could stand those long summer days. In truth, even though she acknowledged the humidity in Louisiana as uncomfortable, she didn't think it was any worse than the humidity of Minnesota summers. It was just different.

She had freshened her drink. Freddy felt comfortable on the porch. It was clearly a southern extension of a northern home. There was the green foliage of several Banana plants. The Hibiscus plants were in bloom. Bright flowers of red, orange, and yellow proclaimed the advent of spring. Starter plants lined the entire southern exposure. There was a wide sill with broad windows. In the spring, sunlight spilled onto the vast expanse of sill, encouraging hundreds of seeds to germinate into flowers and vegetables for the garden.

In the last several years, Freddy and Mildred had both become avid gardeners. Francis managed the kitchen garden, but Mildred and Freddy had put together several extensive perennial flower gardens. As Freddy gazed out the window, she couldn't see the gardens, but she could smell the deep, rich earth that was freshly turned. Just a week ago, Mildred had driven the garden tractor through the areas that could be machine mulched. These were areas that would contain the annual plants. In the perennial areas, they mulched by hand, weeding and cultivating the earth with tender passion.

Quim's voice cut through her thoughts. "What do you think is going on with John and Mildred?" His question was direct and to the point.

She hesitated, not wanting to smash his hopes. The reality though, appeared to be that Mildred and John had come to some kind of terms with their volatile relationship. Freddy has always wondered why the two of them just hadn't worked harder on the differences. She had to admit, though, Emil had been a very good match for Mildred. Perhaps, when they were younger, she and John simply could not have solved the communication problems.

"I'm not entirely sure, Quim. Something is different. I don't want to make too many assumptions, but I think they somehow realized if things didn't change, they would lose what they had. I think Mildred's always been in love with John. The problem has always been his inability to accept her as a self-sufficient human being. It's a difference in how they were raised. Mildred was pretty independent by the time she was four years old. She grew up on a farm and she started in helping her parents when she was really young." She thought a bit. "The other thing is, she's smart. Even as a child, Mildred was off in the dream land of thoughts and ideas. She was pretty creative and was a stellar performer in grammar school. Now a person like that, is not going to take kindly to some guy telling her to stay home and mind the babies."

Quim laughed. "Jesus. I never thought about it like that. I do remember how they used to fight in college. He'd give her a hard time about getting a degree, when a woman's job was to stay at home and take care of the husband and the kids. I thought he was kidding!"

"No indeed. He was not kidding. John comes from a Bohemian immigrant family. His daddy ruled the roost with an iron fist. The girls were always busy with the housework, the canning in the summer, making clothes, basically serving dad and the brothers. His mother was worn out by middle-age. I remember meeting her, when Mildred and I stopped to visit her. She was dying of cancer. I could swear to you, Quim, she looked almost glad to be going. I think she just plain wore out."

"Sounds gruesome." He agreed. "What in the hell kept her with him so long? I don't get it."

"She loved him, you idiot. Honest to God, Quim, sometimes I think you got a lot of brains, but got shortchanged in the common sense department. Why the hell do any mismatched people get together? Why do some of these gals at the shelter stay with some guy for too many years while he beats her? If you can come up with an answer, you let me know, will ya." Freddy admonished.

"I have never understood that kind of violence." Quim said. "Mildred has told me some of the things she has had to assist these women with as they try to extricate themselves from these relationships. I don't know how some of them have survived the abuse. I used to think they were getting something from the batterer. Or, worse yet, that they must like it. My God! I was stupid!"

"A lot of people don't understand the dynamics. The thing is, lots of people think 'you made your bed, lie in it'. They don't understand the women are held in the situation by fear. And they have good reason to be afraid. It's a very dangerous time for a woman when she tells the batterer she's going to leave. This is a crucial period. Most women are at the greatest risk during this time. This is when most of them are severely injured or killed." She paused, "and then you have the people who think, if she's getting hit, she must have done something to deserve it. My God! It's beyond comprehension."

"It's worse in the rural area, isn't it?" Quim asked.

"I don't know if it's worse, but it certainly is more difficult for a woman to get help. If she's isolated on some farm in the middle of Pine County, for example, it's hard to let anyone know you are in trouble. Some of these guys take the phone when they leave the house. Some of the women are locked in so they can't leave. I'll tell ya, Quim, it makes my blood boil." Freddy said forcefully, "that's what pisses me off so much about this situation with Mildred being threatened. Someone is playing 'cat and mouse' with her. It's batterer mentality."

"Jesus, Freddy!" Quim cleared his throat. "We've got to do something. But, what?" He asked. "I feel so helpless about what's happening."

"I know. That's what's driving me nuts. There doesn't seem to be anything I can do to stop the process. Someone really hates Mildred, that's what is going on here. This isn't just some random threat. There's a reason for it. I don't think she knows anything about the mob. I think that idea is a tempest in a teapot."

"Like hide the object in plain sight?" Quim inquired.

"That's exactly what I mean. Look at it this way. Dino Manuchi could have been killed very easily. Why go to all the trouble of setting up this look-alike situation with her accident? It doesn't make sense. I think the real reason is something else. We have to figure out what it is. That's the only way we're going to stop this craziness."

"I don't have the vaguest notion where to start." Quim said. "For one thing, I was gone when the accident happened. So there's a whole lot of information I never knew about in regard to it. You were here, Freddy, what do you think? I know you didn't live here in the house then, but you were in Minneapolis area. You have a much better grasp of the whole mess, and to top it off, you spent a lot of time with Mildred when she was recovering. You must have some ideas." He insisted.

"It's odd. At the time I kept thinking it reminded me of a stalking situation. Except it was different. It's so hard to put my finger on it, but it felt more like a jealousy triangle. It didn't make sense though, because Mildred knew Manuchi's wife real well. Mildred was just getting involved with the women's shelter. Dino Manuchi's wife was one of the executive board members at that time. Still is, actually. Mildred and her really hit it off. Spent a fair amount of time together. It was odd when Manuchi ended up in her psychiatric unit."

"Did she keep on being friends with his wife?"

"Well, I wouldn't say they were friends exactly, but I think it was certainly headed in that direction. They have a lot in common. Crystal is from the south, too."

"Crystal?" Quim asked, "That's her name?"

"Yes, her mother had a thing about gemstones and rocks. I think sometimes people don't give much thought to how the name, might affect the child. As names go, Crystal is a lovely name." Freddy leaned back in the wicker rocker. "Some of her siblings weren't so lucky."

The night was so soft. The black, shadowed edge of the trees, added definition to the manicured lawn. The tree line was only twenty feet from the house on the north side. The porch, which ran the length of the house, featured a bank of windows on that side.

Freddy had candles burning on the porch. No lights marred the beauty of the flickering tapers. Freddy liked atmosphere. She liked the semblance of romance. She had always felt the mood created by your surroundings were a major factor in how you handled life situations.

Her life had changed dramatically the previous summer. Romance has been snuffed from her life within the last year, when her significant other had died in an accident on the freeway. She had been devastated by it. In the ensuing months, her practice had been affected. Freddy had referred many clients to different therapists, as she coped with her own tragedy.

The beginning of this May had marked a major change in her progress. She was taking on clients again and had become very involved with the Women's Shelter. Mildred had brought Freddy home with her a month after the accident which had taken the life of her friend. Freddy had been isolating herself in her apartment, refusing to see anyone. Mildred, who had been worried sick over Freddy's behavior, involved John in the intervention. Between the two of them, they convinced Freddy that her isolation was very unhealthy.

During the months between August and April, Freddy slowly began to revert to her usual optimistic self. Out of the tragedy of her loss, she began to understand the ties that bound families together, and the emotional upheaval caused by the severance of those connections. In truth, she grew up emotionally.

Now, as she sat back reflecting about the current situation, she felt the cold blade of steely resolution take form in her mind. She knew she had to identify the reason behind Mildred's victimization. There was a logical reason for it. Perhaps if she and Quim discussed her ideas, they would hit on something significant.

"Quim," she began, "let's just brain storm about this. What are the reasons why a person wants to kill someone?"

"Whew!" he mulled, "that's tough for me to look at. I have got to be the world's biggest pacifist. I cannot conceive of killing a person. As to why, God . . . . I just don't know."

"Sure you do. Just because you wouldn't hate anyone that much, doesn't mean you don't understand the reasons why someone else might want to do it." She looked at him, "you've traveled extensively. You've been in a lot of counties and all over this one. What are the things you've seen in your meandering? I know you've been in dangerous places. You were in one country when a civil war was igniting. What kinds of things were you aware of there?"

"Well, wars are another thing." He answered.

"No, I don't think so. Wars are just murder on a large scale. What was behind it?"

"Power! Wanting power, I guess." Quim sat back thoughtfully and re-lit his pipe. He drew on the stem and then stopped in disgust. "Damn things. Plug up all the time." He pulled a little instrument out of his pocket and began to clean out the pipe bowl. "Let's see. In the civil war you mentioned, there was a lot of money involved, too. Apparently the current President had helped himself to the government till and had transferred a considerable amount of cash and negotiable bonds to a Swiss Bank. Lot's of good it did him. He was the first one killed."

"That's what I mean. Reasons for killing. Keep going," she ordered as she jotted down his ideas in a small notebook.

"Okay, Greed. Power. Jealousy. Wanting something or someone you can't have unless another person is absent. Love?" He looked to her for agreement.

"No, I don't think people murder for love. If you love someone, you don't kill someone they love. Seems simple to me." Freddy quipped. "What else?"

"I don't know if there are any more fundamental reasons why people commit murder." He answered. "Of course, if you get into emotional thoughts and feelings, sometimes people commit murder because of unstable emotions."

"I'm wondering if this isn't the area we should explore. Mildred has led a fairly blameless existence." She caught his glance. "No, Quim, I am not implying Mildred is bland. My God! What a thought!" She laughed. "Not only do I see her as dynamic and brave, but I see her as a mover and shaker in society. She sees an issue, she deals with it." She readjusted in her chair, "But, she may have inadvertently done something that really upset someone else. Someone unstable, who might have misread Mildred's intentions."

"Sure. What about some of the women she is working with at the shelter? Could it be one of them?" He asked.

"I suppose." She thought it over for a minute. Mentally she ran through the different women Mildred had worked with in the last few months. "I can't think of anyone who fits my idea of a profile of a killer. Most of these women are so threatened in their own lives, I cannot conceive of one that would wish harm to Mildred."

"What about Dino Manuchi's wife?" Did she think something was going on between Mildred and Manuchi?"

"No, I would stake my life on it. Crystal is a very complex person with a lot of interests. She runs those restaurants very well. She has an

MBA from Loyola University in Chicago. She's one hell of a business woman. I think she and Mildred were on the road to forming a very tight friendship. Dino liked Mildred, but my impression has always been, he was besotted with his wife. He really seemed like the kind of person who wanted a happy home-life with lots of kids, dogs and cats, and lots of family hanging around. I think his wife is devastated by his murder. For God's sake, who wouldn't be?"

"There's someone, Freddy, there's someone." His voice drifted off. "It's a matter of whom."

# CHAPTER NINETEEN

Mildred awoke feeling quite refreshed. She got up and walked to the windows. The morning was hazy with fog. Tendrils of gray glided along the slope, from the pond, then wended their way along the ground. The gardens were shrouded in the mist. She could hear the horses nickering to one another through the cottony air. A glance at the bedside clock read 5:45 AM.

The morning trill of a robin teased her ears. She got dressed swiftly and checked Erica. The young girl was still sound asleep. She would leave her for awhile. She went down to the kitchen and started a pot of coffee. Then, she went to the porch and picked up her riding boots. Pulling them on, she gave a satisfied grunt and walked out the door.

Maud was waiting for her at the fence rail. She led the horse into the barn, saddling and bridling her with practiced ease. Within ten minutes she and Maud were enjoying a slow canter down the path to the road.

Unlike two days ago, Mildred did not have a sense of unease. She had somehow resolved her previous fears and determined that she would continue to live as she always had. Dino Manuchi's death saddened her a great deal. He had been a man who loved his family and, in a twisted way, had felt loyalty to 'his business group', as he referred to the mob.

In some way, he had fulfilled his obligations to them and had become dispensable. Mildred did not think Crystal would feel quite the same way about it. As the horse cantered, Mildred thought.

Near the driveway, somewhat sheltered from the road, Emil had placed an exercise ring. Mildred stopped and opened the gate in the fenced area. Maud stepped into the ring and began to tug at the reins. She loved being put through her paces. Maud was an excellent riding horse, but she was also a showman's dream. Her strides, her rhythms, her ability to change diagonals and follow commands, was extraordinary. She had a number of blue ribbons in the barn.

Mildred spent the next half hour riding a set pattern of exercise. When they were finished, she opened the gate, and she then directed Maud to walk leisurely toward the road. Mildred was determined to get the newspaper and return to the old routine. If she didn't face the reality of carnage that greeted her the other morning, she knew she would never overcome the fear. They walked on.

Mildred recognized the young face that peered at her. "Ms. Smythe, I didn't expect anyone up so early. You shouldn't be coming back out here." He said gently.

"You're John's friend from Anoka County, aren't you?" She asked.

"Yeah. I moonlight in security. Helps pay the tuition for grad school." He looked up at her. "I'm studying criminal psychology. We're doing more and more of that kind of thing. Profiling killers, I mean."

He looked so young and earnest, Mildred smiled. "Grad school gets expensive, but you won't be sorry."

"I don't think so. Lt. Jacobs got me this job. Well," he said flustered, "not got exactly. He recommended me to George Bonnaunt. I like the job." He emphasized. Then he looked at her and asked, "what are you doing out here?"

"Came out for the morning paper." She answered him. "Maud and I ride out here every day, rain or shine, to pick up the paper."

He blushed and cleared his throat, "just a minute."

She watched him walk to the makeshift security shed. In a moment he returned, straightening the newspaper. She smiled.

He handed up the paper, "saw the morning headlines and couldn't resist. That lady who was killed, she was a friend of the author who lives here?" His voice rose in query.

"Yes, they were best friends." She answered simply.

"Must be awful for her. My best friend was killed years ago in an accident. We were just kids, but I'll never forget him. We were closer than brothers. We were like, inseparable. If you saw one of us, you saw both of us. I miss him still. We were the Jeremy and Jeffrey duo. Now, Jeffrey is gone."

"I'm sorry," Mildred said gently. "I lost my husband two years ago. I miss him, too. We were married for thirty-three years."

"A long time," he agreed. "Do you still think about him a lot?"

"Yes. Although not as intensely as I used to. I remember things sporadically. I'll be doing something and it will remind me of something else," she answered.

"Yeah! It's just like that for me, too." He sighed, "It's not like it used to be, but more like once in a while. Like you said. I play softball. Sometimes I get the strangest feeling he's there, right next to me. I get this feeling that someone's going to try and steal second base. Sure enough. I've gotten more guys out, than you'd believe. All because of this feeling that Jeffrey is telling me to watch second base. Weird."

"Oh, I don't know if it's weird or not. Just different. In a way it's comforting, to think someone is still there somewhere, keeping an eye out for you." She glanced at the drainage ditch. All the yellow tape was gone. The tall grass had regained it's pristine appearance, not a pathway remained, showing that a body had been carried through it. It was as if a magic wand had passed over the scene, erasing the chaos of the murder squad, with the serenity of a country morning. She shuddered.

Jeremy looked at the ditch. As if reading her mind, he said, "I know what you mean. It's disconcerting to see how quickly things revert to normal. It's doesn't look like anything happened. Yet, your whole world can be turned upside down, and not a hair out of place, when it's over. Now that's even more weird."

Mildred couldn't agree more. She had a fleeting image of the Whitcomb, with it's elegant trappings. She would bet the noon lunch today, would be back to their usual high standards of service, as if a murder had never happened on their premises. "It makes the statement, 'what a difference a day makes', make sense, doesn't it?" She asked Jeremy.

"You said it." He glanced around, "well, I'd better finish up my reports. The day man will be here to relieve me pretty quick."

"Yes." Mildred replied, gathering up the reins. "See you again." She nudged the horse into a smooth canter. Ten minutes later, she was brushing down Maud's coat and cooling her down.

Francis called to Mildred from the house. Mildred waved, indicating she had heard her. She picked up the papers and walked slowly to the porch. The papers headline proclaimed, 'FAMOUS WRITER INVOLVED IN SUDDEN DEATH: MURDER SHE WROTE?'

Mildred put the paper down in disgust. She had a pretty good idea how Alison was going to respond to this, and it wouldn't be pleasant. As if in answer to her thoughts, Alison appeared in the doorway. "Are you going to sit out here for coffee?"

"I think so. There's a nice breeze coming through the porch. It's quite pleasant after my ride."

Alison moved smoothly across the room. She had seen the paper and picked it up. A look of utter disgust crossed her face. "I don't know how they can get away with this kind of thing. Don't they have any regard or sensitivity to people's feelings?"

"Sensitivity doesn't sell newspapers," Mildred remarked. She had missed the headlines following her accident and her husband's subsequent death. The two city newspapers had waxed eloquently about the effects of Mildred's near murder and to her husband's heart attack. She had been blissfully unaware of the whole ménage, as they hung around the hospital, waiting for her to talk with them. When that failed, they laid in wait for her doctors. When the medical personnel refused to talk, they went after her three daughters. Renee, Virginia, and Helene were left to deal with the media blitz.

"Well, I've decided to ignore them as much as possible. Will suggested that I consider going out of town for awhile. Just for the peace and quiet. I don't know if that will be permissible, but I'm going to ask about it. They can only tell me no." Alison stated thoughtfully.

"Is Will coming over today?" Mildred asked.

"Yes, he should be here any time." Alison ran a hand over her smooth hair. "I really slept quite well. Of course, the brandy helped, as did the tranquilizer. I really don't want to get too dependent on those things, but I don't think I would have slept a wink without them."

The wide porch was still cool in the morning shade. Alison picked up the paper and began to read. She was daintily sipping her coffee when Father Will entered the porch. "Morning," he offered. "Alison, I'm so sorry I couldn't get here last night. Did you sleep all right?" his soft, gentle voice addressed her.

"I did. Fortified by some Brandy and Tranquilizers, but I slept." She answered him.

"Good." He turned to Mildred. "How are you doing, Mildred?"

"Better, too. "She answered him. "I was up early as always. Maud and I went for a brisk ride and I blew the cobwebs out of my head. Riding does that for me. How is your parishioner doing?"

"He died last night. That's the reason I just couldn't leave. He was young. His wife is left with a small child and no relatives to speak of locally. She had no one to be with her. She and her neighbor are close friends, but the lady is out of town. We spoke with her friend, but she can't get home 'til later today. So, I called some of the women from the church to be with her until someone can get there."

"What happened to her husband?" Alison inquired.

"He was an electrician. He was at work on a construction job. Apparently someone had cut through an electrical line and he was looking for the break. The current was supposedly turned off. It wasn't." Father Will looked distressed. "It's so hard, when people are young, to understand why this kind of thing happens to them."

"Oh, Will," Alison soothed. "I'm so sorry. I know how hard a time you have with people dying for no apparent reason."

"Seems like you and I are cursed somehow," he directed to Alison. "We've had to deal with loss and death too many times." He leaned down and gave her a hug.

Alison gave him a hug in return. "You'd think we would have developed thicker skins by now."

"I don't know if anyone gets used to death. Especially when it's violent in nature." Mildred added. "I cannot fathom why anyone would commit murder." She sat down opposite Alison. "Did Ashley have any family here?"

"No. She was like me in a way, no family left. I think that was the common bond in college. Her parents had died in a car accident while she was in High School. She came form the suburbs, Evanston." Alison paused, "she inherited a trust fund. It's so odd, all these years she has wanted to write a book. Now that she finished it, she died."

Mildred felt a chill in her spine. "Surely, there's no connection."

"That's not what I meant. I think it's just a terrible loss for someone to fulfill a lifelong dream of writing a book, and then not being alive to find out what happened."

"You said last evening, the book was in your car. It's still there, isn't it?" Will asked Alison.

"Oh, I'm sure it is. I was so worried yesterday that something happened to it. That's not logical. We left it in the car and I'm positive it will still be there." Alison paused, "I've done some thinking about it. I'm going to read that manuscript. If it's any good, I'll edit it and submit it to my publisher. Even posthumously, Ashley's book could get recognition if it's any good. I'm the executor for her estate. So it wouldn't be hard for me to follow up and see. My agent was very interested after just talking with her those few minutes."

"I just don't want you to overdo it, Alison." Father Will admonished.

"Oh, Will, I won't. I've come to some resolutions about all this. I'm going to be okay. My God, I've lived through a lot of shit. I'm still here. I'm gonna find out who wants me dead and then I'm gonna make them pay for Ashley's death.

"You never told me much about yourself, Alison. It sounds like your life hasn't been easy. The other night you talked about your dad being in the mob. Was that true?" Mildred asked her.

"You bet your life, it was. That mean son of a bitch. Dying was too good for him. I felt bad about my mother and my brothers though." Alison's teeth clenched. "He really was selling me to his sleezy friends."

Will reached over and put an arm around her. "Alison, you don't have to go over it again."

"That's all right, Will. Talking about it the other night opened the floodgate. It's like Freddy says, you've got to deal with past pain somehow. Otherwise, I might never get over it." She turned to Mildred. "I used to think death stalked me. First my parents burning to death in the house. Then, I lose my foster parents. She died of cancer, but he had an 'accident' the police said." She paused. "The really good thing out of all of it was, even though my foster father was abusing me, he must have like me. He left me a damn fortune. I don't think anybody knew just how rich that old man was. I sure didn't!"

"What kind of business was he in?" Mildred inquired.

"Numbers. He worked with the mob. Just like my dad, except he didn't want to share me with other men." Her mouth twisted sardonically. "I heard rumors in the neighborhood later, that he was some kind of stellar Hit Man for the mob. I do know he used to go on these trips. Be gone for a few days, then back again. My foster mom always worried about him when he was gone. She was gorked out on pain meds most of the last year of her life. I don't think she knew what the hell was going on around her. When she died it was a blessing. 'Course that's when the old man started screwing me all the time. She wasn't there to intervene."

"Why didn't you leave?" Mildred asked.

"And where was I gonna go? I didn't have no one to take care of me. I was sixteen by then. Of statutory age. Do you really think in the fifties anybody was going to put a stop to it? I was considered to all intents and purposes, of age." The bitterness rolled off her tongue.

"Oh, Alison, I'm so sorry. I can't imagine what that must have been like for you." Mildred felt speechless with rage. "It's just so damned frustrating how women have been treated. I think if there's anything that could cause me to kill someone, it's this kind of abuse."

Father Will spoke up, "she had me. I knew what was happening. I couldn't do anything about it either, but at least I could be her friend and confidant. We did have something going for us. We were both smart. I knew if anything could get us out of that neighborhood, it was our brains. When the old man died, she was rich. It saved our lives." He added forcefully.

"Yeah," Alison lapsed into her Chicagoese. "I had quit high school, but with that money, I was able to support us while we studied for the GED's. Will and I passed, no problem. We applied at a number of Colleges and Universities. But we both got accepted close to home. Northwestern in Evanston accepted both of us. We went to back to school in September of '57. I gotta say, we fit in quite well, considering where we came from." She smiled as she looked at Will.

"Then you went to Grad School?" Mildred asked, "University of Chicago?"

"Yeah." Alison replied. "Course Will here, got religion. He left and went to the Episcopal Seminary. That's kind of it."

"You said you'd been married." Mildred pushed. "Your husband died in Vietnam?"

"Yeah, he did," she replied. "That was a fluke. Gordon was really something. Careless, you know. I was in Saigon visiting him when he died. Will was stationed there as a Chaplain, or I don't think I would have survived."

"Gordon really was careless," Will agreed. "He was into drugs pretty heavy, too. What a waste! The guy was really a brain. He was Summa Cum Laude from the University of Chicago. You'd think a guy like that, would know better than to get into junk!"

"Using has nothing to do with brains!" Mildred quipped.

"He was celebrating my arrival. Can you believe that?" Alison asked Mildred.

"What a damn dumb thing to do!"

"He got some really high quality stuff. Most of the drugs were quite good. But this was pure. He didn't even have a clue how lethal that stuff was." Father Will stated quietly. His hand crept over Alison's and gave her a squeeze.

"I'm okay, Will. It was a long time ago and in another world. I finally went on with my life and started writing. My major was literature, so it was a natural. I sure as hell didn't want to teach. I'd had enough of school rooms to last me forever."

"Did your books sell right away?" Mildred asked.

"Surprisingly, yes," she answered. "You see, I'm really gifted at research. My minor was history. I just put together my two academic loves and viola! They sold. Right off the bat, I had best sellers. It was really quite a heady experience for a young widow. Literary teas, luncheons in New York City with my publisher, oh, yes, it was great fun."

"Did Gordon encourage you to write while he was alive?" Mildred asked.

"Actually, yes." Alison answered. "He thought I should try writing because I was so good at story telling. I had a really good imagination. That's how we met. There was a literary group at the University. I would read my short stories to the group. He was always disappointed that I never did anything with my ability. After he died, I decided to try."

"What did he do?" Mildred asked, "I don't mean to be curious, but I'm interested."

"He was the Stores Keeper for the U.S. Army in Saigon. He was really very organized. He ran a tight ship, so to speak. It always amazes me how a guy could be so organized professionally, and be so screwed up personally." Alison shared. Her face had become strained. "Look, enough reminiscing for a bit. It's getting too depressing. I need to get something in my stomach this morning."

Will broke in, "I'm sorry, Alison, it's probably my fault. I shouldn't have said what I said about Gordon." He turned to Mildred. "Is it possible for a tired guy to get a little more coffee with breakfast?" He raised his cup.

"You're right." Mildred said, "if we're going to dissect the last few days, we need to eat. I'll check and see if Francis up." She got up and walked into the kitchen.

# CHAPTER TWENTY

Mildred found Francis pulling pans out of the cupboard. "What's the plan for breakfast?" she asked.

"Prepared Egg Bake last night, just have to pop it in the oven." She answered. "So much comin' and goin' round here, a person's got to get organized." As Francis spoke, she popped two baking pans into the oven. "I'll bet those two from security are gonna be half starved. Now I've got everything ready to go. Cut up the fruit last night and set out muffins to thaw. You just take some coffee and I'll be out to get things set up on the porch." She assured.

"Can I help?" Erica's voice piped from the doorway. "I'm hungry as a bear."

"Me too," Hunter added, as he came into the kitchen.

"The troops have arrived. Ya'll come in here, an' I'll tell you what to do. How's that?" Francis directed to the children. "Let me check your hands. Then you can set up the table on the porch."

"I'll take more coffee out. Will needs more to get fortified for the day." Mildred took a pot full from the big urn. "He's going to need to get some sleep. He's been up all night with his young parishioner."

"Yes," Francis drawled. "I heard all about it. Poor young woman lost her husband and has young children."

"How in the world did you hear about it? You've hardly been home long enough to talk to anyone."

"Of course I've heard. I'm on the prayer chain from church. I got a call about the time I got settled in bed last night" Francis answered. "Not much I don' hear 'bout."

"Maybe we ought to have you out here helping us figure out this murder."

"Well now, Miz Mil, maybe you ought." Francis replied.

"What's the holdup. We need coffee out here." Freddy's sleepy voice joined the chorus. "I stayed up too late and now I'm up too early. This is not good for me. Mildred, Are you holding things up? Get that pot out here."

Mildred laughed. "It's good to hear Freddy complaining again. I was beginning to think things would never get back to normal."

Francis rolled her eyes. "Normal? What normal? Between you and the good doctor out there, nothin' has ever been normal 'round here." She emphasized.

"Come on, kids, you can help out, bring the dishes." Mildred directed as she held the door open with her foot.

Mildred looked around the large enclosure. The porch ran the length of the house. There were three doorways that opened into the space from the kitchen, the library, and the central hall. When Emil designed the house, he wanted something that would conserve heat in winter, and be a cool haven in the summer. He wanted a comfortable and accessible place where he could kick back with the daily paper and forget his problems. He wanted a summer porch, the way he remembered them.

The porch itself was nestled into the house on the east end of the structure. Once the morning sun has passed by, the majority of the porch was in shadow for the rest of the day. The exception was the south end of the porch. Here is where the long, wide sills were exposed to the southern sun, an open invitation for garden pots to be placed until their resident seeds germinated into a variety of plants.

As Mildred brought the new pot of coffee, she glanced at the sill. At least a couple of hundred pots awaited placement in the gardens. Neither she nor Freddy had given a thought to the task at hand. 'Murder will do that,' she thought to herself. With a resolve to set aside time for some garden work, she sat the pot down on the table.

"I think it would be a good idea if we moved over to the chairs. The kids are going to set the table and we're all in the way."

"Okay," Freddy agreed. She was quiet this morning. Mildred wondered how late Freddy and Quim had stayed up last evening.

"What time did you two head off for bed?" Mildred inquired of her sleepy friend.

"Oh, not really all that late." She answered. "I think there has been so much psychological trauma that we're all exhausted."

"Did you solve anything?" Mildred inquired smiling at Freddy.

"Came up with some ideas," she answered.

"Come over here and talk" Alison said, "Will and I don't want to shout."

Mildred sat down and faced them, "look, during breakfast, let's not get into too much about what we know. I don't want the children to hear all this stuff. It can't be healthy for them to worry about murder."

"Don't kid yourself." Alison quipped, "kids are blood-thirsty little people. They love blood and guts. Look at all those computer games with shooting and knives and automatic weapons. They don't really see it the way we do. To them, this kind of thing is almost like make-believe."

"I think that's just a wee bit strong, Alison." Freddy interrupted. "Children can get hurt by being too close to something like this."

"Hurt by what, Aunt Freddy?" Erica's voice broke though the conversation. "Tell me," she insisted as she placed the place settings on the big table.

"Well, honey, we were just talking about what's been happening here."

"The murders, you mean?" Her clear voice cut the silence which followed. "You know I'm not a baby. I do understand what is going on. Maybe Hunter doesn't quite understand, 'cause he's younger, but I do. I know my grandma is in danger."

"Hon, I don't want you to worry." Mildred walked over and hugged Erica. "I really will be all right."

"I know," the child answered with the steadfast faith of children. "John won't let anything happen to you. He told me so." She resumed placing plates and glasses on the table. "Grandma, I don't want to change the subject, but you said we were going to do some planting while I was here. Francis says there's pots and pots that need to go in the ground."

"That's true. Do you want to work in the garden with me after breakfast? Freddy will help, too. We've got that big garden all ready. All we have to do is put the plants into their assigned places."

"What's this? Don't I have a say?" Freddy asked. "What about my plans for the day? I might just have something else to do."

"I doubt it." Mildred said blandly. "Since we had this project planned for this week. It's probably on your calendar. John wants us to stick close to home. There's nothing quite so close to home as the flower garden."

The kitchen door opened and Francis stuck her head out. "I need some help with the food. Father Will, you can carry out the heavy pans. The rest of you can each grab something."

There was a large variety of breakfast choices. Mildred couldn't believe the spread. There were two large pans of the baked egg dishes, hash browns, muffins, and a giant bowl of cut fruit. Toasted bagels were on a platter with cream cheese on the side.

"I think we just might fend off starvation." Mildred chided.

"Nonsense, it's all these men around here, they got to eat." As Francis spoke, Joel and George entered the porch.

"I knew I smelled something good." Joel said to George. "My nose never fails me when meals are involved."

"I made plenty." Francis assured. "Now let's sit down and eat before it gets cold." She settled into a chair next to Mildred. "If we're going to spend the day in the garden, I'll get the neighbor boy to come and help."

"Which one?" Mildred inquired.

"Zach. He's the one that came over last year. He's really good with running the garden tractor. Hunter's still a little young, but Zach could teach him how to use it, then next time he can help."

"Francis, that's a great idea. For starters, we can have the kids carry out some of the smaller flats of plants. You know which ones go where. This will keep everybody busy and let George and Joel get a break from Hunter. There's not much they can show him now that the fences are mended."

Hunter looked at Mildred. "Grandma, I'm not in their way. Joel would tell me if I was causing any trouble." He brightened, "but I do like to dig in the garden. My mom says I'm a natural. I have my own plot this year. I'm growing tomatoes and peppers."

"Yeah," Erica laughed, "but you don't like to weed them."

"Do too. I've just been real busy at school, and I got a lot of homework right now." He insisted. "You know it too, smarty!" He stuck his tongue out at his sister.

"All right!" Mildred intervened, "that's enough. I'm not going to have you two kids get into a fight about the garden. That would defeat the purpose."

"Well, I've got a few things to do today, too." Alison added to the conversation. "Will has agreed to go into Minneapolis with me to pick up the car. Quim can drop us off on the way to the University. Last night he said he could. I want to get the manuscript as soon as I can. Lt.

Hershey has some statements for me to sign. Then, we'll come home after that. Don't save any of those little plantings for me, darling." She said to Mildred. "I'm allergic to dirt."

"I know, Alison. You can't even keep a house plant alive." Mildred laughed.

Francis pushed back her chair, "I'm going to go call Zach. I know he's saving money for school. Might as well get him over here as soon as he can." She picked up dishes on her way.

Freddy hopped up to help. "Eating sure helps. I feel like a new woman." She looked around, "where's Quim. Usually he's down for breakfast. There's not going to be anything left"

"I saw him upstairs, right before I came down. I think maybe you and Quim, overdid it a little, Freddy. He's looking a little green around the gills. This night life is not what he's used to anymore. He said he'd be down in a bit, but didn't want anything but coffee."

As if on cue, Quim appeared in the doorway. He did look a bit tired, but the freshly shaved face and crisp shirt assured all of them, he really wasn't in too bad a shape. His cologne was subtle, but wafted a clean scent into the room.

Freddy's nose twitched, "Mmm, you smell good. What is that you're wearing?"

"Gucci. Has a nice crisp scent, doesn't it?" He asked no one in particular. "Yes, dear, I am alive and well," he assured Mildred. "It is true, we," he indicated Freddy and himself with a wave of his arm, "stayed up way too late last night. However, I believe I will recover."

"That's reassuring, Quim," Freddy said. "I did ask if I was keeping you up too late."

"That you did, my dear. I think it was just all the events of the day and letting down to relax. One does have to do that once in awhile," he stated as he poured a cup of black coffee.

"What time do you have to leave, Quim?" Alison asked, "Will and I are ready anytime you are."

"No time like the present, to quote an old phrase," he answered. "I have the car gassed, and the chauffeur is ready anytime you are."

"Good, I'll just run up and get my things." Alison replied. She finished her coffee and left the table. A faint scent of floral perfume was the only reminder she had been there.

"Grandma, what are we going to do today?" Hunter asked. "I don't want to be bored. You told us you had things for us to do."

"The garden, my dear. We're going to put in all those plants you started from seed. You have about twenty of them on the sill over there. They're all set to go into the ground."

"I guess that'll be okay, but what are we going to do after?" Hunter asked.

"Son, if you finish with that job, I'll find something for you to do." Joel assured him. "I don't think there will be any chance you'll get bored. Maybe later today we can visit your mom in the hospital. She'll be there until Monday. She might like to see you. It would cheer her up. We could take her some flowers. How about that?"

"Wow! She'd like that, I know she would." Hunter's enthusiasm was contagious.

"Can I go?" Erica inquired. "I miss her, too. He's not the only one."

"Yes," Mildred said, "you'll get to go and visit with Hunter and Joel." She turned to Joel, "I'm making an assumption it's alright?"

"Sure, one more kid isn't going to be any big deal. We can stop for burgers on the way home. That way you won't have to worry about supper for them."

"Cool," Hunter exclaimed. Then he thought it over and added, "Maybe we could have spaghetti instead. I like that place over in Andover near the hospital. We go there a lot. Mom says it's the best!"

"Whatever," Joel agreed. "I won't let you starve."

Alison arrived back in the room. "I'm all set." She directed her statement to Mildred, "I'm expecting a call from my agent. You know, Ronnie McDougal. I left the main number because my machine isn't picking up messages, the way it should. Let him know I'll call as soon as I get a chance to look through the manuscript. He's just dying to know if it's any good." Alison grinned. "So am I, actually."

"I'm ready if you two are," Quim rose from the table. "I'll just bring a mug of coffee along with me. I don't need breakfast, we have a department meeting this morning. They always have a big spread. The English Department likes its food."

Mildred's eyebrow lifted and a smile teased her lips.

"I know what you're thinking, Mil," Quim answered. "They don't usually serve that, this early." He grinned back at her. "Besides, I'm not into the 'hair of the dog' thinking."

"That's good, my dear," she gave him a peck on the cheek. "You'll be back for dinner, won't you?"

"Should be, I want to take a good look at Ashley's manuscript before I go to bed tonight. If I don't, Ronnie will be in a fit. He's raring to go if it's any good." Alison answered for both of them. "He thinks any publisher would love to get their hands on a manuscript written by a murder victim. I have misgivings about it. She was my friend." She emphasized the word, "I don't want to exploit her. I'll just have to see what I think."

Mildred gave Alison a hug. "You take care of yourself. It's hard to lose a friend under any circumstances. This has been an appalling experience."

"Later," Father Will stated as they all three left the room.

# CHAPTER TWENTY ONE

Mildred pushed the garden cart to the center of the freshly dug garden. She and Freddy were starting a new perennial bed just south of the porch. It was just to the east of the pool and cabana area. A thick hedge separated the two areas. The new garden was a large oval and the central section would bed the tallest of the plants. It was here that Freddy planned to put the hollyhocks, delphinium, and foxglove.

On either side of the central circle, were two oval beds. The center of each contained a fountain. The water was pumped through brilliantly colored pottery fish. Mildred had a close friend who was a potter. The two of them had designed matching fish whose blues, greens, and yellows, in the two fountains, would balance the central portion of the garden. Mildred liked symmetry. The fish faced each other from opposite sides of the center, their mouths aiming the jets of water into the deep bowls of the fountains. The sound of water cascading into the pools offered a mystical peace to the setting.

Freddy said, "If we're not careful we could end up with a southern garden." She was kneeling on a small, wooden garden board, whose padded surface offered little comfort to her knees. "I'm not sure if I'm going to be able to walk after today." She leaned back and stretched out her legs. "I'm stiff already."

"You'll get used to it," Mildred assured. "A couple of days out here, and you'll be an old hand at this. Think of how beautiful this will be in just a few weeks."

Gardening was one of Mildred's passions in life. When she and Emil had lived in Bald Eagle, they had a wonderful cottage garden. She always allotted at least an hour a day to spend there with the plants. Rarely did she miss this special time.

Now, it seemed, all kinds of things interfered with her commitment to her garden. This year, she decided, things would be different. Mildred, Freddy, and Francis had organized the garden project. Previously, there had been no overall plan. Now, the three of them had created a blueprint of what needed to happen, and when. Even the choice of the plants had been determined.

Two of the side sections were to contain herbs. Mildred loved herbs. Their heady scent would bring back memories of her mother's garden. When Mildred was a child, she used to sit with a book under a huge, spreading oak tree. Spanish moss hung above her head, as she avidly read one of her childhood heroines. The scent of freshly dug earth would reach her nostrils, offering reassurances that all was right with the world, when her mother was in the garden.

This familiar sense of belonging to the earth was intrinsic to her. It was the earth, which had sustained her family for generations, and even now, continued to support their lives. It didn't matter to her if the flora was native to Minnesota or Louisiana, what mattered was that she had her hands in the soil and was cultivating the earth.

Her cell phone rang. The insistent, clarion tones cut through the sunny morning. Mildred answered. "Hello, Mildred here."

John Jacob's voice penetrated her ear. "Morning, Mil. Outside, already, huh?"

"I won't even ask how you knew." She answered crisply. "We're in the garden getting the seedlings in. I don't have a lot of time right now to gab."

She listened with a frown to what he was saying, then spoke wearily. "I'll call you back from the house. This connection is not good and you're talking too fast. What number are you at?" she asked. "It'll be just a minute. Stay put!"

Mildred closed the cover on the little phone, "I have to call him back. Apparently they have a suspect in the poisoning. I have a feeling I know who he is thinking about, and I don't agree. I'll be back."

She got up a walked briskly to the porch. Within minutes, Francis and Freddy looked at one another. Mildred's voice penetrated the air with her protests. The two women rolled their eyes and Francis spoke first, "those two are gonna kill each other before it's through. I never knew two people who could disagree more about everything. How they gonna live together, I ask you?"

"Maybe they don't plan on living together." Freddy reasoned. "Just 'cause you love someone, doesn't mean you gotta get married."

"You think . . . ?"

"I'm not sure what I think, yet." Freddy answered. "I just know, those two can't seem to be together or apart. I think they like the conflict. Otherwise, they would find some other way to problem solve these issues." It sounded reasonable, but Freddy knew, relationships were not always reasonable.

Mildred reappeared suddenly. Her face was flushed, but she looked determined. "I called him back, to have him tell me he's going to pull Crystal in for questioning. Can you believe it? He thinks she may be responsible for the waiter's poisoning. By the way, the waiter's name is Darryl Everest. He's originally from Chicago. Only been here a year. Worked in the Manuchi restaurants the entire time. He picked up casual at the Whitcomb to have money to send home to mom. Sounds like a devoted son, doesn't he?"

"So," Freddy said impatiently, "what else? We could hear you out here. What's the disagreement?"

"He thinks Crystal may have had something going with the guy." Mildred sighed deeply, "God almighty, John is going to drive me nuts! I don't know why?" her voice drifted off for a minute. "Anyway, this is the gist of it. The waiter really liked Mrs. Manuchi. Everyone at the restaurant says so. John has apparently talked to all his co-workers. They said there wasn't anything he wouldn't do for her. Apparently Dino used to tease her about it."

"So that means, she killed him?" Freddy's voice rose inquiringly.

"Apparently. I didn't get the whole story. John's going to stop by to check on us. He should be here in about an hour." She pulled in her breath sharply, then released it. "Let's concentrate on the garden. Maybe I can cool down a little before he gets here." She went back to the row of pots sitting in the herb section. In a few minutes they were all back at their task.

*     *     *

Two hours later, John and Mildred were faced off in the study. Mildred sat on one side of the large coffee table and John on the other. This room was just off the library and offered a more secluded space to disagree with one another.

"I don't know why you are so pig-headed!" Mildred hissed. She saw the set look on his face. "Let me fill you in a little on Dino and Crystal's marriage. I do know something about it." She leaned back a little in the chair. "This is one of the big things he bent my ear about while he was in the hospital. It's also what I remember most clearly. I was struck by how much he loved his wife and family. It didn't seem to fit with what my stereotype of a mobster was."

"Mil," John tried to interrupt.

She cut him off. "You just give me a little time to talk, then you can talk all you want. I just want to have some input, before you go off half cocked and destroy that poor woman's life. She's suffering terribly right now. I talked to her, remember?" She asked.

John's face was cloudy, his eyes were as penetrating as lightning bolts. "Mildred," he tried once again to interrupt.

"Never mind with your rationalization, John. I want you to listen to me." Her voice was cold and intense. "I know this woman. You do not! I am telling you, she is incapable of killing him. Crystal loved him so much, it was almost scary. She savored his presence when they were together. No," she saw the look in his eyes change, "it was not a jealous relationship. When they were first married, he almost died. They had been going together since they met as toddlers. Their parents were friends. Crystal's mom was kind of a spiritualist, but her dad was pretty with it. He owned a business in Lafayette, Louisiana. Dino's mom was a single parent, waited tables in Lafayette. She grew up with Crystal's mom. They stayed close and saw each other as often as possible. The kids were together all the time.

They have ties to one another. He was not just a husband. He was a brother, a friend, the person you tell your most intimate secrets to, knowing they will never tell. That's what the relationship was, John. Deep, committed, and above all, loving. They have two of the most wonderful and dedicated children you could ever meet. I'm telling you, it's not her."

"Will you let me talk?" He hissed. "I don't know if she did it or not. It's my job. What little time I have left in this department, I will do in a professional manner. Do you get it?"

"Don't be insulting to me, John. I am not an idiot! I am your ally. But I will not sit idly by, why you torture this wonderful woman with your suspicions."

"They aren't my suspicions. I do have a reporting network, you know. The County Attorney is insisting we bring her in for questioning. I have to do my job. That's what it is, Mildred, my job!" His voice rose belligerently.

"Him? That pipsqueak? That's who's behind this? I should have known. His entire understanding of life is that he breathes in and out about eighteen times a minute." She peered at John's face. "Alright. I give up. Tell you what. She is allowed to have her attorney present, right?"

"Of course." He answered with less intensity. "We always let people bring their attorneys in when they're questioned. If they want them," he added.

"She wants, you bet your sweet bippy, she wants. And," she added, "If she wants me there, I'll be there, too."

"Jeez, Mil, will you give it a rest?" His chin lowered, changing his appearance from charging-bull to a willing partner.

She looked closely at him. There was no question he appeared tired. She wondered if he had indeed, gone home to bed last night, like he said he would. John had a habit of getting side-tracked by a new idea, and changing plans mid-stream.

"Did you go home and catch up on your sleep, John? Or, did you go tooting off on some new idea?"

He looked guiltily at her. "I thought of some things after I left here. I spent most of the night at the office going over my notes."

"Why did I know this?" She asked sarcastically. "I don't know if you're ever going to change. You realize, if we go into this partnership, I hold to a belief that people need to rest at night. This isn't going to be a twenty-four hour a day business for me. I have a life. I think you need to start thinking like that yourself. It's not healthy to keep pushing yourself. You never seem to take the time to look at where you are and let yourself enjoy life. That's got to change or you won't live long enough to be retired. You'll be like all those cops who work for forty or fifty years and die within a year or two of retirement."

"I know, Mildred, I know." He agreed. "I will work on it."

"Work on it! It sounds like you'll make work of it. That's not what I had in mind. When is your last day?" She inquired gently.

"The end of this month, May 31$^{st}$." He told her.

"Good. I think we should take some time and just do nothing for a couple of weeks. Then we'll start with setting up this partnership. I'd like there to be a distinct break in between this job and our new enterprise." She reasoned. "Here," she handed him his refilled cup, "let's drink to the plan," she lifted hers up and towards him.

He responded, bringing his cup level with hers. "Cheers."

"Now," Mildred said, "here's what I have in mind. I think there was someone who was really pissed at Dino. Not his wife or family. It's just a sense I have of," she fumbled for words, "of . . . it feels like stalking. I can't explain it exactly. Crystal said some things to me in the last year. We met at the Women's Shelter. She's on the board and so am I. When she realized who I was, she was very kind. I think Dino always felt responsible for my accident somehow."

"Who else . . . . ?" John started to say.

Mildred pursued her train of thought, not letting him interrupt her. "Now, he wasn't of course, but someone was. Who, that's always been the question. I feel like they killed Emil, too. He wouldn't have had that heart attack if I hadn't been hurt. Well, you know how I feel about that whole scenario." She gathered her thoughts. "The way I see it is this. Someone thought Dino was interested in me. Thought maybe he was paying too much attention, and all that. I wracked my brains for who or whom. I can't think of anyone. Crystal can't either. Dino never was much more than a fairly superficial business connection to the mob. The whole trial thing, was a farce. He told me he didn't know shit about drugs and dealing and the mob. I believed him, John. He was in that damn unit for three months. We talked a lot. He was intelligent, he was a lot of fun and had a great sense of humor. He did all kinds of really nice things for the other patients."

"I know, I know," he threw up his hands, "the way to your heart is to be nice to the people with mental illnesses." John said.

"Absolutely. People just don't understand these illnesses. They're as physical as heart disease, but for some reason society doesn't recognize it. Oh well, now I'm getting side-tracked. The thing is, he was a really nice man. It was obvious his children liked him, his neighbors who visited liked him, his wife liked him. It goes without saying, they all loved him, too."

"A paragon of virtue, right?" John quipped.

"John," Mildred's voice started to rise dangerously. "Don't push it! I agreed to listen to you, now it's your turn."

"Alright! Alright! The guys practically a saint. Okay, you made your point. His wife loved him. She wouldn't kill him. So who," he asked, "do you think killed him?"

"Well," she said thoughtfully, "I have thought about it, quite a lot, in fact. It's someone, who for whatever reason, also doesn't like me."

# CHAPTER TWENTY TWO

John and Mildred continued to discuss underlying motives for the attempts on her life. Neither of them could think of any reason, someone would want her dead. It made no sense. No matter what context they put the facts into, nothing surfaced that could have any meaning to the case.

Mildred felt as if she were in a dream state, where the villain has a logical reason for the chase, and the victim hasn't got a clue. Like all dream states, this was frustrating and offered no answers.

As for John, he had spent the last two years trying to figure it out. Unbeknownst to Mildred, he had examined her life and career with a fine-tooth comb after her accident. He had followed up on every client and family complaint; every disgruntled employee, and had come up with nothing more than minor disturbance. In truth, Mildred had led a somewhat blameless life. Even the nurse forced into Chemical Dependency Treatment after stealing drugs from the hospital, had nothing but good to say about Mildred.

As for Mildred, she had given up worrying about it. Her philosophy of life had undergone a great change after the accident. She now considered each day a gift of life and believed everyone should feel that way. So, they acknowledged stalemate.

"What do you suggest?" Mildred asked after considerable silence. She couldn't remember when they had spent this much silent time together. They were usually arguing about something. This was different.

"Well, I don't know. I have literally thought about this situation until I have no other conclusion to come to, except, we are dealing with someone who is not logical. There is no plan, other than killing you, at some point."

"It does seem that way, doesn't it? Do you think Freddy might have any ideas? We really haven't used her expertise in this. She does a lot of work with the St. Paul Police Department and Hennepin County. She's an expert profiler for them on cases that seem to have a psychological basis. Why don't we ask her?"

"At this point, we have nothing to lose." John answered grimly. "Where is she?"

"Still in the garden, I assume." She grinned, "Where I'm supposed to be, I might add."

"Why don't we tell her to take a break and see what she thinks." He rose. "You stay put, I'll go and get her. I need to make a pit stop on the way."

While he was gone, Mildred got a pitcher of iced tea. At this point, she thought this might be more welcome than the hot coffee. She was right.

Freddy settled into the chair opposite Mildred. She poured a glass of tea and drank deeply, then added more. "My god! It's hot work out there." She leaned back in the chair. "Okay, you didn't bring me in to discuss how sweaty I'm getting in the garden. And by the way, I have got a lot of your," she emphasized the your, "herbs planted. This was going to be a joint venture. I seem to have lost one of the joints. I hope this isn't starting a trend for our gardening moments."

Mildred laughed. "No, I don't think so, dear. I wouldn't do that to my best friend." She looked at John, "we need your help, Freddy. John and I have reached the conclusion that we don't have a clue what the hell is going on. You have said you think Dino told me something I don't remember. I don't think that's true. My memory surrounding the time of the accident, is much clearer. My recollections of my job, of professional interactions at the hospital, of projects I was involved with, have surfaced. There is no pocket of lost memory. I just don't believe that exists. So," she leaned forward, "that kind of indicates there may be a different motive for the attempt on my life."

"Well," Freddy's brows furrowed in thought, "if you're right, and I don't entirely admit you are, then there is obviously another reason. You don't have any enemies that I know of just offhand of course. You've never been a nasty person to anyone. In fact, I've always thought of you as . . . ."

Mildred cut in, "Miss Goody Two-Shoes. I know, Freddy. This is serious though."

"What if," Freddy speculated, "the accident was not part of the plan? What if, it was an accident? What if, everything we've believed for two years, is not true. But, what if now, the killer is using the accident as a means of frightening you?"

"But why?" Mildred asked. "Why would somebody do this? There's gotta be," she fumbled for words. "There's got to be a reason for Manuchi's death."

"Yes, but maybe his death is the real plan. Just think about it. We've have always assumed your accident was planned. It is possible that something else caused the truck driver to hit you, and then not stop." Freddy reasoned.

"Of course," John interjected, "he could've been drunk." He sat back and thought about it. "My God! If you're right, then maybe all this need for security is a result of my fertile imagination."

"Could be, John," Mildred agreed simply. "Although, from what you've told me, it certainly looked like the crash had been planned. It would be something to find out the driver was under the influence and didn't have any plan, except to not go to jail for vehicular homicide. Could be a guy with a long list of drunk-driving charges. Drives truck for a living, and stopped for a cold one on the way home."

"Shit!" Freddy said explosively, "that means now, there really is a danger. I mean, look at it this way, why was Manuchi's body dumped in the ditch in front of your house. Now, for whatever reason, there is a connection. See what I mean?"

"Yeah." John agreed. "One thing I can do, is to get records to check out guys who have a long list of drunk-driving arrests or convictions, who drive truck for a living."

"Better check out women, too." Mildred interjected, "you never know." She said to his look of disbelief.

"Damnation! It would be somethin' to find out, we've been wrong all along. "Freddy quipped. "It never occurred to me it really could have been an accident."

"It means looking at this investigation from a different point of view. I'm just not sure, which one." John spoke slowly, as he thought out loud. "Manuchi's killer must have known two years ago, whatever he had to say in court, was not worth the powder to blow it to hell. That's what he told you, Mildred. My God! Wouldn't you think the Prosecutor would have caught on, there was no case?"

"Fred Gorman thought there was enough data for a case, too. He was nobody's fool." Mildred added. "You know, John, Emil was named as the executor for Fred. Of course, when he died, that wasn't possible. Somehow, even though Emil was gone, Fred's possessions were put aside for me to go through. I guess it was interpreted that I would take Emil's place as Executor. No one else was named. It was weird. No family, no close friends but us, so the things were brought here. I have all his files in storage. Maybe there's something there he overlooked. Fred was tenacious, but he was also stubborn. He may not have let it go, because of his own inability to see the truth. What do you think?"

"It's possible alright. I'm gonna get some help from the department on that. My young partner loves research. I'll let him tackle those files.

"I have them under lock and key." She saw John's odd look of query. "I know, it's odd to say the least, that I have these files. You'd think they would have gone to his office or something. The thing is, he worked a lot of the time out of his office at home. His partners' saw him as an old fossil. They didn't give a shit."

"That may be to our benefit." John said, "I'm going to put a call in to Glenn Becket. He's the young guy I was telling you about. I'll have him come over and pick up the files. It may take a bit of time, but if there's something there, he'll find it."

"You know, John, if we've been looking at this backwards, then it opens up all kinds of possibilities. Look at the trail of bodies here: Dino, Ashley by mistake, Daryl Everest. If Mildred wasn't the original victim and Dino Manuchi was, then what are we left with?" She paused, "I think we have a very highly skilled and deadly murderer. This is a person who knows exactly what they are doing and how to go about it."

"Except, Ashley was killed in error." Mildred said.

"True, but think about it. Two of the victims, Dino and Alison, were people you know fairly well. I don't think there's any doubt, Alison was the intended victim. So," She sighed, "that leaves us where?"

"What the hell do Alison and Dino Manuchi have in common other than you, Mildred?"

"Nothing that I'm the least bit aware of," Mildred answered swiftly. "It doesn't make any sense."

"It does to somebody." Freddy reasoned. "Dino knew what he didn't know. You didn't know what you did know. I still think the man said something to you that seems inconsequential. Now, I haven't a clue what that could be. What in the hell did the two of you talk about? You must remember some of the conversations. What was the topic of most of them?" Freddy drilled.

Mildred put her hands to her head and pulled on her hair. "I can't remember! You know how I am, Freddy, the harder I try to remember something, the more befuddled I get. I'll just have to let it go. If there's something important, it'll come to me, but it won't if you keep pushing it!" Her frustration carried her to her feet. "I'm gonna go and lay down for awhile."

With that statement, Mildred got up and left the room. Freddy and John looked at the closing door.

"Well, I'll get over to the county building. I need to check in. I'll call Glenn before I leave and have him come and pick up those files. If you can get the key from Mildred before she takes a nap, I'd be thankful." He picked up the phone.

Freddy got up and went after Mildred. She returned in a few minutes and gave him the key. "She said they are all in the files to the left of the door. There's a few boxes, too. The contents of his desk." Freddy touched John's arm. "We have to figure this out. I don't want to scare Mildred, but I do think she is the intended victim. Maybe it's not logical, but my guts tell me there's more here than meets the eye. I'm gonna keep a close eye on her."

# CHAPTER TWENTY THREE

The next two days passed in a blur. John was as good as his word. He had Glenn Becket sifting through Fred Gorman's files, which had been taken to Anoka County. John was in and out of the house, but in general, just said the investigation was continuing. Of Crystal Manuchi's interview, no more was said.

Mildred felt relief. Someone else was reading trial materials. She didn't have to bring herself to face that period of time again, as the trial notes would have done. She didn't have to do anything but putter in the garden and read. She did both.

Alison was holed up in her rooms. She had Ashley's manuscript, and after the Minneapolis Police had completed the search of Ashley's home, she brought her computer to the house. Alison said it was so much easier when she had the original hard drive contents. Ashley had done a lot of research which she had transferred to her hard drive. Alison edited and Mildred and Freddy gardened.

It was actually peaceful. Erica and Hunter were gone with Virginia to pick up Renee from the hospital. They would all be at the house tonight for dinner. Francis was already in the process of creation of some divine meal.

Mildred had stopped by Alison's room. She knocked, when she heard the reply, she entered. "How's it going?" she inquired.

"Slow," was Alison's terse reply. "Her style is different from mine, so it's hard to determine exactly what I should do, when something needs to be edited. Still," she reflected, "it's really not going too bad. I think the book is very good. Certainly it's marketable. Ronnie is ecstatic about the prospect. He keeps calling and pushing for me to let him see it." She sighed.

"You're tired. It's got to be a lot of work editing something like this."

"It is. When it's your own book, you have another set of problems. It's hard to see fault with something so near and dear to your heart. It really takes a ruthless character, to shred a book to it's bones, then build it to where it will be meaningful. You know what I mean, Mildred, I see you doing that very thing. You just do it in a different context."

"So what do you think about her book? Is it good?"

"Oh, yes, I'd say she would have had a best seller here. There is no question the material is excellent, the research flawless. It would have sold. She would have given me competition. And that's saying something!" Alison stated emphatically.

"Wow!" Mildred reacted, "just like that? A best seller?"

"Mildred, I've been in this business the better part of twenty years. I have sold millions of books. I know what sells and what doesn't sell. Believe me, I would've taken the back seat to her. I can hardly believe it."

"Whew!" Mildred looked at Alison's desk. Although it was neat, it was quite apparent she was busy with a writing project. "I'll let you be. I just wanted to check on you and see how you are doing."

"It's okay. I was at a point where I could take a break. I needed one, too. When I'm writing I don't want any interruptions at all. That's not always good, though, you can get so immersed you stop eating and sleeping. A little interruption is good." She smiled at Mildred and then turned back to her work.

The dismissal was clear and Mildred obeyed it. She backed out of the room and felt amazed. She didn't have any concept how someone could take an idea and then put together a thousand page saga about some fictional person's life. It just didn't make any sense to her. She didn't even understand why someone would want to do that. She shook her head and went on down the stairs.

She heard voices on the porch and wandered out there. For the first time since the 3rd of May, she felt somewhat relaxed and peaceful. Freddy and John were on the porch.

"I didn't hear you arrive." She stated to him, as she crossed the room and sat down near them. "What are you two talking about?"

"We found some background data on our waiter. Interesting fellow." John said expansively. "Alison here?" he inquired. "No point in me going over this twice, if I can avoid it."

"She editing. I don't think it's a good time to disturb her." Mildred answered.

"Well, this is pretty interesting stuff we found. I think you'd better give her a call." He insisted.

"Okay." Mildred agreed. She got up to get her, but just at that moment, Alison entered the porch. "I couldn't get back to it." She said. "It's what happens when I'm interrupted." The accusation sounded flat. "Usually I get cranky. Today, I just feel relieved. I must be tired and need a break."

"I was just going to get you. John has information on the waiter," she stated. "He figured you'd be interested to hear what he's learned."

"Shoot!" Alison said, "I can't stay away from the work for too long, or I'll lose my motivation. When that happens to a writer, it's death."

"For starters, his assumed name was Daryl Everest. In reality, it was Marco Giovanni. This'll interest you Alison. He's from Chicago all right, and he's from your old neighborhood. He's not as young as he looked. Dental records and fingerprints marched for one Marco Giovanni. However, he's used the Everest name for years." John leaned back in the chair. "He was in a lot of trouble as a kid. Fires mostly."

Alison leaned forward, "Fires?"

"Yep!" John answered succinctly. "That's it!"

Alison's face underwent a transformation. She stared at John with an interest she hadn't felt previously. "What fires?"

"Well, some of it is pretty sketchy." He said, "Mostly he was a suspect. It was hard to prove that he started some of the fires. It was when he was about fourteen, they were able to nail him. They had evidence and a witness. Someone was in the building he torched, so the cops had an eye witness."

"What fire?" Alison kept asking persistently.

"A large warehouse, on the southwest side of Chicago. Supposedly empty." John drew out his pipe and began filling it. "There was a homeless man living there. It was good digs. It was certainly dry, but it also had running water in one of the bathrooms. That's where he was when the arsonist was pouring out the gasoline. In the shower. Saved his life. The bathroom had a small window. He was looking out just before the fireball went up. He saw our boy Daryl, or Marco as he was then, running away with a can in his hand."

"Why wasn't he killed?" Alison asked.

"He was soaked to the skin," John said. "I mean literally. He had been in the shower and was soaped head to food. The blast didn't destroy the bathroom wall, but it got pretty damn hot. His words exactly from the police report." John took a few puffs, then continued. "He says he damn near flew out the window, stark naked and ran for his life. The cops found him hiding down the street after they arrived on the scene. Took him a few days to convince them he wasn't the torch who started the fire."

"My God!" Alison was trembling. "It's like a nightmare . . ."

"How old are you Alison?" John's question seemed to have no bearing on the conversation.

"Why?" She asked. "What the hell does my age have to do with this?"

"Not a whole lot, but I've got some information on some of the fires Marco was suspected of setting. One of them was your parents house." He watched as this information sank into her consciousness. "He was pretty young, but then a lot of fire-bugs are."

"Jesus! Are you telling me that piece of shit is the person who burned up my family?" She turned to him, here eyes blazing. "You can be damned sure of this. If that son of a bitch was alive, I'd kill him."

Mildred put her hand on Alison's arm, but she shrugged it off. "Don't! Don't touch me! I don't want your damn pity!" She turned to John. "Tell me. Tell me, dammit! Do you think this creep is the one?"

"I think so," his voice sounded weary. "I think he was twisted as a kid. Probably did a lot of things, they couldn't trace to him."

Alison's head dropped on to her chest. She sat for several minutes. Freddy was getting very concerned when Alison's head came up again. She looked at each one of them in turn. "There's not a damn thing I can do to change the past, but I can do something about the future. That bastard killed my best friend. We don't even know why. But I'll tell you this, I'm not one bit sorry that he's dead! I hope he rots in hell." Her eyes flashed fire. "I can't do anything to him! God!" she smashed her fist on the coffee table. The cups rattled. "I could just kill someone!"

Freddy got up and went to Alison's side of the table. "Look, Alison, you have a right to be pissed. I don't know what the hell I'd feel like if I'd just gotten this news. But don't let it destroy you. Ashley's dead. Nothing is going to bring her back. You can still keep her spirit alive and let others know how talented she was. Bring her book to life. Get it published. Use the notoriety to sell it. I know that sounds crass, but the money could be used for crime prevention somehow. You're the executor of her estate. Make it mean something."

Alison looked at Freddy. Her eyes were wide with confusion. She reached out to Freddy and let her put her arms around her. "I don't know what to think." Her voice was muffled. "I know I lost the best friend I ever had. She never did any harm to anyone. Why her?"

"I don't know." Freddy said simply. "Come on; let's go up to your room. This is one time when I'm going to prescribe something for you." She pulled Alison to her feet and let her out of the room.

Mildred turned to John, "My God! I can't believe it. It almost looks as if there is some kind of logical motive for all of this."

"It's hard to find, Mil. Even with the connection. I have a lot of work to do, to try and find out what Manuchi had to do with all of this."

"Why are you so convinced he had something to do with it?" Mildred insisted.

"Mildred, look, the guy wasn't so bad. Okay? But he did have some connections. We know he and his wife were paying some insurance to the mob. We've traced it. Mrs. Manuchi did the books, she had to know something was up. Now, let's face it. Nowadays its insurance coverage, nice and legitimate, but it's still protection against something bad happening. Like a fire, a gas explosion in the kitchen after hours, you know what I mean."

"Well, he did tell me once, he knew a lot of the players. He also insisted he was legitimate. He didn't want any part of it. I was never clear on what kind of information he had on the mob. He kept insisting he didn't know shit!" She said.

"Well, maybe he didn't." John admitted. "He really does look pretty clean. I was so pissed when I thought he was responsible for your accident, I wasn't exactly level headed."

It was the first time John had ever admitted he could be wrong. Mildred was afraid if she said anything, it would jinx the moment. Still, she felt she had to acknowledge his admission.

"Something changed your mind. What was it?" she inquired.

"Logic." He said briefly. "I really took a long hard look at myself and some of the things I have never wanted to admit." He grinned at Freddy, who had just returned to the room, "Dr. Fredericka here helped me over the rough spots."

"Freddy?" Mildred looked at her friend. "You didn't tell me."

"Physicians don't talk about their clients." She answered smoothly, "what the client wishes to share is none of my business."

Mildred looked from her best friend to John and back again. She smiled. It was a smile so broad, it lightened the already bright room. "When did all this take place?"

"The last year or so." John answered her. "I decided I needed to work on some issues besides the alcohol. I've been sober for years, but it didn't seem to be helping our relationship much. I decided I had better do something about it, before I lost you to Quimby. That," he muttered, "would have been a bitch to take."

"I can't believe it."

"You can't believe that I could see what Quim was up to? Or are we talking about the therapy?" John asked her.

"Both." She answered him. "I don't know that I agree about Quim, but I have always thought you needed to take a look at your insecurities about me and my career."

"Don't kid yourself, Mil, that guy is looking out for himself. I probably shouldn't say this to you, but I'm gonna anyway. He's looking for a nice berth. It's pure and simple, like the soap. He wants a nice, cushy old age. His retirement from the University will be quite nice, but to keep up the lifestyle he really wants, he needs more money." He looked sheepish, "and, of course, we investigated him, too." The words were quiet.

John didn't quite know what he expected, but Mildred stared at him and then, burst out laughing. "Quim, a gold digger. I don't think so, but I do agree with you, he does love luxury. Nothing but first class all the way, and the devil take the hindmost."

"That's Quim." Freddy agreed. "All the way. So, what's next?"

# CHAPTER TWENTY FOUR

Dinner that evening was a successful venture. Francis had outdone herself and everyone seemed to groan with gastronomic happiness. Even Renee, who didn't have much appetite, ate quite a bit. Though tired, she had asked about the investigation and appeared relieved to think perhaps her mother might not be the primary victim.

After dinner, Renee and her children went upstairs to spend time together. Joel kept them company, mostly to be near Renee, for whom he had developed an attraction. It must have been obvious, George teased him about it mercilessly. However, Joel persisted and Renee was happy for the company. She liked him, too.

Mildred sank with great relief onto the couch on the porch. She and Freddy had come out to rest after dinner. Father Will was once again in attendance with Allson, in her room. It was peaceful. The cool air of the evening penetrated the porch and for the first time that day Mildred really relaxed.

Mildred had come to distrust any sense of peace and quiet. Each time she had acquiesced to those feelings, all hell had broken loose. Now, she was not so quick to think the quiet would last. In this she was right. Quim had returned home late from the U. It had not been his finest hour. One of the English Professors had confessed to him an affair with one of her graduate students, and he was fearful of the repercussions. All in all, it had not been a stellar day.

When he arrived on the porch, the mood was not exactly shattered, but it was slightly compromised. Mildred tried to analyze later just how a mood could be changed so completely by another person's aura. She liked to tell herself she was in charge of setting her own emotional state.

Certainly Freddy preached personal responsibility for how one feels about the world around them. One thing was impressed on Mildred's mind. She didn't want any kind of deep, personal relationship with someone who could so effectively impact her mood. UGH!

"Quim, for God's sake, take it easy. It's not the damn end of the world." Freddy tried to help him to realize there was nothing to be gained by his being so upset.

"Fat lot you know about it Fredericka dear. The point being, my English Department could be shattered by this."

"You said the couple has every intention of getting married."

"Yes." He said abruptly, "but you see, they should not have been in any relationship except the professor-student relationship. These things should always be set aside while one strives for academic success. Why if every one of the professors behaved this way, we'd have all kinds of legal issues. The men certainly have learned this is not acceptable."

Mildred took the bait. She wondered later if it was just an excuse to prick his pomposity balloon or what. "This is over it being a woman professor, isn't it? You could really give a shit, except it's your token woman. Quim," Mildred accused, "you're being a sexist pig."

"I beg your pardon. Did you say what I thought you said?"

"I did indeed!" Mildred shot back, "you sit here as arrogant as can be, holding forth on the virtues of the male professors in your department. I think you have conveniently forgotten that little incident of three months ago."

"That?" he inquired. "Why the two of them worked through all those issues. The student got a very large settlement from the University, too."

Mildred interrupted, "getting a settlement means everything is alright? What planet are you from, Quim? This is not the day of male supremacy. That young woman was not only sexually harassed by your colleague, she was also physically assaulted. You think that's okay because she got paid?"

"Mildred, I see where you're going with this. No, I do not approve of violence. I think you don't have quite all the facts. The young women in question, pursued my colleague constantly. He finally lost patience with it."

"They went to dinner and had a few drinks while he lost patience. This man knew he couldn't handle liquor, so he just conveniently took her out for dinner and drinks? Come on, Quim, you can do better than that!"

"Mildred, I have come here as your friend. I did not come here to be insulted for the behavior of my colleagues." He sat rigidly in his chair. "I'm not so sure I feel welcome here."

"Quim, I've known you for almost forty years. You consistently react the same way to adversity. For god's sake, don't pack up and run this time."

"I had no idea you felt that way about me, Mildred. I can only say I'm shocked at your attitude." He set his coffee cup on the table. "I came here hoping to get a little understanding, and instead, I'm feeling attacked."

"Look, it's not just you, Quim. It's the general attitude that somehow a woman shouldn't do what men have been doing for years, that's all. You're not so much pissed off at me, as you are for the fact that you've been set up by your colleagues, men and women. You're the head of the department. Who hears about it from the University Board? You do. Of course, you're going to be angry. This is the perfect place for you to come and vent your feelings. We're your friends, for better or worse."

"Well, perhaps in that light, I can overlook your crass behavior."

Mildred kept her mouth shut. Albeit she had to bite her lip, she persevered. Quimby was Quimby, and nothing was going to change how he interpreted the world. She knew, however, she did value his loyalty and friendship. She didn't want to lose it either.

The letters he had sent from England, every day of her confinement, were still read and savored for their deep, almost spiritual meaning and support. She treasured his friendship, like one locks away golden memories in the heart, gently lifting them from that secret place, when she most needed warmth and caring. No, she did not want to lose either his friendship or his presence in her life.

He was grumbling, "I suppose you think I'm just an old fool, wanting to carry on tradition at the University.?"

"You've lost me, Quim. What are you driving at?" Mildred inquired.

"It just seems like there have been so many changes, one never knows what is coming next." He answered quietly. "I used to think if I became a professor at an established institution, I would have the world by the tail. Alas, the world has changed far too much. There is no longer that genteel quality that made University life such a bastion of middle class security. I no longer feel I have it made, as my students would be apt to say."

"Quim, you're just facing what the rest of us have accepted. Life changes things. What we once valued no longer seems to have merit. But what's even stranger is things we wouldn't have given a second thought to in our twenties, are now precious realities." Freddy answered his statement.

"That's for sure," intoned the voice from the doorway. George stood there. "Mildred, John and I have talked. We've decided we can close up shop here. I think I'm going to leave the Security Person at the front, but as long as you use the security system in the house, you'll all be fine. Just remember to set it at night. Joel plans to stay tonight, but I'm leaving for another job. You don't need both of us here. Anubis is on patrol and the other two hounds are locked in the kennel." He gave her an inquiring look as he finished speaking.

"I appreciate everything, George. I think we're all set, too. There's really not much to do here. Go ahead, we'll be fine." She assured him.

"Well, I'm off. Tell John if he needs me, to call my cell phone. He has the number." He backed out of sight.

"Is he really sure it's safe?" Quim asked. "The last few days have been the most harrowing of my life. Is he sure you're really safe?"

"Reasonably." Mildred answered him. "It is beginning to look as if Alison is the intended victim of the murder attempts. We don't know why, but at times there are fanatic people who focus unwanted attention on movie stars, or authors for that matter."

"That doesn't explain Manuchi's body in your ditch." He reminded her.

"I'm aware of that. It makes me uncomfortable, too. It's as if a piece of the puzzle is missing. Or the lynch pin is absent in a piece of machinery. Something doesn't seem right, but yet I can't exactly determine what it is."

"How's Alison doing?" He veered off topic.

"Will's with her. She was pretty upset this evening."

"Well, when isn't she upset?" Quim inquired sarcastically. "The woman is a hysteric."

"There have been developments in the case. The waiter has been identified as a possible arsonist. He's got a history that indicates he has set some fires. It seems, as a juvenile offender in Chicago, he may have been the person who torched Alison's parent's home."

"How did you find this out?" Quim asked. "That's . . . . that's fantastic," he stammered, at a loss for words.

"John received the information today. The waiter had an alias, Marco Giavonni. He was living in the neighborhood where Alison grew up. Had a long history of setting fires, as a juvenile offender. It was difficult for

Alison to hear. She's been repressing that stuff for years. Hell, I'd repress it, if it was me." Freddy stated flatly.

"Is she all right?" He asked in a subdued voice. "I mean really?"

Freddy sighed, "It's really hard to say, Quim. Alison is a person who reacts to stress. She's temperamental and high strung. I'm never sure how much is real and what is projected, but she's definitely hurting."

"What's really so difficult is why Marco would want to poison Alison. I don't think there's any question that she was the intended victim at the restaurant. If she hadn't changed seats, so they wouldn't have cross conversations at the table, Alison would be dead. It's a lot to handle emotionally."

"Especially when there doesn't appear to be a motive." Mildred added.

"That's what is frustrating John. There doesn't seem to be a motive. Unless," Mildred paused in thought, "it has something to do with her childhood." She fell silent, puzzling it in her mind.

"That's a thought." Freddy agreed. "Look, I'm going to check on her. If she's doing okay, I'm going to suggest they come back down here for some brainstorming. We've got nothing to lose and maybe she'll remember something."

"It sure as hell can't hurt to try." Mildred said. "I think underneath all the fluff and drama, Alison is pretty damn strong. No one can be as successful as she is, and be totally frivolous."

"I couldn't agree more," Freddy said as she got up from her seat. "I'll see if they'll come down and join us."

She left the room.

Quim turned to Mildred, "I suppose this isn't the time to ask this, but it may be the only chance I have . . ."

"What?" Mildred asked.

"I wanted to discuss our future relationship," he paused. "I have been thinking about . . . ."

His words were lost as Hunter and Erica came into the room to say goodnight. He wondered later, if perhaps their entrance saved him from feeling a fool. Quim wasn't sure what kind of grandfather he would have been.

# CHAPTER TWENTY FIVE

Freddy returned to the others on the porch. "They'll be down. I'm wondering if we should go into the library. There's a thunderstorm coming and it might be more comfortable in there." She started closing windows.

It was true. Mildred couldn't believe how black the sky had become. "I agree. I'll take the coffee things into the kitchen. Would anyone object if I brought in the Brandy and Scotch?"

"Not me, that's for sure." Quim answered.

"I'll give the kids a bedtime snack and then I'll be in." Mildred replied. She gathered up the dishes from the coffee table. Erica grabbed the coffee pot and Hunter took the cream and sugar bowl. They vanished into the kitchen. Quim raised his eyebrows as the sound of squabbling arose from within.

"That's enough," Mildred's voice rose slightly. "I know you two have been cooped up all afternoon, but this is not the place for that!"

What 'that' was, Quim was left to surmise, as he went into the library from the porch. He and Freddy settled into their favorite chairs. "Those children are certainly boisterous," Quim stated.

"That's how kids are." Freddy answered him.

"When I was a boy, my mother would never have let me behave like a ruffian."

"Quim, when we were young, parents didn't let kids do a lot of things. Times have changed." Freddy said.

"Well, I'm not so sure it's for the better." He answered levelly.

Freddy looked at him intently, "this really doesn't have much to do with kids, does it?"

He felt disconcerted by her gaze. He cleared his throat, "I was thinking of talking with Mildred about some personal things. Our conversation was interrupted by the children. I don't believe children should be given such free rein. If I would have interrupted my parents, or any elder for that matter, when I was young, I would have been sent packing to my room."

"I'm not so sure the interruption is what is so upsetting. I think you're having a hard time adjusting to the fact that Mildred and John seem to have reached some kind of agreement."

"Oh, I don't know," he said quickly. "Have they reached an agreement?"

"I think you have to talk to Mil about that Quim. However, I am aware there is a change in that direction. Besides, think about it Quim, how would Mildred fit into your lifestyle. She's a homebody. You travel all the time. You'd like nothing better than to go back to Britain and spend another year or two there. She's got all her interests here, the women's shelter, the construction company, her ideas for group living for elders, and the kids. Where would she have time to go off cavorting to Europe or England?"

"I suppose you're right. I just don't like to think about it. I think she and I have a lot in common." He paused, "it's just that she's so . . . ."

"Assertive?" Freddy queried. "I admit, Mil's not the meek and shy type. Look, Quim, she really cares about you and I know for a fact, she has always valued your friendship."

"But that's all it is, isn't it?" He asked quietly. "That's all it ever was."

"What are you saying? Are you telling me, you don't think friendships are important? Holy shit, Quim. Without friendship what is there?" Freddy sat forward with her intensity. "I can tell you, she's the best friend I ever had. When I was a kid, nobody wanted anything to do with me, 'cause I was different. They were scared of me. Probably thought being a lesbian would rub off on them. Mildred didn't act that way. She just seemed to accept we were different, and so what?"

"I'm not sure you understand."

Freddy gave him one of her penetrating looks. "I understand all right. You're in love with her. You have been since college. I've always known it. What you have not been able to see, is that Mildred is someone you have idealized. I'm not sure you see the real person, but more the woman you think she is."

"Don't you think I know her?" Quim answered heatedly. "I've been close friends with her since then. We've seen each other almost weekly since college. Of course, I know her."

"No, it's not that. Of course, I agree with you, you know her. What I'm saying is, I don't think you really know how she thinks and feels about issues. You know the passion she exhibits, but I'm not sure you fully understand the woman behind the feelings." Freddy studied his face. "Quim, she's in love with John. Surely you see that?"

He sighed. "Perhaps, I don't wish to see it. He seems so barbaric, somehow. I'd like to think she would prefer someone more refined in their thinking."

"She likes people who aren't afraid to get dirt under their fingernails." Freddy said. She heard the others coming, "Think about it, Quim, have you ever thought about gardening or going up north and fishing all day? She isn't just books and philosophy, she does things."

He looked up startled. "She does things . . ." he mulled as Will and Alison entered the room. He unconsciously rose and offered Alison his chair.

Mildred entered with a tray loaded with bottles, glasses, and ice. "Who wants what?" she asked, and then began to serve.

Within minutes the conversation resumed. Will spoke first, "when is John going to know if this Marco character is definitely involved?"

"He didn't say. He was in touch with Chicago Law Enforcement. They're going back through records and data. They do have a file on Marco Giavonni. John wants to make sure we definitely have the right guy."

"So, if it is him, what then?" Alison inquired. "What can happen? The guy is dead."

"It will answer some questions. It will also indicate what danger, if any, still exists for you, or for that matter, me." Mildred answered her. "He may be the one who executed Manuchi. If that's the case, then in all likelihood, there is no longer any danger to me."

"I want to be damn sure," Alison said. "I'm exhausted in body and spirit. When this is all over, I plan to go back to the south of France and stay there for awhile. I'm even thinking of taking a sabbatical from writing. I've lost my energy for it. If all this happened because I had some fanatical fan, then I'm not sure I could ever write again." She looked sad. "Ashley lost her life because of it, I'm convinced of it."

"You shouldn't make that kind of decision now, Alison," Father Will said quietly. "When it's over, then think about it. You're a great writer. It would be a terrible shame to give it up. It's like you're letting Marco win."

"I just can't deal with any more loss." Alison said quietly. "I think it would kill me if anyone else is hurt."

"Hopefully it's done with," Mildred interjected. "I am ready to get out of the house. I truly feel like I have cabin fever." She poured drinks as she talked. "I talked with Crystal. She has set another date for the memorial service. It's next week on Wednesday. Dino's body has been released by the Coroner, so she's made arrangements for cremation. I'm glad she canceled the earlier date. This gives everyone a chance to prepare emotionally. Dino's parents are elderly. His mother had a terrible time accepting what happened. By waiting, Crystal has given them a chance to recover their composure somewhat."

Freddy stood up, "I'm going to get some chips. Anybody want anything else?"

When no one responded, she went to the kitchen and returned within a few minutes. "The kids finished their snacks. Francis is taking them upstairs. She said for you not to worry about them." She directed to Mildred.

"I wasn't worried." Mildred lifted her eyes to Freddy. "She loves to spend time with them. They'll sit up there and play cards or scrabble. Those kids are spoiled rotten by her. Did she say how Renee is feeling?"

"She's asleep." Freddy answered, as she dipped her chips in salsa. "When did John say he was coming back?"

"He should be here now. He said around eight-thirty." Mildred turned toward the windows, "I think I hear him now. That muffler is a dead give-a-way."

Minutes later, John entered the room. "Anything left to eat?" he inquired.

"This just proves my theory: Law Enforcement moves on it's stomach."

"No time for a break today. I do have news." John settled into his favorite chair with a sigh of relief. "I am one tired cop. I hope I never see another computer screen."

"Does it beat the old way?" Freddy asked, as she got up to get him a plate of leftovers. "I remember you complaining about how long it used to take to get information. Now, you have the information super highway. You should be happy."

"Well, I admit, technology is good. In this case, it's even superior."
He looked smug.

"What have you learned?" Alison leaned forward. "You know
something. Tell us!"

"We've got the data on Marco Giavonni."

"Is he behind the murders?"

"He was involved. All his movements have been pretty well
documented. He's been busy. His co-workers have been interviewed. He
had taken time off from the Manuchi's On Main. That's the restaurant he
was assigned to on a regular basis."

"Have you been able to tie him in with Manuchi?" Mildred inquired,
her voice low and intense.

"He was seen with him on Tuesday evening. Crystal Manuchi was
able to give us specifics on time. The two of them had an appointment
with a wine merchant. Apparently Dino was thinking of bringing in a
new line of domestic wines. The two of them were going out to Taylor's
Falls to check out a Winery. That's the last time anyone saw Dino."

"If ya'll want to eat, you've got to promise to not talk 'til I get back,
hear? Ya'll want a Coke, John?" She smothered him with the drawl she
reserved for special people.

"Yah." Was the terse reply.

"Have you determined that he killed Ashley?" Alison insisted. "I've
got to know."

"Wait until Freddy is back, you heard what she requested," Quim's
baritone voice commanded. "All of us are dying of curiosity." He leaned
back pulling his pipe from his pocket. All eyes focused on his ritual pipe
cleaning and filling.

"God! You'd think that pipe was the most interesting thing in the
world." Mildred laughed. "We're all sitting here watching Quim like he's
the star attraction."

"All I want to know, is what you've found out!" Alison's voice was
strained.

"Here we are," Freddy breezed back into the library, setting a small
tray of food in front of John. "Now, at least let the guy eat some of it."

Five minutes elapsed before John wiped his mouth with the napkin.
"That'll hold me for a while. Okay," he slowly leaned back and lit his pipe.

"For God's sake, will you tell us what's happening?"

John's voice was steady as he began reciting the facts he could tell
them. "Marco Giavonni, alias Daryl Everest, has lived in the Twin Cities

for the past twenty years. He's fifty-five, grew up in Chicago on the South Side. As near as the Chicago Department can determine, he's been an active felon since he was a kid."

"I want to know if he set those fires." Alison's voice was steely. "Did he kill my parents and my brothers and sister?"

John was somewhat evasive, "they're not quite sure. Apparently that fire was a little different from others he set. Arsonists tend to use the same procedure in settings fires. It's thought the fire that killed your parents had a very intense starter fuel. Not the usual thing Marco used."

"Does that mean he didn't do it?"

"No, it doesn't. It means he may have had access to another type of solvent or fuel that he didn't usually have available."

"Oh, God!" Alison hissed. "I just can't believe how upset I am. My parents died years ago. I was just fourteen. I thought I had worked through this shit!"

"It's not so easy to get past that kind of trauma, Alison," Freddy's voice was soothing. "Violent death leaves some serious emotional and spiritual scaring. We don't just work it through. It's always there with us in one way or another. Some people are more able emotionally, to process tragedy."

"Well, Damn it, I've had more than my share of it!" Alison hissed. "I just want it to go away. I don't want Ashley dead." Her sobs filled the room.

John's voice was more gentle than usual. "We will figure it out. We can't change it, Alison, but we can at least identify who did it."

"That's not much consolation, but at least it will bring some closure to the wound. You'll have a face to hang the blame onto, and know they are being held accountable."

"But, John," Quim's voice interrupted, "this Marco fella, he's dead. Look's like he was poisoned. Who did that?"

"We don't have all the answers yet." He drew on his pipe. "Marco had a couple of close buddies. We're in the process of tracking them down. We think, and this is only surmise, that Marco may have told them something. He was somewhat of a braggart. He never really hit the big time in crime."

"Aren't fires big time?" Alison asked angrily. "It seems to me, murder is murder."

"Your parents house was an exception. The fires he lit were mostly storefronts, warehouses, stuff like that. We think he arranged fires to collect insurance for the owners. Paid accidents, so to speak."

"Like a hit man?" Mildred asked.

"Now that's another topic." He puffed vigorously, then pulled the pipe stem from his mouth. "Those foster parents of yours. What did your foster father do for a living?"

"The Dennison's?" Alison looked at him. "He ran a local candy and tobacco store. It was a real Mom and Pop operation. When I was a kid, there weren't a lot of supermarkets in the neighborhood. It was all little stores and ethnic groceries. Why?"

"Seems your foster dad was more than he appeared to be. You did say he was killed. Did you ever hear, why he was killed?"

"I did." Father Will stated. "I told Alison what I heard. He ran numbers for the mob. Did collections, that kind of stuff. He had lots of money. He was different than most of those guys, he didn't flash it around. That's why he had so much to leave, when he died. A conservative investor!" He finished sarcastically.

"He was a little bit more than that." John stated, "He was a Hit Man for the Mafia."

The room became totally silent. Every eye was on John. Alison's jaw dropped open. Will gaped. Quim squirmed uncomfortably in his chair.

The thunder clap filled the room. Every one of them jumped. "My God!" Quim roared over the din, "even the gods are into the act."

Alison jumped up, as she moved, her brandy spilled on the table. "Oh Jeez! What else? Give me a napkin, or something. Hurry up, this is dripping all over the damn place."

"Here," John handed her his crumpled one. He cleared his throat. "I really need to spend some time talking to you, Alison. I know this is upsetting, but I have to ask questions about the past. About the Dennisons and whether or not you ever saw or met Marco back then."

"You really expect me to remember if I met a guy, what, five, six years younger than me? Jesus! I was in such a bad place back then, I don't know if I'd remember my own grandmother."

"Think about it. We'll talk either later tonight or tomorrow, whichever you prefer."

"Tomorrow. Like Scarlet O'Hara, tomorrow sounds like it could be better time for me."

"What do you think happened to Dino after he went off with Marco?" Mildred brought the subject back to the present. "Do you think he killed him, or what?"

"Looks like it was a setup. We did have Crystal in, to assist us in our investigation, Mil. She was really very cooperative. I guess you were right. That's a lady who is going to take a long time to recover. Our esteemed County Attorney met her and fell victim to her charms. His parents are here to lend support to her. They came with her. It's pretty obvious they think a lot of her. Turns out, the County Attorney is Italian, and his parents know Dino's parents. Does this sound like a soap opera? He's never been married, so he's eyeing the distraught widow. It was something."

"Well, didn't I try to tell you she was a lovely lady? I know it's your job to be suspicious, but there are people in this world who don't murder their husbands."

"Some spouses deserved to be murdered. Those are the ones who never are. What do you suppose is going to happen next, with your County Attorney and the widow?" Freddy smiled. "I hope the tension can be balanced with a little humor. This has really gotten difficult around here. Everybody's walking on eggshells."

"For what it's worth, I'm reasonably convinced we have Manuchi's murderer identified. There is too much coincidence for it not to be Marco who was involved. Now his murder is the troubling one. We're not ever going to know why an attempt was made on your life, Alison. I don't think there's any question, you were the intended victim. He's the only one, who could have poisoned that wine. The fact that he died so soon afterwards, really bothers me. At this point, I'm convinced you have more to fear than Mildred."

"But why was Dino's body a parody of my accident?"

"Not sure. Glenn and I wonder if it has to do with the woman's shelter. Some kind of message from the murderer, that you aren't safe. Maybe you should keep your nose clean and not get into some batterer's space. God knows, Mil, you know how some of these people think. If Marco had a hand in his death, and it looks like he did, he may have done it to scare the shit out of you."

"Well, he did that!" She replied.

"Scared the shit out of all of us." Alison added. "Look, I'd like to go up to bed. Will and I are going to take a look at me getting away for awhile. I won't go until you tell me it's okay, but I think I want to get out of this place. I don't want any more reminders of what has happened."

"I agree with her, John." Will corroborated. "When I think of all the tragedy Alison has dealt with for most of her life, I'm amazed she's been able to function as well as she has. Ever since Gordon's death, she's done nothing but work to deal with her emotions. I think a respite is in order. She's asked me to go along. I'm not sure what the parish council is going to say, but Alison has been my friend through thick and thin. It's my turn to return the favor."

Freddy got up and put an arm around Alison. "Sleep is the best thing you can do for yourself. If you need anything, just let me know," she gave her a hug.

The two of them left the room. Quimby and John re-lit their pipes and eyed one another. Mildred leaned back in her chair. Freddy observed all of them.

"Well, what do we look at next?" Freddy finally spoke. It seemed to break the spell cast by Alison and Will leaving the room. "If we're just going to sit here and look at one another, I'm going up to bed."

"I was just thinking that I'd better be on my way. This is the first chance I've had for a good night's sleep in a week. I'm going to take it." John leaned forward and tapped the contents of his pipe in the ashtray. He rose from the chair.

"I'll walk you to the door," Mildred told him. She got up, too.

"You don't have to see me out, I know the way." John kidded her.

"It's a blatant excuse to spend time with you alone."

"Why Mildred," John teased her, "I wondered how, in this crowded place, we would arrange to see one another." He reached over and pulled her close. "I do think, when all this is over, it would be nice to take a couple days off and go to the North Shore or something. Somewhere," he jerked his thumb toward the library, "where the troops aren't in attendance. I think we have some things to talk about," he paused, "alone." The tone was significant.

"When this is done, I promise, we'll go up north," she agreed, "Just the two of us."

# CHAPTER TWENTY SIX

Before she returned to the library after letting John out, Mildred proceeded to check all the doors and windows, locking any she found open. Afterwards, as she set the alarm system for the lower level of the house, Mildred felt uneasy. It seemed as if the answers to the puzzle were falling into place nicely. 'Perhaps too nicely,' she mused to herself. She stared out of the front windows towards the long driveway. It was black as pitch out there. The sky had clouded up and the clouds were hanging low and sultry in the sky.

She returned to the library. The first clap of thunder roared as she entered the room. "It's getting bad out there. I hope John gets home before it lets loose."

"He's a country boy now, Mil." Quimby said through pipe clenched teeth," he's lived here so long."

She laughed. "Oh, I know, you're right. It's just this storm seems ominous. Probably the state of my mind." Mildred sat back in the chair she'd vacated. "It's almost a letdown in a way."

"What's a letdown?" Freddy asked. "Not being the primary victim? I've been worried sick about you, thinking some killer was planning to annihilate you; don't you even hint you miss the excitement!"

"That's not what I meant."

"Sure sounded that way," Freddy said in return.

"I just feel at odds, somehow." Mildred replied thoughtfully. "it's so pat. Everything has worked out nicely. It's just . . . . oh, I'm not sure."

"I hope you're not getting one of your infamous feelings about this."

"What infamous feelings?" Quim inquired, leaning forward in his chair.

"Oh, Mildred gets this sense of something not being right sometimes." Freddy said to him. "Kind of like, gut feelings."

"Okay, be a poop about it. But, you've got to admit when I get these feelings, I'm usually right?" Mildred said emphatically. "I just don't feel right somehow."

"It's probably the effects of the storm. It's starting to blow out there." He tapped his pipe on the ashtray. "Tell you what, I'd like another glass of Scotch on the Rocks. What about you two?"

"Sure," Freddy passed her glass to him. "Mildred?"

"I guess a small one. Then I'm going up to bed. I have to take Renee and the kids home tomorrow. She's actually getting around pretty well. I suspect Joel will be there, too. He's really smitten with her and the kids."

"She could use a little fun in her life. Since her husband died, she hasn't really had much social life." Freddy reasoned.

Mildred sipped her Scotch. "Quim, I guess you really don't have to stay here any longer. If you want to get back to your apartment, I should think it would make your life easier."

"Well, if you feel safe, I'd really appreciate being able to go back to the city. This situation in the department has been on my mind a lot." He agreed.

"My gosh," Freddy said, "if Alison leaves for the south of France, Quim goes back to the city, and Renee and the kids go home, we'll be ambling around this place by ourselves. How nice."

"I'm so glad you're going to miss my presence," Quim quipped. He finished his drink and rose. "I'm heading up to bed. If I get up early, I can pack and leave right after rush hour. I hate all that damn traffic from out here. I don't think I could get used to it."

"Sweetie, if you value privacy, you can get used to anything." Freddy threw him a mock kiss. "I've learned to enjoy the commute. It gives me time to gear up or wind down, depending on the destination. It's a good window of quiet solitude in my busy world."

Quim air kissed her back and left the room.

It was quiet for a moment. Mildred and Freddy looked at each other over the table. "Okay, let me have it, Mil. What is going on?"

Mildred leaned back in her chair. "I keep thinking it's all so pat. I mean, I'm glad we have some closure on Manuchi's death. I don't doubt that Marco was responsible for killing him. Whether he had help is another thing. I don't suppose we're ever going to know the entire truth. I think that's what is disturbing to me. It feels like there's more to it, but I just can't tell you what."

"You need to just let it be," Freddy said.

"Let my subconscious work?" Mildred asked. "I know. The more I try to concentrate on figuring it out, the more confused I'm going to be. I know that." She sighed.

"What I feel bad about is Alison. I've been harboring all these negative feelings about her, and she's been through hell in her life. I had no idea she had been abused so bad."

"It's not exactly as though she told us anything about her life. When John recommended I get a housemate, I thought she sounded like a great candidate. She's a published author, travels a lot, is really very intelligent, and when she's not swooning like her heroines, she's a lot of fun."

"I agree. I actually have come to like her quite a bit." Freddy mused. "I wouldn't have thought that was possible a couple of months ago. She has dealt with so much loss in her life. It's incredible she's able to function as well as she does!"

"I know. When she came to talk to me about living here, I thought it would be fun to know an author. I mentioned to Will that I was thinking about getting a housemate. He's the one who told her about it." Mildred shared. "I met him at the shelter. He does spiritual counseling for the women."

"He's an attractive man. I wonder why he never married."

Mildred looked at her. "Freddy. Just think about it. Will's available to Alison every waking moment. He has a congregation, but really almost every time she needs him, he comes. The other night was an exception."

"I don't suppose he could have left when someone has just died. It doesn't look good if your priest leaves at the time you need him the most."

"Exactly. But other than that, he's here anytime of day or night. To my mind, that means she's pretty damned important to him." Mildred answered.

"Yeah. You're probably right. Look at how long they've known each other. He said they met way back when he was a kid. It sounds like he was someone she could take care of and love, who didn't take advantage of her."

"I don't think it was one-sided, either. He probably supported her when she was being sexually abused." Mildred said quietly, "you know something? You and I have led much insulated lives. Sometimes when I hear some of the women's stories of their lives, I have to pinch myself to believe it's real. I think about the homes we were raised in, and it's hard for me to believe what other women have lived with compared to you and I."

"I know. In my practice I've heard so much pain I sometimes wonder why I want to continue in this profession." Freddy shared. "Reality is sometimes very nasty."

"Reality is a pisser!" Mildred hissed. "You know I really liked Dino Manuchi. John can say what he likes, the man was a good person. We did have a couple of pretty interesting conversations about the mob. That's when I began to have serious doubts about his connection. It almost seemed," she paused in recollection, "as if what he knew was more book learning, than real experience." Mildred was fishing for words.

"Like when you study something, but haven't done it yet?" Freddy asked.

"Exactly! I don't know it is, but there was that quality about it. He talked about his involvement as if it was someone else. You know what I mean?" she asked.

"Sure do." Freddy answered. "It's like the first time in your psychiatric residency when the patient is suddenly yours and you have to apply everything you learned. I was scared shitless. But then, you know me, blunder into it and hope the shit doesn't fly too far."

"As I recall, with your psychology background, the stretch wasn't too difficult."

"You know what I mean, Mil. At that point I was responsible for prescribing the meds. Now that's an awesome responsibility."

"But you did it. That's my point. I had the feeling, Manuchi had never done it. I'm not even sure what 'done it' means. I'm not saying I don't think he had some connection. I think he did. I just don't think he was important."

"So, why is he dead?" Freddy asked.

"That's what mystifies me. All I am left to believe is he was killed for another reason."

"What are the classic motives for murder? Jealousy, greed, love gone amuck, hate, anger, these are classic reasons. You don't think Crystal did it. Who else would have a motive?"

"You know, it's odd. We talked about that kind of thing one evening. I had stayed late getting ready for the annual licensing inspection. I was so damned tired, I stayed at the hospital. We talked for a long time." Mildred leaned back in recollection.

"Just relax Mil. You know how hard it is to remember some thing when you try too hard." Freddy advised.

"I am. We were talking about the shelter and how most battering victims are women. He made some inane remark about sometimes men are victimized too. I really bit on it. We got pretty heated in the discussion. You know how I can get about this topic." She stated to Freddy. "I think, for all my disagreement with him, he might have been right. I thought about it quite a lot."

"There must be some little thing he said that stuck. That's probably the piece you aren't remembering."

"I know, it's so damn frustrating. It's there, but it's not." She yawned. "I think I need to go up to bed. A good night's sleep is in order. My best thinking time is early in the morning. Maybe I'll take Maud out for a ride and just relax. It's been so tense around here." She got up and put the bottles and glasses on the tray. "I'm going to clean up a little and go up to bed."

"Are you sure you're all right?"

"I'm fine, Freddy. John and I talked about going up north after this case is done. He's definitely leaving the department and he wants to talk about a joint venture with the Retreat Center. It's the first time I have felt interested in anything, since Emil died. And, you know, I feel better, too. It's like my life is just starting, instead of supposedly ending."

"Sixty-two is a great time, Mil, if you aren't infirm or incapable of doings things."

"Right. My surgeon can't believe I did really did what I said I would do. Ride Maud again. He's thinks I'm off my nut, for even doing such a thing. My answer to him was simple, if you can't or won't do anything, what the hell is life for?"

Freddy picked up the ashtrays and followed Mildred into the kitchen. She went back quickly and wiped off the table in the library. "That's done. No sweaty glass marks on the high gloss. Francis will be proud of us."

The two of them put the glasses in the dishwasher and cleaned up the counters. "I think we're done. Time for beddy-bye. You sure you're gonna sleep?" She asked Mildred.

"Like a baby, my dear." As the two of them left the kitchen, Mildred switched off the lights.

The two of them ascended the stairs and parted at the second floor landing. The house was eerily quiet.

# CHAPTER TWENTY SEVEN

Mildred, true to her word, was up early. It was barely light when she walked to the pasture where Maud stood at the fence. The horse nuzzled her hand looking for treats. Mildred led her out of the gate, closing it securely behind her. Anubis trailed after them. He was up for a morning run. Mildred saddled and bridled the horse, and with a practiced movement hoisted herself into the saddle. She mused it wasn't as simple as it used to be.

The three of them worked out in the ring for a half hour. When it was time for a ride down the drive, Anubis was the first to head out. He enjoyed the leisurely pace set by Maud. It gave him a chance to sniff the trees and bushes, while they meandered down the path.

The morning was sultry. The sky hung with dark clouds, their seeming intention to drop buckets of water at any moment. Still Mildred was happy she was able to ride before the storm broke.

Before she left the house, Mildred had picked up the phone. It was dead. She knew last night's stormy invasion had done some damage, knocking down trees and power lines. The house had no electricity either. Neither of these things bothered her. A cold breakfast with juice, instead of coffee, was fine. She wasn't sure if the others would agree.

There was a paper this morning. She said hello to the security guard still on duty and returned to the house. Renee and the children were at the front door.

"Mom, I wondered where you were, I should have known." Renee said with a smile.

"Where else would I be on a day like this?" She looked at her daughter.

Renee was pale, but had a determined look on her face. "I'm gonna go home, mom. I really appreciate coming here yesterday, but I want to be in my own bed."

"I don't want to go!" Erica made her wishes known. "I don't want to leave Grandma."

"Honey, your grandmother has her hands full here. She needs some peace and quiet." Renee insisted. "Joel offered to take me and the kids home. He's leaving this morning. George thinks now that Manuchi's killer is dead, things will be fine here."

"Hon, don't worry about me." Mildred assured her. "Freddy and Francis will be here. Alison and Will are planning to leave if they get approval and Quim is going back to town."

"See!" Erica insisted, "If everyone's gone, Grandma will be lonely. Can't I stay, Grandma, please?"

"I don't see why not," Mildred agreed with Erica. "She's no problem, Renee. We've still got plenty of plants to put in, and she can help me with a couple of projects."

"I don't think you're gonna do any planting. It looks like the sky is gonna open up any minute. That's another reason I have to go home. I'm sure my power is out, too. I need to take care of the food. There's really not much in the frig, but we need to use up what's there."

"I'll help her out, Mildred." Joel's voice joined the conversation. "Her neighbor is coming over to stay with her and I'm taking Hunter with me. He's no problem. He's rarrin to get home and tell all his friends about the body in the drainage ditch."

Mildred sighed. Little boys liked adventure. She wished it felt like an adventure to her. Instead she felt sadness for a life gone for no apparent reason. "Erica can stay. We'll be fine. I'm sure by this evening we'll have power again. You just make sure you rest!" She admonished her daughter, as she kissed her cheek. "Home to bed. Only get up for bathroom runs, and a little exercise. And remember, I said a little exercise, not a lot."

"Mom, I'll be fine." Joel helped Renee into the car. He put her suitcases in the truck and got into the driver's seat. "I'll call you, mom. Erica, you behave." She admonished.

"I will mom," Erica answered. She waved at them as they drove down the driveway.

After they were gone, Mildred turned to Erica, "come and help me with Maud."

The two of them went to the stable and brushed her down. After Erica fed Maud carrots, they put her back in the pasture. Maud joined the other horses and began to graze.

"Oh, Grandma, the horses are so nice. When can I ride with you?"

"I've got to give you some more lessons in the ring. Maybe in a couple of weeks we can go out on the trails. How's that?"

"Great!" Erica whooped. "That'll be fun."

Quim was just leaving when they got back to the house. Francis and Freddy had set out breakfast on the porch and Quim had just finished eating right before the two of them got there.

"You're ready this early?" Mildred's eyebrows rose. "You must be ready to go back to town."

"Want to beat the storm. I called in on the cell phone. It's supposed to get really nasty today. We're in a Tornado Watch right now. So, I want to get out of here before it gets close with another deluge. There was a lot of rain last night in town. The power's out here. They still have power in the cities, but who knows if that will last. They even closed Twin City International Airport for awhile during the peak of the storm last night."

"I guess," Mildred said, "we aren't going to be doing anything outside today."

Francis came onto the porch with some coffee, "How in the world . . . . ?" Mildred looked at her.

"You light the gas stove with a match" Francis retorted. "Works fine." She set the pot down on the middle of the table. "If ya'll want somethin' warm, I'll cook it up. Looks to me like the weather's fixin' to get bad."

"Well," Quim said, pushing back his chair, "I'm outta here, as they say." He got up and walked over to Mildred. He stood looking at her for a minute. "You need to take care of yourself. This is a lot of stress, Mildred." Then, without further words, he reached down and hugged her close. He said something quietly to her and then abruptly left the room.

Mildred looked stricken. Freddy leaned over and took her hand. "What's the matter? You look like you've seen a ghost. What did he say?" Her voice pitched higher.

Mildred turned to her friend and spoke quietly. "He said, he loved me too." She turned at the sound of Quim's car reving up, in the driveway. Then the sound of the engine slowly faded as he drove the length of the driveway. He was gone.

"He was a little shaken up by the turn of events with John. That was apparent last evening." Freddy said. "I thought he was actually handling it pretty well."

"He would never be anything but a gentleman." Mildred murmured to her friend. "I think that might be one of his fatal flaws. He's always so correct, one gets the feeling he's perfect. It's damn hard to live with perfection. Most women have sense enough to stay away from it."

"Still, he's intelligent, funny, and socially correct. A mother's dream." Freddy said.

The two women looked at each other. Each knew what was in the other's mind. A memory so clear, it could have occurred yesterday, popped into their heads. Freddy's mother, talking to the two of them, one afternoon late in the day. She had met a delightful classmate of the two girls and was extolling on his charms. "Oh Freddy, he'd be so perfect for a date for you. You still haven't been asked to the Prom at the Academy. This young man is so charming."

That memorable afternoon had ended with her mother in tears. It was the moment when Freddy told her the truth. Their relationship took years to recover. Mildred had thought it so peculiar, Freddy's dad had been so understanding, but her mother never quite accepted the truth.

Mildred looked at Freddy. "Let's walk out to the garden. I want to see what we have left to do." She opened the door and held it for Freddy.

"You aren't thinking of doing anything out here today, are you?"

"No, my dear. I just thought we could see how much is left to do. Come on," she urged Freddy.

"I'm coming, I'm coming. Just let me grab my coffee. Erica," she asked the girl, "are you going to come out?"

"Nope! I'm staying right here. It's too icky out there for me." She was curled up on one of the couches, reading a book. "I'm fine. I saw enough plants yesterday. Besides, we planted all of the ones we needed to, didn't we?"

"Most of them. We'll be back," Freddy shut the door behind her.

Mildred was standing in the center of the garden. The pottery fish looked gloomy without water spurting from their mouths. It had gotten so dark, Mildred wondered if being out here was a good idea at all.

"I think we should listen to the weather report. I've got that transistor radio in the car. I'll go and get it. Take a quick peek here, and we can go in and plan out the rest of the layout. It's gonna pour any minute." Freddy left.

Mildred took a quick walk around the garden. Most of the plants were in the ground. At least, with all this rain, they didn't need to water them. They were getting almost too much water. She felt the sprinkling of rain on her face. It felt good, even cleansing somehow. She didn't realize when she started to cry, but as she returned to the house, tears mingled with the drops of rain on her cheeks.

"Grandma!" Erica got up and came to her, "are you all right?"

"Yes, Hon, I'm really okay. It's just been a strain." As she spoke, the sky seemed to open up and rain fell in a deluge. Once again, it was so dark; it seemed as if night had descended again.

Freddy came in from the front of the house, "Whew, I just made it to the front door. I sure hope Quim isn't driving in this. The freeway has got to be a mess."

# CHAPTER TWENTY EIGHT

John's head had barely hit the pillow, when the phone rang. It was a Sgt. O'Mallory from the Chicago Police Department. He filled John in on some of the developments they had uncovered and suggested John come to Chicago immediately.

"There is a major storm here," John protested.

"I think you will find what we have very interesting. I also believe it will be very helpful."

"Can't you just fax the material?" John asked, already suspecting the answer.

"I can fax you the material. That's not a problem. However, there's someone I think you should talk with about the case. It's a retired cop who lives in the old neighborhood. Ordinarily, he'd like nothing better than to come to Minnesota and see you, but he just had surgery on his leg. He ain't going nowhere." The man paused thoughtfully, "I think you'd better talk to him. You won't regret it."

John sighed. He seemed destined to not get any sleep. "Okay. I'll see if the department can get me a plane connection. I'm not sure anything is flying, it's so shitty here. We're in a major storm system."

"Let me know when you'll get here, I'll meet you at the airport. All I can say is, you won't regret the trip."

"Yeh." Was John's grumpy reply.

An hour and a half later, John boarded a Northwest flight to Chicago. He had lucked out and they were still flying. Later he described the flight as the worst in history. It should've been canceled. He no longer considered the good connection, luck. He spent the next hour and a quarter feeling like he was riding a Wells Fargo Stagecoach up the Rockies. When he stepped on solid ground at O'Hare, he felt like kissing it.

Sgt. O'Mallory was waiting for him. The weather in Chicago was fine. Apparently the system was moving to the northeast. John prayed he would have a smoother flight home.

"Where we going?" he asked.

"Little Italy," came the terse reply. "I got a car waiting. Let's go!"

"Can I grab a sandwich?"

"Yeh. We'll pass a couple of spots where you can pick something up. We really gotta get going."

In five minutes they were in a squad car with the flashers on. O'Mallory had called and ordered sandwiches, they would pick them up on the way. "You'll need coffee, too."

"So what's this about?" John asked. "You have some secret font on information squirreled away somewhere?"

"In a way, you might say that. We're going to see a retired copper name Lucci. He was assigned to the old neighborhood years ago. He grew up here. This place has had it's ups and downs. Now it's enjoying the ups. For awhile, the place was practically a slum. Well, to make a long story short, he is living in the house he grew up in."

"I gather where he lives is important?" John asked.

"Yep." O'Mallory drew out the word. "Next to a major arson scene almost fifty years ago."

"Arson?"

"Yep."

"So, can you fill me in?" John inquired.

"I'd rather wait," O'Mallory replied "That's the point of bringing you out here. To talk to Lucci. He was the man on the scene."

The squad pulled up to an all night diner. "Be right out." O'Mallory got out of the car and returned within a couple of minutes. He handed a brown bag to John and kept one himself. "Go ahead, start in. I'm drivin'. Besides we'll be there in about a minute." He deftly wove the squad through a narrow street and then turned into a driveway by a three-story brownstone apartment.

John looked around. Even in the dark, he could see the well kept lawn and garden. It was almost picture pretty in the light from a corner streetlight. He got out of the car, holding his bag tightly. He had waited, too. "This where he lives?"

In answer to his question a voice came from a side door. A dim light spilled onto a set of stairs leading to an English Basement apartment. It silhouetted the man who was speaking. John could see he leaned heavily on a cane. As he approached, it was apparent the man was slender and very muscular.

"Good to see you, O'Mallory. Sorry about the timing here. I've gotten to be quite a night owl. Can't sleep, so I might as well do something constructive." He stepped aside as the two men came down the stairs. "Come on in." He waved indicating the direction.

John was astounded at the room they entered. The furnishings were antique. Every piece of furniture was a thing of beauty. He looked around, unsure of where to sit.

"Don't worry, you can't hurt this stuff. It's been around so long, getting used by generations of Lucci's, that it would feel abused not to be used. Know what I mean?" He indicated a seat at a Chippendale table that wrung John's heart. "Sit! Sit!"

John sat. He placed the bag gingerly on the table. Before he could empty the contents, a lovely Spode plate was set in front of him. "There you are. Enjoy." A cup was placed next to the plate.

"I'm Benjamin Lucci," the man put his hand forward. John took it and shook. "Glad O'Mallory here, got a hold of you. I've been thinking about this case, ever since he called me about it. I've been praying for a chance to maybe," he paused, "rectify a couple of miscarriages of justice. Sometimes, you know, you have a case you just know was deliberate murder. You know who did it. You know why, even, but you can't prove it." He shook his head.

John shook his head in agreement, as he ate his extremely good Cheeseburger and Fries. He sipped some coffee and cleared his throat. "Sorry. I feel like I'm being anti-social. I know what you mean I've had a couple of those cases myself." He agreed.

"Yeah, it goes with the territory of being a copper." Lucci said.

"So, tell me what you have in mind." John leaned back in his chair.

Lucci settled into his chair. "I was born in this house. First floor, back bedroom. Been here ever since." He cleared his throat. "I have loyalty to the people who live here, and in this case, to those that lived here a long time ago. I know your suspect Alison."

At the word suspect, John leaned forward. "Suspect? She was the victim! Her friend died by drinking a glass of wine intended for her."

"Well, now . . . . Maybe you're right. Certainly I wasn't there to observe what happened. Have your coppers figured out a motive for this friend's death?" He inquired.

"It's a problem. Doesn't seem like she had an enemy in the world. Her background is impeccable. Never had a speeding ticket, much less any event in her life which would indicate someone would want to kill her. It's a problem." John agreed.

"Let me give you a history lesson. I was seven years old, when Alison Lipinski was born. She was the baby next door." He watched John's face register surprise. "Yep. I was the next door neighbor. The house stood on the corner, right where my big perennial flower garden is standing today. But, I don't want to get ahead of myself. She was a cute little girl. When she was old enough, she was toddling after me all over the place. I got teased about having a shadow. She had an older brother. He was three when she was born. He was a smart cookie, too. The parents were wonderful people. Dad was Polish and Italian. Mostly Italian. His grandmother had married a Pollack back when the girls from this neighborhood didn't do such things. It was a great union though. They had a bunch of kids, raised 'em Catholic, and started a family business."

"What kind of business?" John inquired.

"You gotta stop interrupting me, young man. If you want to get back to Minneapolis, or where-ever you're from, you got to listen sharply." He admonished. "When I'm done tellin' you this story, you're gonna want to get back home. Pronto."

"Alright. I'll shut up and use my recorder, okay?"

"Right, turn the damn thing on and just listen." He settled back in his chair.

John turned on the recorder and sat back.

"Now, where was I? Okay. Alison. She grew up here. My whole family knew her, all my friends knew her, she was here all the time. See?" He questioned, as he made an expansive gesture with his arm indicating the apartment house. "Anyway, she was smart. Lots smarter than most of the kids in this neighborhood. She went to Catholic School, didn't have to read a book even, she just knew the stuff. When she started Kindergarten she was already readin'. Her dad said he was readin' The Three Bears and she started correcting his reading errors. He told her if she was so smart, read the book herself. Damn, she did it. Picked up that book and started readin' to him. He said, "Shit", that's it. If the kid's so damn smart, put her in school. The nuns took her early. None of that birthday shit then." He leaned forward and continued.

"This kid was always into mischief. The notes came home regularly. She was precocious and very smart. Her behavior was always kind of adult, you know?" He questioned. "Her mom and dad despaired of doing anything with her after awhile. She got around the neighborhood a lot. Took the bus downtown to the Loop when she was just a little thing. Her ma was worried all the time. Said the kid was gonna get kidnapped, raped, beaten up, you name it. Alison was into mischief. Now, there was one place she went all the time. The Candy Store. She spent all her free time there. The couple who owned the place was childless and they really took a shine to Alison."

John leaned forward, "the Dennison's?"

"Yeah." Lucci said. "The Dennison's. They were a nice couple, you know. They were in their mid-forties then. The Candy Store was just part of the operation. They had a bigger business in the antiques. They sold American stuff, but the big sellers were the European and British antiques. They had customers up and down the North Shore. People came to this neighborhood from all over the damn place. Put us on the map." He cleared his throat.

"Successful folks, I take it?" John interjected the question.

"Yeah, they were. Now Dennison, he traveled all over the world. He was a good lookin' guy. The neighborhood women, single and married, young and old, they doted on him. My God, when his wife got sick with the cancer, then the hot-dishes and cakes arrived, I can tell ya. He was invited to dinner in more homes than you can shake a stick at. But, he turned down most of 'em. You know why?"

John answered in the negative.

"Cause he had a little admirer, name of Alison Lipinski. She was there all the time. Doing housework, cookin' for the Mrs., running errands. You name it, she did it for them. Became indispensable, understand? Well, while all this is happening, her dad is taking exception to the behavior. This is a little kid, you know? He don' like havin' his kid practically livin' at the neighbors. It don' look good. I mean she's doin' this stuff for several years," he sat taller in his chair. "Even the nuns were talkin' about it. Jesus Murphy! Some people thought she was their daughter."

"Is this the couple that became her foster parents?" John asked.

"Yeah! That's them. Now's here's how it happened. I was about twenty at the time. I was already in the Department. Back then no Rookie School, you learned the job on the streets. I was sharp, I grew up with knowin' the mob was here to stay. Capuche? They existed. If you lived in Little Italy, those people were family. Right?"

John nodded.

"So, here's little Alison, only she's not so little anymore. She's got these pointy boobs and a figure you could get lost in. She's fourteen or so. Like I said, she's seven years younger than me. All right, where was I? Oh yeah. Her old man, he starts tellin her 'NO', she can't be spendin' all this time with the Dennison's. It ain't right, you know?" He cleared his throat, which had become husky. "Oh God! This brings it all back. I gotta stop for a minute. Let me make some coffee, okay?"

"Sure," John turned off the recorder. He watched the older man deftly make a pot of coffee. When it was done, he pored three cups and returned to the table. "There, now I got the grease to run on. Okay, where was I? Flip on that recorder, we're in business. So, her old man is pissed. He sees his little princess practically livin' at the neighbors. The wife's got the cancer, she's bedridden. Here's the daughter, makin like a little wife. You got me?"

"Yeah," came John's terse reply.

"So, the next thing happens, the old man has a damn fit about it. Tells the kid she's forbidden to go there. Whew. It's like tellin' the lava to stop flowing on Mount Etna. You know Etna? Well, I don need to tell ya, it don stop jus' cause you tell it to." He drank some coffee. "Keeps me oiled, you know? So, little Alison is poutin' and carryin' on to everyone, how her dad is mean to her. He makes her do things, and you know what kind of things I'm talkin' here? Right?"

Another nod, from both listeners, indicated their understanding.

"So, she spreads this shit about her old man being connected. Jeez. The real mob guys, the wise guys, they know better. But what can they say? If they talk, they're in trouble. She's saying the old man is sellin' her to guys, that he's drunk all the time, it was bullshit! Her old man, he was havin' one hell of a time, tryin' to deal with this kid. He even came to me. Now, I don want to tell him, she's been hot to trot since she's been about nine years old. She was one hot little pussy. You know what I mean? I think she's been seducing old man Dennison since God made little green apples. His wife don see it. She's sick, for God's sake. Took her a couple of years to die, it was real shit, she dealt with." He sipped more. "Well, all this time, the kid is lyin' about her father, tryin' to get me to arrest her old man. Now her brother, who's three years older, he calls her a whore. Me, I never would have said that word, but in hindsight, I wondered about it. He probably had some personal experience, you know? That happens sometimes, but usually it's the girl being abused. In this case, I was real torn. I mean, she was a god damn goddess to look at her. Beautiful, butter wouldn't melt in her mouth. And smart, Jesus Murphy, this kid remembered every damn thing she ever read. Holy shit, how do you deal with a kid like that?"

John squirmed uncomfortably as he thought of the Alison he knew. "So what happened?"

"What happened, was the fire! Jesus! It was horrendous. You could hear them people screamin' all over the block. They were trapped in the hottest, fastest damn fire we ever had in this area. Rigs came from all over the damn place. Couldn't do a damn thing, but watch it burn."

The old man sighed as he recalled that night. "Now, Alison wasn't home. She had snuck out to visit the Dennison's. Later, she claimed it was a miracle she escaped. Yeah, right." He looked so fragile, John was worried recalling all this would be unhealthy for him. After a few minutes, he continued. "There's some other pieces to this. Alison had taken a shine to a couple of kids. One was her cousin, Marco Giavonni."

"Who?" John sat bolt upright. "Marco was her cousin? Jesus!" He shouted.

"Yeah! Her cousin. A bigger slime-ball you could never meet. Even as a kid he was twisted. A fire-starter. Had a problem since he was real little. He's another one her old man didn't want her hangin' with. He was pulled in for questioning more times than anybody in the neighborhood. Alison was his alibi lot's of times. We couldn't break the story with either one of 'em." He paused and drank more coffee. "Her other friend was Vittorio Mancussi. He was several years younger. God knows, she probably was boffin' him too. I mean, it's real crude, but at the department we had a name for girls like her. All I can say is this, she acted like her crotch was on fire, from the time she was about eight, nine years old. She used to make those gooey eyes at me when I was about sixteen. Would rub up against me and ask if I didn't want to spend time with her. Jesus! She was somethin'! A real piece of work."

Lucci's face was glistening, as if the exertion of memory was difficult. "Now Vittorio, he was a street urchin. Like Oliver Twist. I sometimes wondered if he wasn't a little twisted. Anyway, he was at her beck and call all the time. She talked the Dennison's into givin' him a little room at the back of the store. He used the bathroom in the shop to clean up in. He lived there for a long time. He left school when he was about twelve. We could never catch up with him. Don't get me wrong, this was another very smart kid. Like Alison, he never forgot anything either. It's probably what drew them together. Their still hangin' out together."

When John looked puzzled, he spoke again.

"You know him as Father Will." Lucci spoke quietly.

The three men took a short break from the conversation. John walked outside to clear his head. Lucci followed with his cane. "That's where the house stood. It was on the corner lot. I grew up in this brownstone. My grandparents were from Italy on my father's side. They bought this place during the depression. Both of them were frugal and property was somethin' you could get cheap at that time. They both worked their asses off, but they left a hell of a legacy."

John nodded as he listened.

"They were both gardeners. They liked antiques and Pa liked nothin' better than refinishin' some beautiful old piece. Nowadays, they say you ruin the value. I say, if it looks like shit cause it has the old finish, fix it. Anyway, the brownstone came with two lots. After the fire on the corner, the house was razed. Pa and Ma bought it, cause no one wanted to live there ever again. Now, the corner lot is flowers. I put in a memorial garden for the Lipinski's. The least I could do. Alison, she could give a shit."

It was evident Lucci was going to talk again. John turned the tape and started the recorder. "After the fire, she went over and sweet talked the Dennison's. Next thing I know, they're goin to adopt her. Happened right away. Chicago Social Service got real busy. Next thing you knew, Alison was livin with the Dennison's. Now I know she sleepin with the old man. Soon after she moves in, the old lady dies." He cast a meaningful look at John. "Now, I can't prove nothin' you understand, but that old lady had been doin' pretty good for several years. I heard she was in remission. Suddenly, she's gone. There's Alison, pretty as a picture, livin' right out in the open with Dennison. Then he dies. Surprise, surprise! Alison inherits everything the old guy owned. Millions. Nobody even knew he had that kind of money, livin' in this neighborhood." He waved his hand indicating the surroundings.

"My God" John's adrenaline kicked in. Alison was home with Mildred. "Oh shit! She's there! She's living with Mildred and Freddy. Oh my God! Let me use your phone." He ran to the house. He tried and tried. The same results kept being repeated. The phone lines were down. There was no connection to the East Bethel Property.

He tried Mildred's cell phone. No answer. She had the annoying habit of leaving it in her car. When he got the chance he was going to wring her neck for being so stubborn about carrying the phone. In this he was wrong. The phone was in Mildred's purse, the insistent buzzing not catching anybody's attention, because Mildred was up in her room, just waking up.

"I've gotta get back there. Now!" John yelled at the two of them. "I need to call the Anoka County's Sheriff's Department. Someone needs to get out there, quick. Where's your phone?"

Lucci told him. While he called Anoka, O'Mallory lined up a flight on Northwest. They could just make the connection if they left from Midway, instead of O'Hare.

"I'll ride with you, then I can finish what I think is goin' on. Lucci got into the squad car with the two men. Turn on the recorder, John. It get's better." He settled himself on the back seat. "My God! I don't know where to begin again. It's like grabbing an amoebae. No matter where you grab, it changes shape. Don't Native Americans have something called a Shape Shifter? Okay, here's my last thoughts on it. A couple of months went by, after Dennison's death. This word began to trickle back to us; he had been a Mob Enforcer. A Hit Man. While I'm hearin' about this, our friend Alison is getting enrolled in college. She had a great track record. Who wouldn't, with that memory of hers? Vittorio, or Will, as you know him, did just as good. Marco, did some jail time, as a juvenile offender. Fires again. This guy couldn't stay away from matches. I think what finally happened is this, Alison sent him to a shrink. Somehow, they got this loser to stop setting fires, and he got training in the food business. Alison had some good connection."

Lucci shifted position again. "Jesus Murphy! These god damn back seats are shit. Okay, let me see. Alison ships him off to Italy to learn about wines and Italian food. He comes back pretty damn civil. Really fits in to society. Get's some real good jobs, builds a food service dossier. It's sure as hell better than his previous record. He follows her to the Twin Cities last year. She moved there from here. Father Will got a call in your Anoka County. So, she follows him. That's how she gets to her present address with your friend."

John was trying once again to get through to Mildred. No luck.

"Back to college. Alison and Will go to Northwestern and then she goes on to the University of Chicago. He starts there, then leaves and goes to Seminary. He's close though, in Evanston. She meets her husband, Gordon. He was at Grad School with her. Literature student, another smart guy. Although, I'm not so sure it's smart to get too close to Alison Lipinski. Lot's and lots of deaths. You know what I mean? They get married. He goes into the Army by choice, goes to Vietnam. Then stationed in Saigon, then poof! She goes to visit this successful guy, and next thing you know, he's dead of an overdose of Heroin. She cries about all the grief's she's suffered. Lost her family, her adopted family, her husband. And, I can tell you, I think there's more grief's back there, I just don't know who they are. You see, the word is this; she took up where old man Dennison left off. There are people who think she's the new Hit Man. That he taught her all he knew, then she snuffed him. Took his job. Convinced the Mob she was hot shit. Of course in this day of feminism and such, she'd be called a Hit Woman. Whatever! Word is this, she's a hired Mob killer and she's damn good at it." He finished with a deep sigh.

They were speeding into Midway Airport. John pulled all his possessions together. Looked at Lucci, "anything else?"

"Yeah. She probably aced Marco. How she did it, I'm not sure. Why she had a motive to kill this friend of hers, I don't know. That's your job. Figure it out."

John turned off the recorder and opened the door as soon as it stopped. He thanked O'Mallory and ran into the terminal. He just made the connection to Minneapolis.

# CHAPTER TWENTY NINE

Mildred didn't feel much better an hour later. There was a sense of great sadness in her heart, which she couldn't connect to just the current circumstances. In many ways, though she was very intelligent, Mildred depended on her intuitive nature to assist in dealing with difficult situations. No connections were being made.

Freddy knew she was upset, but was wise enough to let her sort through the feelings. Mildred checked on Erica and was assured the child was settled in with her books. She certainly seemed contented, so Mildred told them she was going to lie down for a short while. Both agreed they'd survive without her company for awhile.

She went up the stairs. As she was starting up the flight to the third floor, Alison spoke to her, "Mildred," her voice was eager with anticipation. "I finished editing what little had to be done on Ashley's book. I wondered if you could glance through it and let me know what you think."

Mildred thought, perhaps this might be just the thing, to ease her mind. Reading had always soothed her when things were rough. She agreed and Alison handed her the book. "It's important to get another opinion. I usually had Ashley proof read my manuscripts before I sent them in."

Mildred had every one of Alison's books. They were on a shelf by themselves, prominently displayed in a place of honor. All were signed first editions. Mildred had been very pleased when Alison had given them to her. She had never known an author before and was astonished to discover how bright and funny she was. Alison also had a wonderful sense of humor. There were times when the two of them had laughed at situations until their sides ached. All in all, Mildred had found Alison to be great company.

There were also times, when Alison's emotional barometer seemed to fail her. Then she would seem very unstable and her moods were changeable. This was when Mildred would find her difficult to deal with or understand.

Underlying Alison's persona seemed to lurk a different person. When Mildred had asked her about it, Alison's reply would be full of excuses about a writer's difficult personality. It seemed to fit. Alison had mood swings. Freddy would not be as generous as Mildred in accepting these changes. She believed the woman had a very tight, emotional control. Still, Mildred liked her. She had discovered shortly after Alison had moved in a year ago, that you took things a day at a time with her.

Now, as Mildred took the book from Alison, she saw the bubbly, personable façade that indicated excitement. "You look as if Christmas is coming. What's happening?"

"I think we'll be able to leave this evening. I know it's not socially the thing to do, but I have just got to get away from here for awhile. Ashley's death has really upset me so much. I just can't deal with all the feelings. I feel like I'm on overload. You ever get that way?" Her eyes seemed to take on a queer light, as she asked the question.

"Of course I have," Mildred said soothingly. "Everyone feels like that at times."

"I have started to make arrangement for Ashley's Memorial Service. There are some of our friends that can't be here for another month. So, I decided to wait until then to schedule a service. I know I'll have better emotional control if I wait."

Mildred could see the strain in Alison's face. Her mood seemed mercurial, from anticipation to despair. She was glad that Father Will was planning to go with Alison, at least for a short while. Mildred did wonder how his congregation would cope with his sudden departure. However, she figured he'd do it somehow.

She held the manuscript close to her chest. "I'm going to go up and lie down. I'm not feeling very well myself, this morning. I have a headache and just feel . . . ."

"I know just what you mean. I'm so up and down, I feel like a yo-yo." Alison's assurances eased Mildred's departure.

As she ascended the stairs, she spoke over her shoulder, "I'll read this as I'm lying down. I'll let you know what I think."

"That would be wonderful, Mildred. You're really one of my most trusted critics." She went back into her room and closed the door.

Mildred continued up the stairs. When she reached her room, she entered and closed the door behind her. She began to relax right away. This was her hideaway and special place. When she furnished these rooms, she had taken care to put her most treasured possessions here. There were special pieces of pottery and art work. Mildred had found she had no special preferences for what she collected, other than it needed to please her eye.

Her glance fell on a display of Sagerware Pottery. The rough surface of the collection of bowls and containers, always filled her heart with satisfaction. The potter was someone she knew. When she had first seen his work, and admired the pieces he created, she couldn't make up her mind what to purchase. She ended up buying every one of them she admired. Now, she used them for a variety of functions from serving food, to bathroom accessories. The larger pieces were prominently displayed in her sitting room.

Her thoughts lingered on her friends. She too, seemed to have a mercurial temperament this morning. Her emotional range had been everything from happy, while riding Maud, to the overwhelming sense of despair, while she was in the garden. It scared her. Mildred liked to think she was stable, especially since the accident. She hadn't suffered any head trauma, but she worried about it anyway. The fear that some new difficulty would arise was always at the back of her mind.

Her physicians had assured her that at this point in recovery, there was not much danger of this happening. She worried anyway. She crossed the room and sat down in a chaise lounge under the broad sweep of windows. Though it was dark outside from the storm, there was enough light to read the manuscript. She began.

An hour later, Mildred drifted off into an uneasy sleep. There were a parade of images which drifted across her unconscious mind. When she awoke, she sensed something different in the atmosphere. She had experienced a dream sequence wherein Dino and herself were sitting in the lounge area of the psychiatric unit. He was laughing and talking about the progress of women in today's world. She knew his words were significant, but she couldn't quite make them out. He faded and so did the excitement of discovery. She awoke fully to the sound of thunder. The noise was so overwhelming, it scared her out of the chaise. She peered out of the window. The trees were blowing, as if in gale winds. Freddy's car was gone. She felt a sense of fear, wondering why Freddy would leave in this weather. It didn't make sense.

She wondered where Erica was. The fear that coursed through her body became hot and electrical. Mildred wasn't sure why, but she sensed incredible danger. The darkness wasn't as intense as previously. Rain was pouring copiously from the sky. Now that the skies had opened up with the deluge of water, it seemed to have lightened outside.

She saw the manuscript on the floor. The pages were mussed as they had slid from her hands. 'A writer's style is as identifiable as their fingerprints'. The thought was as clear in her mind, as when Alison had stated it to her in one of their first conversations. Freddy had agreed. Freddy thought, a book produced by a writer, gave major clues to their personality style. She felt the characterizations were projections of the writer's persona. Each character took on an aspect of the writer's own hidden belief systems and spiritual commitment.

Mildred had disagreed. The argument came unbidden to her mind. Mildred felt intuitively that writers also used creative license. She believed they produced a person from their fertile imagination, projecting characters that met the needs of story, as it unfolded in their minds.

Now, she wondered, who was right. If what she perceived was the truth, then the reality of the past year, was questionable. Manuchi's words surfaced. "There's equal rights everywhere, even in the Mob." He had laughed and put off her request for clarification. With the chill of realization, she leaned over and picked up the pages. As she straightened them, Alison's voice penetrated her mind.

"You know, don't you?"

The words were spoken quietly, but without passion. Mildred turned to face a triumphant Alison. One of her tightly closed fists held Erica captive. The child's face was ashen. The other hand clutched a revolver. New, smooth, Mildred thought it was a 9 mm Glock. She wasn't sure however. What she knew was her granddaughter was in grave danger.

"Alison, I'm not sure what I know. I do know however, you are far too intelligent for me to dicker about this. Don't hurt her. In your plan she doesn't have to be a hindrance."

"I know that." Alison answered smoothly. "I won't hurt her if you cooperate."

"Can I trust that promise?"

"I'm done with killing innocent kids. I do have a couple of regrets." An odd smile played around her mouth. "My kid sisters. I think about them sometimes. They really never did anything to me." She sighed deeply, "however, they were there, and there was no way I could have gotten them out without warning my dad."

Mildred looked at Alison closely. Her eyes were deep set with darkened rims. She looked as if she had been crying. It was even more frightening to Mildred, as she realized the depth of Alison's emotional confusion. The woman was suffering a great deal from Ashley's death. Mildred realized that Alison had never formed any attachments to another person. Perhaps Will, but certainly no one else. Now it appeared she had been deeply connected to Ashley.

"You miss her." Mildred stated simply.

"Oh God," Alison's anguished voice rose, "I didn't know. I just didn't know."

"Alison, can we sit down? You said you wouldn't hurt Erica if I cooperated. She's scared shitless. Look at her."

Alison's head turned to look at the child. Her grip loosened slightly, "all right. You just sit tight right here, next to me." She indicated the couch behind them. "Any funny stuff and I'll shoot your grandmother. You got that?"

Erica shook her head from up and down. She didn't say anything. She looked totally white faced and in shock.

Mildred sat uneasily across from Alison on another couch. "Do you want to tell me about it."

"What the hell is there to tell you? You think you're going to be a fuckin' psych nurse with me?" Her voice grew steely and nasty.

"No, that's not what I meant. Tell me about Ashley."

Another sigh, "I miss her. I shouldn't have killed her. It was one of those really stupid impulse things you regret as soon as you've done it." She looked at Erica again and spoke, "you just stay put, kid, I meant what I said."

"I heard you," Erica said emphatically, but quietly. She sat back against the couch.

"You know, Ashley was the first girlfriend I ever had. She was so damn nice to me. I really couldn't believe it when I first met her. I thought she wasn't for real, you know?"

Mildred nodded.

"We were in English Literature classes together. Kept running into one another. Finally one day, she asks if I wanted to have coffee or something. So, I thought, 'why not?' and I went. We really hit if off. She had this really interesting, dry sense of humor. She knew a lot and had traveled with her parents all over the world. She grew up in Evanston down by the Lake." She looked at Mildred. "I don't know if you've ever been there, Evanston I mean. It's a really cool suburb north of Chicago. She told me so many stories about growing up there, I began to think maybe I could belong, too. I know that sounds crazy, Mildred, but I kind of rewrote my life when I met her. I pretended sometimes, I didn't have my life history, but I had one like hers. It helped."

"She must have been a very good person to have affected you so much."

"I'll never be able to replace her friendship." Alison sighed again, "She became like a sister to me." She leaned back against the couch. Her grip loosened again on Erica. The child leaned back with her and put a tentative hand on Alison's arm.

Alison looked Mildred in the eye. "You know I hate your guts, don't you?" Her voice was once again cold with something Mildred couldn't identify. "You are another one of those people who have everything. You know what I'm talkin' about. People who take things for granted." She settled into the couch. "I didn't have that kind of childhood. Oh, yeah, it wasn't like I told ya," she thought a bit, then added, "but really it was. My old man never let me alone about stuff. He was always preachin' and bitchin' at my behavior. I kept tellin' 'em, I wasn't him. Leave me the fuck alone. I wanted to do my thing. He didn't get it. Always getting' in my face about how I was a bad kid. He was worried about me getting' in trouble. You know, sex stuff. He got downright fixated on it. Always givin' me lectures on what I couldn't and shouldn't do. Jesus! He nearly drove me fuckin' crazy, I'm tellin' ya."

"Parents get worried and do things sometimes, in ways they shouldn't." Mildred said quietly.

"I used to wonder if he was so damn worried about me, why was he always lookin' at my crotch." She saw Mildred's look. "Yeah, it's true. No, he never did nothin', but he was thinkin'."

"Tell me about Ashley." Mildred said, "It sounds like things got a lot better after you met her."

"She was really cool. She grew up with a lot of money. Now, I've got lots of money, but I didn't have that kind when I was a kid. I just daydreamed about it and finally figured out how to get it."

"Money was that important to you?" Mildred asked.

"You bet! I grew up in that stinkin' neighborhood. All the time the smells of sauce and italian meats. I can hardly stand it, when Francis makes the stuff. I don't know why," she said in reply to Mildred's look. "Sometimes, you just don't know why you are the way you are. There isn't a psychological reason for everything, is there?"

"I honestly don't know," Mildred answered. "I've thought about it, but I don't know."

"Well, I don't think there is. I think we are who we are. And," she added, "if we get reincarnated, I think we just continue on the journey, til we get where we're supposed to go."

Mildred looked closely at Alison. It had never occurred to her Alison thought about spiritual issues of that nature. She didn't want to get side-tracked though. "Tell me about Ashley. I'd like to hear about her."

Alison's face softened again. "She was wonderful. I told you, we met in class. I had never really ever read real literature. You know the kind of things, I mean. Shakespeare, Keats, Shelly, Hemingway, even. In that sense, I was socially deprived. The nuns at the Catholic school didn't teach that stuff. Of course, they were worried about my immortal soul, too. I could have told them some stuff. That old priest they had there. He was in his seventies. He was hot for me. You want to really know when I lost my Cherry. In was in the damn Priest's office with that old goat. I tried to tell my mom. She beat the shit outta me for talkin about him like that. That's when I knew, enough of this shit. If I'm gonna survive, I'm gonna have to do it on my own." Alison's face closed in remembered anger.

"He raped you." Mildred stated. "And then nobody believed you."

"Yeah," Alison agreed. "That's when I decided, no matter how damn good my parents seemed, they didn't really even listen to me. So, I decided if I had to survive in that neighborhood, where Priests could rape you, and parents didn't trust you, then I'd find a way to take care of myself."

"How'd you meet the Dennison's?" Mildred inquired.

"They had the Candy Store." She related. "Well, it wasn't just a Candy Store. The two of them sold antiques. They traveled a lot. To Italy, France, Germany, even England. It seemed like they were gone a lot. I knew they had a lot of money. So, I decided I was gonna get to know them better. They never had any children. She couldn't have em. So, I made myself indispensable to her. It wasn't hard to do. He was gone a lot more than she was. He traveled all the time. Not just for antiques. He went to lots of cities around the world. I used to listen to them talking about it. He would tell her who and what he had seen. He always seemed wired when he came home. I used to wonder about it. Then, one day I was there when he came back and I asked him why he traveled so much. He answered me. 'Little lady, that's how I make my living. I travel and do jobs for people. They pay me a lot of money. So, I keep doing it.' Then he laughed and talked a little more about how life was short and a person should get everything they could out of it. That's when he started lookin' at my boobs. The thing is, with him, I felt tingly."

Mildred looked at her. "Is that when he started making moves on you?"

"Nah! You got it wrong, Mildred. I shouldn't say this in front of the kid, but really, it was me wanted to mess around. I'm the one who got him interested in the first place. When his wife got the cancer, she couldn't have sex no more. That's when I got into his pants."

"How old were you?" Mildred was shocked and hoping her obvious response wouldn't upset Alison.

"Old enough" Alison said smugly. "I got that old man started and nothin' could stop him after that. I was careful, though, I didn't want to get pregnant. We screwed all the time. You see, I like it. I woulda made a great whore. Oh well," she recalled, "between him and Will, I kept pretty busy."

"Will?" Now Mildred was shocked.

Alison just laughed. "Yeah! Will. He was a kid, but he was only a couple of years younger than me. He started getting friendly when he was about thirteen. It was after the old man and me were doing it. He figured out what was going on and wanted some too. I thought, why not? What's the difference? Then, of course, there was Marco."

"Marco?"

"Yeah!" Alison answered. "He was a cousin, but we had some stuff going. He was more into fires. He set these fires and then get off on 'em. He was really crazy, you know?" As she leaned toward Mildred, she let go of Erica's arm. "You don't move! Got that?" She demanded.

Erica quietly nodded her head and leaned back into the couch.

"Alison, I'm confused about this. Marco was your cousin?"

"Yeah. It don't matter. He was always a damn pain in the ass. Those fires! My God! When I think how many times he almost brought that shit home to me. I coulda killed him. Believe me, I thought about it. Then he got sent to Juvie Prison. That's when I said when he got out, he was gonna learn a trade. I sent him to Italy to study cooking. He did come back more civilized. Only problem, he knew too much about me," she paused and lit a cigarette. "I don't give a shit if you don't smoke up here. I'm doing it!"

She looked at Erica hovered in the couch, then got up and picked up one of Mildred's bowls. "A great ashtray." She moved back next to Erica. "Now, where was I? Yeah, Marco had stopped setting fires. I told him if he did any more, I was gonna fix him permanently. He believed it, so he quit. Goes to show you, Mildred, ya can do anything you set your mind to, it just takes practice."

"Threats don't hurt, either. Tends to make one want to cooperate."

"That's it exactly. Threats work. Only person they didn't work on was that stupid husband of mine. He didn't listen. He was so smart, he got himself killed over it." She paused and took a drag of her cigarette. "That was his problem; he just couldn't leave anything alone, once it captured his imagination. The son of a bitch had an idea of writing a novel about a female 'Hit Man'. I told him, 'don't think about it. That wouldn't be healthy.' I get to Saigon; he's got a damn novel written. I don't have much choice. He's gotta go. Too God damn arrogant about everything. He didn't even blink when I gave him that great Heroin. It never crossed his mind he was about to die. He was happy, though."

"How many people have you killed?" Her voice came from the end of the couch. Erica leaned toward Alison, "killing is against the law."

"Yes, sweetie, I know. But, you know what? Some people deserve to die. I just help them out a little. I don't kill innocent people. I kill people who are no good." Her face clouded, "except for one." Her voice quivered.

"Alison," Mildred's voice was gentle, "it's done. You can't go back and change it. I think what's important is this, you're sorry about it. I think somehow, Ashley understands. She cared about you and probably knew you better than any other human being. When she wrote that book, she had to know she would be in danger."

"Why did she write it?" Alison's voice was angry. "Why? Why did she do it? That's why she had to die. Nobody could find out about it. What was she thinking?"

"My guess is this, she wanted to have a book in her own name. She wanted recognition for her talent. She wanted people to know, she could write great fiction, too. Unfortunately, she didn't realize it would put her life in jeopardy. If the public read her book, they would recognize the style. Your ghost writer would have been exposed, and your cover as a Gothic Romance Novelist would have been gone."

"When did you figure it out?"

"You let me read the book. It was evident you hadn't had enough time to really edit this book. If that were true, then it would mean the writer was Ashley. If your style was so blatant in Ashley's book, then the natural conclusion is, she wrote your books as a ghost writer. It would be too much to believe the two of you were so similar, that your writing would be basically the same. That's why she had to die. Her style was her fingerprint. It would have been much smarter to tell you what she wanted to do and ask your help to get published. You could have found a way, she couldn't."

"You're just too, too bright, Mildred. That's why you have to die. Don't you agree?"

"It would seem that's your plan. However, I would like to know why you killed Dino Manuchi. What did he do to you?"

"It's what he wouldn't do, Mildred, it's what he wouldn't do . . ." Her voice trailed off.

# CHAPTER THIRTY

Freddy and Francis left the house. Alison's request for help seemed appropriate for a change. Besides, if anything would help to get Alison away for awhile, Freddy would have done it. The woman was such a pain in the ass. Since Ashley's death, Alison's mercurial mood swings had become more than any of them wanted to deal with, on a day to day basis. A trip was a great idea.

Francis didn't make any bones about what she thought. "That woman's screwy. I never know if I'm gonna serve dinner to a sophisticated writer or a shrew. She's a changeling. I know Mildred's lost patience and wonders why she ever let her move in with us."

"The good thing is she travels. Hell, she's hardly been around the last year. The problem is, when she's home, you can't miss her. If she'd stay up there and write, things would be okay. God Almighty! She just drives me to distraction." Freddy pounded the dashboard. "I'm afraid I'm gonna lose it one of these days. I'm the shrink! I'm supposed to be sane and in control. You bet I'll go and pick up her shit at the cleaners. I'd do just about anything to get her going."

"Well, if you wanna get anywhere, missy, you better slow down some, or neither of us is gonna get there." Francis said dryly. "This road is a mess."

They had just turned onto Highway 65 at Viking Blvd., when Freddy's cell phone rang. She answered, "Dr. Beaudreaux here." She paused and listened.

"John! Where are you? You sound like you're on another planet." She listened. "What?"

Francis turned toward Freddy. It was obvious something was wrong. Freddy's had gripped the phone until her knuckles turned white. She listened intently to the voice on the phone. Every so often she would interrupt, "are you sure?"

Freddy had stopped the car at the East Bethel Theater parking lot while she talked. Before the conversation ended, she had turned the car around and was heading back to the house.

Francis was very uncomfortable. Freddy wasn't paying any attention to her driving, she was so engrossed in the conversation. She hung up. "Jesus! We gotta get back there!" She floored the car.

Francis grabbed the door handle, "what's going on?" She demanded.

"Alison's the killer, that's what's going on. Mildred and Erica are back there alone with her. She's nuts! John says she's probably killed a hundred people in her life. He told me to wait for Anoka County, but shit on that!"

"Freddy. Don't you be thinkin' of doing somethin' stupid!" Francis shouted at her above the roar of the engine. They were going eighty on Viking Blvd. It scared Francis. "You slow down, girl, or I'm gonna drive this damn car." She insisted to Freddy. "If you run us off the road, ain't nobody gonna help Mildred, you damn fool!"

Freddy heard her and slowed down the car. They turned on East Bethel Blvd. at the Fire Station. "Okay, is this better?" She had slowed to sixty.'

Francis nodded. "What did John tell you?"

"Alison's been lying to us. Well, twisting the truth would be more accurate. Jesus Christ! He figures Alison hates Mildred because of Dino Manuchi. John's on his way back here from the Airport, but he'll never get here in time. He said his partner talked with Dino's wife Crystal again. She remembered Dino telling her something about Alison coming on to him. He told Crystal that Alison was a stalker. She wouldn't leave him alone. He was thinkin' about calling the cops. Then he was killed. She never thought too much about it until John's partner Glenn called her and began ask more questions. Then she began to wonder about it and asked him what he thought. When John called him this morning and the two of them shared information, it was clear who killed Manuchi." She had reached the driveway.

She pulled in and stopped the car at the Security Shack. Young Jeremy was on duty. Freddy got out and talked with him at length. Francis saw the young man's face blanch as Freddy told him what was happening. Then Freddy came back to the car.

"We have to go to the house on foot. The car would tip her off that we're back. Jeremy is contacting George and Joel. The Cops are coming on silent alarm status. They know a siren would be Mildred's death warrant."

"How we gonna get to that house without her seein?" Francis asked. "It's all open an' if she has a gun, we're sitting ducks."

"We'll have to go through the woods. Mildred hasn't used the Bridle Path Emil put in. It needs mowing, but it's passable and will get us to the other side of the barn. Then we can move from there to the guest wing. That's the only place we'll be exposed at all. We'll have to take the chance. It's the only way in without going across the back or front lawns."

"What about the dog?" Francis asked. "Should we bring Anubis?" "I don't honestly know. He's trained, but he was trained to obey Mildred. I don't know if we can take the chance. Actually, Francis, I want you to stay in the guest wing. There's no point in any more people being involved than necessary.

The two of them walked rapidly through the woods. The edge of the barn loomed ahead. Freddy peered up at the third floor. Mildred's windows were open on the east end of the house. If Freddy was correct, the three of them were in the south facing rooms. They'd have to take the chance. She indicated to Francis they should hurry across the space of lawn between the two buildings. It didn't take but thirty seconds to accomplish their goal, but Freddy's heart was in her throat the whole time. One look at Francis indicated she had felt the same way.

Once they were inside, Mildred told Francis where to stay. Francis didn't like it, but decided Freddy was probably right. Two of them were likely to make noise. After Freddy had gone into the house, Francis sat and thought. She had an idea, but wasn't sure exactly how it would work. The house was equipped with a sophisticated sound system. Mildred had not used it at all, but Francis had spent time with Emil before he died. He had explained it to her and given specific details on how it could save her a lot of running to find people for dinner and other things. He had also equipped the system with an emergency generator. Francis had not thought about it until now because it was only available for the security system.

She quickly thought about what he had taught her about emergency power. She checked the batteries. Everything was ready. She was surprised at how much information she remembered. She turned on the generator and smiled. It came to life as easily as it did when Emil first showed it to her.

Emil had been discussing his ideas for future changes, when he died. He had enjoyed teaching Francis and had shared his considerable knowledge with her. She was smart and liked the challenge. She spent hours playing with the system and understood it far better than Mildred. She loved electronics and gadgets. When she was a child, she had developed interests in a variety of areas. Machinery and electronics were fascinating to her. However, her culinary skills were foremost in her repertoire. It was also the easiest means of success in her strive for independence.

Francis hadn't spent all her time cooking. She had spent a lot of time with Emil when he devised the security and sound systems. Mildred hadn't the time to become adept at the complexity of it. Emil felt one of the members of the home needed to understand it, so he taught Francis. She had been an apt pupil.

Now as she decided how she could help, she moved rapidly to the control center for the sound system. It would take her a few minutes to find what she was looking for in the file of audio tapes. Though Mildred was unaware of it, Francis had at times, used the audio system. She felt she needed practice to keep her knowledge base current. She taped various conversations. One day, Alison had requested her to audio tape a conversation with a friend. Freddy had done so. Alison had used the tape in an editing process. Her friend had read the manuscript so Alison could hear the flow of conversation, instead of just reading it. Alison said she had found reading aloud helped her to check dialogue. Francis quickly checked the files of tapes.

At the same time, Freddy was moving silently up the back stairs of the house. She knew if she went up the front way, Alison would see her coming. The back stairs opened into Mildred's sitting room. She could hear them talking. Her spine stiffened. How in the hell was she going to get in without being observed?

Alison's voice was cold and level. "It's what he wouldn't do, Mildred, it's what he wouldn't do." Her voice trailed off.

"What do you mean, what he wouldn't do?"

"I liked him. You understand. I liked him. I wanted him to come out and play like a big boy. Do I have to spell it out in front of the kid here?"

"I know what you're talking about," Erica said. "I'm not stupid."

"These kids, they know everything, right?" Alison looked at Erica. "Course, when I was your age, I was already involved with a few things." She smiled the corners of her mouth drawn up in remembrance.

"I don't think you have to go into that," Mildred's voice cut into her thoughts.

"Aw shit! Maybe this kid needs an education. I could see to that, Grandma Mildred. She could learn stuff you never had a chance to learn." Her voice took on a nasty tone.

"Look, you obviously have a problem with me. Let Erica go."

"Are you crazy? This kid is my insurance no one is going to try and stop me. I may or may not let her go, when I'm done. But sure as hell, you aren't going to be around to care one way or another. I hate your fuckin' guts. When I'm done with you, you're gonna wish you were dead!"

"Alison, I don't understand. What have I done that you hate me so damn much? There must be something. I haven't a clue."

"You really are stupid! He liked you, don't you get it?" The woman sneered at her.

"Liked me? You are talking in riddles, just tell me. If you're planning to kill me, I'd like to know why."

"He didn't like me. All I wanted was a little roll in the hay with the guy. Nothing serious, just a diversion. My job gets pretty hair-raising at times. Great pay, but the benefits suck." She laughed. "If you live, you can enjoy a lot. You can also die young. So," she added, "diversion is nice once in awhile. I wanted Manuchi to pay attention to me, he wouldn't do it. So, I killed him."

Mildred felt the chill spread through her bones. Alison simply had no conscience. There would be no reasoning with her. The only way to survive was to find a way to overpower or disarm her. It seemed quite unlikely.

Then, unbidden, came the surety that Freddy was in the back stairwell. Alison didn't know she was there. Any sound, however, would give her away. The iciness of fear became hot in Mildred's veins. The next few minutes were lost in confusion. The one thing which stood out was the sound of a voice cutting through the fear and tension of the room.

"Alison, what have you done?"

The voice was clear and galvanized Alison into action. So many things happened in the ensuing minutes, it was difficult to recount later to John.

Alison froze, "Ashley! Oh God Ashley. I didn't mean to do it. Oh God, I'm so sorry." Tears began to spurt from her eyes.

Erica grunted, and then her right foot connected with the gun in Alison's hand. It flew across the room. Freddy burst through the door, a 357 Magnum leveled at Alison's chest. Mildred leaped toward Erica, propelling her out of the room to safety. Anubis, released by Francis from his kennel, raced into the room and sat down on top of Alison. He growled when she moved.

Later, When Mildred tried to explain what happened when, she couldn't.

John arrived thirty minutes after Glenn Becket and the Anoka County Sheriff had taken Alison from the house. She had been hysterical and unable to comprehend the reading of her rights. The cops were taking her to the Anoka County Jail, but planned to have a psychological assessment done immediately.

Mildred was shaken by the vehemence exhibited by Alison. Father Will arrived just after Alison was taken away by the authorities. He came earlier than Alison had asked him to because he had a bad feeling something was very wrong.

Within the next half-hour, a large group of people had convened on the porch. The rain continued, but the skies had lightened considerably and the wind was absent. When Francis entered the room with coffee and food, everyone flocked to the table, then settled in on various chairs and couches to talk.

Mildred sat on the end of a couch, her arm protectively around Erica. It was this scene that John perceived as he arrived. Right behind him was Quim.

"Mildred!" He exclaimed as he moved to her. "My God! I thought I'd never see you again."

"I was afraid I wouldn't see anyone either. I can't believe she's gone. I can't believe she did all those things. Killed all those people. It's unbelievable!"

"It's true," he assured. "I'm not sure we'll ever know the extent of her violence."

"It was considerable." Father Will stated. "I can't tell you everything I know. She confessed to me at various times. I can tell you that knowledge has damaged my own soul. I believe in the seal of the confessional with all my being. But you see, she abused it. Taunted me with things she had done." His face was ashen. "I loved her, you know. But, I don't think she had the emotional capacity to comprehend love. Everything was twisted." He began to sob. "I've loved her since we were little kids. She saved my life."

"Will, I've been to Chicago. I talked with a Sgt. Lucci last night. He told me a great deal about Alison's childhood. I heard how she took you in and found you a place to live." John said compassionately. "I also heard quite a lot about how you and Marko were her side-kicks. It must have been hard to say 'no' to her."

"It was impossible. I owed her everything. My parents didn't die; they just didn't give a shit about us kids. My sister died of malnutrition in the streets. Does Lucci know that?" He said defensively. Then he sat back, "I don't suppose that's fair either. One cop can't change the world. He did try to help Alison. I think he was very clear on what she was doing. After a while, I just gave up trying to change her. When her parents died in that fire, I just couldn't believe she had anything to do with it. It took me years to believe she did it. She and Marco." His eyes glistened with tears. "Those poor people, dying like that."

"Well," John said softly, "they've been gone a long time. I know you didn't have anything to do with it. One of the things Lucci told me was that you were involved in some petty crime. He also said he knew you never took part in any nasty shit. Those were his words. He said he thought you had a conscience. He didn't think Alison did."

Mildred added gently, "you can't change people. The only thing you can do is to try to show them a different way to do things. It doesn't guarantee they will change, or even try to change."

"No," Will add thoughtfully, "sometimes there is nothing that can be done. As a priest I like to believe anyone can change their life. As a person who has seen true evil, it scares me to realize sometimes they can't."

# CHAPTER THIRTY ONE

A week later, relative calm had descended on the East Bethel house. Francis was preparing a picnic in the yard. She said it was to celebrate the Memorial Day weekend and the beginning of summer. Mildred thought it was because Francis simply would use any excuse to cook for a crowd.

Francis had invited everyone who had been involved in the traumatic events of the previous month. Each of them had their own viewpoint. Freddy saw it as a chance for catharsis; Mildred as an opportunity to gain closure. John, saw it as a final outcome for a criminal who had eluded justice.

He had invited Sgt. Lucci to visit. He felt the man had a vested interest in the incarceration of Alison. Without his input, much of the case would have been difficult to believe.

When the guests arrived, they were treated to not only southern cooking, Jambalaya and Cajun Sausage, but to the hospitality as well. The house had never looked more inviting. John and Mildred had mentioned their joint venture as an Investigative Service. Their focus would be the psychological aspect of criminal activity. John had connections throughout the State of Minnesota, as well as some national ones. He felt they had a solid basis for the business.

George and Joel would be adjunctive services for any security endeavors. Freddy was a partner as a Psychiatrist. The project had been supported by John's colleagues in the Twin Cities and Anoka County. The planned opening of the Retreat Center was scheduled for a month away. There was a lot of work to do.

In the meantime, Mildred had been aware of all the mixed feelings surrounding Alison's arrest. First, it was difficult to believe they had lived with a murderer. Secondly, she was so famous as a novelist, the crime had increased her sales.

"I think there are people who think it's just a publicity stunt." She mused to John, as they sat across from one another at the table. Sgt. Lucci was there and gave a snort when she said this.

"I think she has lived with more killings than we'll ever know. A week ago, an informant in Chicago said the word on the streets was that one of the best Hit Men, I use the term loosely, has been arrested. He recounted this person has in all probability killed at least two hundred persons around the world."

"That's what all the travel was about, not writing." Freddy injected. "She probably went there as a writer, stayed in the same hotel or area as the intended victim, and then, 'BOOM' dead as a doornail. Who in the hell would suspect Miss Milk Toast, faint in your arms, Alison Lippencott?"

"Who indeed?" John added. "We have found a number of odd things. She owns a lot of property all over the country and in France, Britain, and Italy."

"All the better to elude justice, my dear." Freddy quipped.

"Not just that," John replied, "she has many identities. We found she had established at least twenty-five distinct persons with records, social security numbers, credit cards, and Drivers Licenses. It's really quite incredible."

"I told you she was a smart child. It didn't stop with growing up." Lucci added dryly. "After Dennison died, there was a lot of supposition about his death and who caused it. He was executed, mob style. There was no question about that fact." He paused, "the thing that was so puzzling was, it appeared the only person who fit all the requirements to have pulled it off, was this sixteen year old girl. The Captain wouldn't buy it. I knew she did it. Anyone who could snuff out her family like she did, could kill anyone."

"Where did Ashley fit in all of this?" Quim, who had been silent, inquired.

"Now that is interesting! She knew who Alison was. She knew about her identities and she knew about her profession. My God! When I think about it, it boggles my mind. Here's this nice college coed who meets Alison, they like one another and form a friendship, and this woman eventually becomes part of the biggest literary scam in Gothic Novel history." John reported. "Can you believe it?"

Freddy nodded.

"I was floored. In all my years in Law Enforcement, I have never met anyone like these people. All of them who touched Alison in any personal way, became tainted."

Father Will, who had listened silently, looked crest-fallen.

Mildred noticed his reaction and addressed him, "you knew her best. What do you think drove her to do this?"

"I'm not a Psychologist," Will answered. "I've thought about it over the years. I knew I loved her. Since we were little kids, she was always foremost in my thoughts. All the time. I've never understood why. In a way, the kind of idolatry I have felt is sick. I know it. I couldn't seem to help it. I just loved her." His eyes glistened.

"It happens. Falling in love is sometimes chemistry. There is no rhyme or reason. It just is." Freddy answered.

"But why Ashley? She came from a solid family background. She had education, money, security, everything. Why?"

"Probably Alison was so different and exotic. I don't think we'll ever know. She left every nickel she had, which is in the millions, to Alison. There is a stipulation that if Alison should predecease her, the inheritance is to go to support health and welfare programs for women and children. At least that's something good coming out of this mess." John said. "Criminals cannot inherit from their victims in Minnesota, so the stipulation will probably be held up by the Probate Court."

"She wrote all the Alison Lippencott books, didn't she?" Francis inquired. She had slipped quietly into the room with Renee and Erica. They had just arrived.

"Yes, she did. Well, almost all of them, I should correct myself." John shared. "It seems Alison started the first book, but got too busy with her primary career. She asked Ashley if she would consider being a well paid Ghostwriter. And," he added, "I do mean well paid."

Father Will cleared his throat, "I know everyone thinks I should have seen what was happening. Do you know, I never suspected Alison didn't write the books. I can't believe how blind I've been"

"You're in good company, young man," Lucci said. "There are a lot of people in the old neighborhood who will never believe their golden-haired darling of forty years ago would be this viscous. Some of those old ladies remember how good Alison was to the Dennison's when Mrs. Dennison got cancer. They can't see beyond it. For them to believe she was having sex with him, probably murdered both of them, and then hired someone else to write her successful books, is more than their imagination could handle. For God's sake, Dennison taught her the business. On a couple of his trips, he took her along with him. Supposedly, to take her on the vacation she never had as a kid. The reality was, he was probably teaching her the ropes and grooming her to follow in his footsteps."

"That would almost mean his wife knew what his business was. Did she?"

"I'm sure she did," Lucci answered. "How could you live with a person all those years and not know. I don't think it's possible. She covered for him."

"It's unbelievable." Mildred added. "However, I know that people have a hard time looking at a possible dark side of their friends and neighbors. It happens all the time, unfortunately."

"I agree," Freddy said, "most people can't see past a person's façade. They think what they see, is what they get."

"What I can't understand is how she pulled off the maneuver with the wine that killed Ashley." Quim said.

"It's really simple. Alison arranged the luncheon and the seating. She had her agent sit across from Ashley. The waiter, Marco-Ernest served the wine. As, per Alison's agenda, Ashley and the agent were talking across the table. It was not a good arrangement for them to talk to one another. Alison suggested that she and Ashley change places. The wine was already poisoned. She was always in control of the seating at the table. She met Marco in the hall before the luncheon. She gave him the poison, instructed him in what to do, and then told him to leave after he had served the wine." John paused thoughtfully. "Then, here's the clincher, Alison had given Marco some really good Cocaine. He thought it was pretty damn nice. He had, among other vices, a very well-established drug addiction. What he didn't know, when he stopped for a little snort, was it was laced with Cyanide. Bingo, number one witness and black-mailer of Alison, is history. She wanted him gone, anyway. She really understood her cousin. She knew he'd use the second he had a chance. He had become too much of a liability. He would have black-mailed her forever if she hadn't killed him."

"It sounds so simple," Will said. "She was such a complex person. What's going to happen to her?"

"She'll do prison time here in Minnesota. At least that's our hope. The thing is, she's got a hell of a great attorney. God knows! We know how she probably murdered Ashley, but proving it might be damn difficult. She did threaten to kill you, Mildred, and she essentially confessed Ashley's murder to you. Still, a good attorney could distort that and try to prove she was distressed about her friend's murder by that no-good, drug-addicted waiter. Who knows? We're gonna try to make it stick."

Renee had joined the group. "I'm glad Erica is okay. I never dreamt Alison was dangerous. She seemed like such a wuss to me."

"Speaking of Erica," Freddy asked, "where did she learn that kicking maneuver she used?"

"Tai Kwon Do classes". Erica answered for her mother. "I've been learning a lot of things there. One of them is how to disarm someone. Of course, our instructor told us we'd never have to use it. I knew she was going to kill Grandma. And when she heard that voice talking to her, she lost her concentration. That's what our instructor said you should watch for in an opponent. I did it 'cause I thought she would kill us anyway. I sure didn't want to go anywhere with her. Yck!" She added distastefully.

"All I can say is, I'm glad you're all okay." John put his arm around Mildred. "You and I can start the business as partners and concentrate on something else for a change. It won't be as dangerous either."

"Oh," Renee said, "I forgot to tell you, Mom, that forty acre parcel of land on County Rd. 74, has been approved for the Senior Housing Project. We can start construction in a matter of weeks. That'll keep you plenty busy, too."

"See, John," Mildred smiled at him, "something that won't involve criminal activity. Finally, we can do something for the elderly in the community that won't involve murder."

"Here! Here!" Quim raised his glass in a toast, "I'll drink to that!"

Everyone laughed